SALAMMBÔ

A ROMANCE OF ANCIENT CARTHAGE

BY

GUSTAVE FLAUBERT

WITH A

CRITICAL STUDY ON FLAUBERT

BY

GUY DE MAUPASSANT

———

VOLUME III.

———

SIMON P. MAGEE,
PUBLISHER,
CHICAGO, ILL.

CONTENTS

ILLUSTRATIONS

GUSTAVE FLAUBERT

A STUDY

———

GUSTAVE FLAUBERT was born in Rouen on the 12th of December, 1821. His mother was the daughter of a physician of Pont-l'Evéque, M. Fleuriot. She belonged to a Low-Normandy family, the Cambremers of Croix-Mare, and was allied to Thouret, of the Constituent Assembly.

Flaubert's grandmother, Charlotte Cambremer, was, in childhood, a companion of Charlotte Corday. His father, born at Nogent on the Seine, was of a family originally from Champagne. He was a surgeon of great skill and renown, a director of the hospital at Rouen. A straightforward, simple, brusque man, he was astonished, though not indignant, at his son's choice of a vocation. He considered the profession of writing an occupation of idleness and uselessness.

Gustave Flaubert was the opposite of a phenomenal child. He succeeded in learning to read only with extreme difficulty. It is doubtful whether he knew how when he entered the Lyceum, at nine years of age.

His great passion in childhood was to have stories told to him. He would listen motionless, fixing his great blue eyes upon the narrator. Then, he would remain quiet for some hours thinking, one finger in his mouth, entirely absorbed, as if asleep.

His mind was at work, however, for he composed dramatic pieces before he was able to write, which he acted all alone, representing the different personages, and improvising the long dialogues.

From his early infancy, the two distinctive traits of his nature were great ingenuousness and a dislike of physical action. All his life he remained ingenuous and sedentary. He could not see any one walking or moving about near him without becoming exasperated; and he would declare in his sharp voice, sonorous and always a little theatrical, that motion was not philosophical. "One can think and write only when seated," he would say.

His ingenuousness continued until his last days. This observer, so penetrating and so subtle, seemed to see life clearly only from afar. When it touched him, when it was busy in his immediate neighborhood, one would have said that a veil covered his eyes. His extreme native frankness, his immovable honesty, the generosity of all his emotions, of all the impulses of his soul are indubitably the causes of this unchanging ingenuousness.

He lived beside the world, but not in it. Better placed for observation, he did not have the impression of downright contact.

To him especially could one apply what he wrote in his preface to the *Last Songs*, of his friend Louis Bouilhet:

"Finally, if the accidents of the world, when they are observed, appear to you transposed for the sake of an illusion in description, so that all things comprise a part of your existence, nor seem to have any other use; if you can be unmoved by any injury, ready for any sacrifice, breastplated against any trial, rush in and publish!"

As a young man, he was of surprising beauty. An old friend of the family, an illustrious physician, said to his mother: "Your son is the God of Love grown up."

Disdaining women, he lived in the exaltation of the artist, in a kind of poetic ecstasy which he preserved by daily association with him who was his dearest friend, the brother heart which one never finds twice. This was Alfred Le Poittevin, who died young of a disease of the heart, brought on by overwork.

Then Flaubert was struck with a terrible malady which his other friend, M. Maxime Ducamp, had the evil inspiration to reveal to the public, in trying to establish a relation between the artistic nature of Flaubert and epilepsy, explaining one by the other.

Assuredly, this frightful disease could not strike down the body without overshadowing the mind. But is that to be regretted? Are happy, strong and self-reliant people fitted, as it is generally understood, to penetrate and express our life, so tormented and so short? Are these exuberant persons made for discovering all the misery, all the suffering which surrounds us, to perceive that death strikes without ceasing, everywhere, each day, ferocious, blind, and fatal?

So it is possible, it is probable, that the first attack of epilepsy left an imprint of melancholy and of fear upon the ardent mind of this robust man. It is probable that, as a consequence of it, a sort of apprehension of life rested upon him, a little more sombre manner of looking at things, a suspicion before the event, a doubt before apparent happiness. But to those who knew that enthusiastic, vigorous man who was called Flaubert, to those who saw him live, laugh, rejoice, feel and vibrate each day, there is no doubt that the fear of a crisis, which disappeared in ripe age and re-appeared only in the last years, could not have modified, except in an imperceptible degree, his manner of being and feeling and the habits of his life.

After some literary essays which were not published, Gustave Flaubert made his *début* in 1857 by a masterpiece called *Madame Bovary*.

Everyone knows the history of this book, the lawsuit brought by the Public Attorney, the violent speech of M. Pinard, whose name will be remembered by this case, the eloquent defense of M. Senard, the difficult, haggling acquittal, the reproach of the President in severe words, and then, success, the avenger, resounding, immense!

But *Madame Bovary* has also a secret history which may be a lesson to beginners in this difficult trade of letters.

When Flaubert, after five years of wearisome labor, had finished this unusual work, he intrusted it to his friend M. Maxime Ducamp, who put it into the hands of M. Laurent Pichat, editor-proprietor of the *Revue de Paris*. Then it was that he found how difficult it is to make oneself understood at the first blow, how one is misunderstood by those in whom he has confidence, and by those who pass for the most intelligent. From this epoch dates that scorn which he had for men's judgment, and his irony for absolute assertions or denials.

Some time after taking the manuscript of *Madame Bovary* to M. Laurent Pichat, M. Maxime Ducamp wrote the following singular letter to Gustave Flaubert, which may perhaps modify the opinion one has formed from the revelations of this writer of his friend, and in particular of *Madame Bovary* in his *Literary Souvenirs:*

JULY 14, 1856.

"DEAR OLD FRIEND: Laurent Pichat has read your romance and has sent me his approval of it, which I am to address to you. You will see on reading it how much I should share it, since it reproduces nearly all the observations that I made before your departure. I sent your book to Laurent without doing more than to recommend it to him warmly; we had no understanding that we were to see you with the same eye. The counsel he gives you is good, and I would even say that it is the only counsel you can follow. Leave us *masters* of your romance that we may publish it in the *Revue;* we will make such cuttings as we judge indispensable; you can then publish it later in book form as you think best; that concerns you alone. My most friendly opinion is that, if you do not do this, you will compromise yourself absolutely and will make your appearance with a perplexing work whose style is not sufficient to give it interest. Be courageous, close your eyes during the operation and pride yourself, if not upon your talent, at least on the experience acquired in these things, and upon our affection for you. You have buried your romance under a heap of things, well done but useless; one cannot see it plainly enough; but try to uncover it and it is an easy task. We shall have this done under our eyes by an experienced and skilful person; we shall not add a word to your copy; we shall only prune it; this will cost you a hundred francs, which will be reserved for you on your rights, and you will have published a thing truly good in the place of an incomplete work too much bolstered. You may curse me with all your might, but remember meanwhile, that in all this I have looked only to your interest.

Adieu, dear old chap; answer, and believe me

Yours always,

MAXIME DUCAMP."

The mutilation of this typical and henceforth immortal book, performed by an "experienced and skilful person," would have cost the author only one hundred francs! Truly, that is nothing!

Gustave Flaubert was stirred with a profound and natural emotion on reading this strange counsel. And he wrote in his boldest hand, upon the back of that carefully preserved letter, only this word: "Gigantic!"

The two collaborators, Messrs. Pichat and Maxime Ducamp, now put themselves to work to extricate their friend's book from that heap of things "well done, but useless," which damaged it; for one reads in a sample copy of the first edition of the book, preserved by the author, the following lines:

"This copy represents my manuscript as it comes from the hand of Sir Laurent Pichat, poet and editor-proprietor of the *Revue de Paris*."   GUSTAVE FLAUBERT.

    20th April, 1857.

On opening the volume, one finds from page to page, lines, paragraphs, and entire scenes cut out. The greater part of the new or original things are cancelled with care.

And one reads further, on the last page, from the hand of Gustave Flaubert, this:

"It was necessary, according to Maxime Ducamp, to retrench *all* the nuptials, and, according to Pichat, to suppress, or at least abridge considerably, and to make over the meetings from one end to the other! According to the general opinion of the *Revue*, the club-foot is considerably too long, 'useless.'"

This was also the origin of the coolness which arose in the ardent friendship between Flaubert and

M. Ducamp. If it were necessary to produce a more definite proof of this, it could be found in this fragment of a letter from Louis Bouilhet to Flaubert:

"As for Maxime Ducamp, I have gone fifteen days without seeing him and should have passed another week in the same fashion if he had not appeared at my house on Thursday of last week. I must say that he was very amiable both as regards my welfare and your own. This may have been policy, but I state the fact simply as a historian. He offered me his services in finding an editor, and later in finding a library. He is well informed about you and your work. What I told him about *Bovary* interested him very much. He said to me, in incidental phrases, that he was very glad the wrong was on your side for never having pardoned him the matter of the *Revue*, that he saw with happiness your works in his magazine, etc., etc. He seemed to speak with conviction and frankness. . . ."

These small details are important only from the point of view of M. Ducamp's judgment of his friend. A reconciliation took place between them later.

The appearance of *Madame Bovary* was a revolution in letters. The great Balzac, forgotten, had shown his genius in some powerful books, stuffed, taken from life, observations, or rather revelations of humanity. He divined, invented, created an entire world, born of his mind. Little of the artist, in the delicate sense of the word, he wrote strong language, full of imagery, a little confused and laborious.

Carried away by his inspiration, he seemed to be ignorant of that difficult art, the giving to ideas their true value through words, sonorousness and context of phrase.

He put into his work the weight of a colossus; and there are few pages from this great man which can be cited as masterpieces of language, as one cites Rabelais,

La Bruyère, Bossuet, Montesquieu, Chateaubriand,
Michelet, Gautier, etc.

Gustave Flaubert, on the contrary, proceeding more
by penetration than intuition, makes use of an admirable new language, precise, sober, sonorous, for a study
of human life, profound, surprising, complete.

This is no longer the romance such as the greatest
have made, the romance where one always feels a little
imagination, a little of the author; a romance that can be
classed among the tragic kind, the sentimental kind, the
passionate kind; the romance where the purpose, the
opinions of the author and his manner of thought show
themselves. It is life itself made evident. One would
say that the personages arose under his eyes as he
turned the pages; that the landscapes unrolled themselves, with their sorrows, their gaieties, their odours,
their charm; that objects surged before the reader, as
he called them forth with an invisible power, concealed one knows not where.

Gustave Flaubert, in fact, was the most ardent
apostle of impersonality in art. He would not admit
that the author ever should be surmised, that he should
let fall in a page, in a line, in a word, a single particle of
his opinion, nor any appearance of purpose. He should
be the mirror of facts, but a mirror which should repro-
duce them by giving to them that inexpressible reflection, that, I know not what of something almost divine
which is called art.

It is not "impersonal" that one should call it, in
speaking of this impeccable artist, but impassible. If
he attached considerable importance to observation
and analysis, he laid still greater stress on composition
and style. For with him these two qualities were
the essentials of an imperishable book. By composi-

tion, he meant that vexatious labour which consists in expressing only the essence of actions that follow each other in an existence, in choosing uniquely the characteristic traits and grouping them, combining them in such a way that they concur in a manner most perfect for producing the effect one wishes to obtain, but not with any purpose of instruction whatever.

Nothing so irritated him as the doctrines of the pawns of criticism upon moral art or honest art. "Since humanity has existed," he would say, "all the great writers have protested through their works against such impotent counsel."

Morality, honesty, and such principles are indispensable things in the maintenance of established social order; but there is nothing in common between social order and letters. Romance writers have as their chief object the observation and description of human passions, good and bad. Their mission is not to moralise, nor to scourge, nor to teach. A book with these tendencies ceases to be an artistic book.

The writer looks at and tries to penetrate the soul and the heart, to sound their depths, the propensities, shameful or magnanimous, together with all the complicated mechanism of movable mortals. He observes according to his temperament as a man, and his artistic conscience. He ceases to be conscientious and artistic if he systematically forces himself to glorify humanity, to gloss things over, to attenuate the passions that he judges dishonestly to the profit of the passions he judges honestly.

Any act, good or bad, has importance for the writer only as a subject for writing, without any idea of good or bad to be attached to it. It is worth more or less as a literary document, that is all.

Beyond the truth, observed in good faith and expressed with talent, there is nothing except the powerless efforts of the pawns.

The great writers are not preoccupied with either morals or chastity. For example: Aristophanes, Apuleius, Ovid, Virgil, Rabelais, Shakespeare and many others.

If a book carries a lesson, it should be in spite of the author, through the very force of the facts it relates. Flaubert considered these principles as articles of faith.

When *Madame Bovary* appeared, the public, accustomed to the unctuous syrup of the elegant romances, likewise to the unlikely adventures of the chance romances, classed the new writer among the realists. This is a gross error and stupid folly. Gustave Flaubert was no more a realist because he observed life with care than M. Cherbuliez is not an idealist because he observed badly. The realist is he who occupies himself only with the brutal fact without comprehending its relative importance or noting its reverberations. To Gustave Flaubert, a fact in itself signified nothing. He explains himself thus in one of his letters:

"You complain that the events are not varied,—that is the plaint of a realist, and besides, how do you know this? It may be necessary to look at them more closely. Have you ever believed in the existence of things? Is not everything an illusion? There is no truth except in its relation, that is to say, the fashion in which we perceive the objects."

No observer, however, was ever more conscientious; and no one strove more to comprehend the causes which led to the effects. His process of work, his artistic process held much more to penetration than to observation. Instead of displaying the psychology of his personages in explanatory dissertations, he simply made it appear by their acts. The inward was thus unveiled by the outward, and without any psychological argument.

In the first place, he imagined his types; then, proceeding by deduction, he gave to these beings the characteristic actions which they would naturally accomplish, following their temperaments with an absolute logic. Life, then, that he studied so minutely, could serve him only as a title of instructions.

Never does he announce the events; one would say on reading them that the facts spoke for themselves, so much importance did he attach to a visible appearance of men and things.

It is this rare quality of *scene-setter* and impassible portrayer which baptized him a realist by the superficial minds who know how to comprehend the deep meaning of a work only when it is spread out in philosophic phrases.

He was much irritated over this epithet of realist, which they pasted on his back, and pretended to have written his *Bovary* only out of hatred to the school of M. Champfleury.

In spite of a great friendship for Émile Zola, and a great admiration for his powerful talent, which he qualified as genial, he could never pardon him his naturalism. It is sufficient to read *Madame Bovary* with intelligence to understand how far removed he was from realism. The plan of the realistic writer consists in simply relating the facts that have happened among personages whom they have known or ob-

3—2

served. In *Madame Bovary*, each personage is a type, that is to say, a *résumé* of a series of beings belonging to the same intellectual order.

The country doctor, the provincial dreamer, the chemist,—a sort of Prudhomme,—the curate, the lovers, and even all the accessory figures, are types, endowed with a *relievo* much more energetic than are they in whom are concentrated great powers of observation, and much more lifelike than those represented by a pattern, or model, of their class.

But Gustave Flaubert continued to grow great up to the hour of the blossoming of romanticism; he was nourished by echoing phrases of Chateaubriand and Victor Hugo, and felt in his soul a lyric need which could not completely expand in such clearly-defined books as *Madame Bovary*.

And this is one of the most singular sides of this great man: this innovator, this revealer, this man-who-dared was, up to the time of his death, under the dominating influence of romanticism. Almost in spite of himself, almost unconsciously, driven by the irresistible force of his genius, by the creative force shut up within him, has he written these romances in a style so novel, and a note so personal. From his own taste, he would have preferred epic subjects, which unrolled themselves in a kind of song, like tableaux in an opera.

In *Madame Bovary*, besides, as in the *Sentimental Education*, his style, constrained to the rendition of common things, has often some flights, some sonorousness of tone, above the subjects it expresses. It makes departures, as if tired of being held back, of being forced to such platitude and, in speaking of Homais' stupidity or Emma's silliness, it becomes pompous or confusing, as if he were translating the movement of a poem.

Not being able to resist this need of grandeur, he composed, after the fashion of a Homeric recital, his second romance, *Salammbô*.

And is that a romance? Or is it rather an opera in prose? The tableaux are developed with prodigious magnificence, with a surprising pomp, colour and rhythm. The phrase sings, cries, has the fury and sonorousness of the trumpet, the murmur of the hautboy, the undulations of the violoncello, the artifice of the violin and the finesse of the flute. And the personages, built for heroes, seem always on the stage, speaking after a superb mode, with an elegance strong and charming, with the air of moving about in antique and imposing garb and decorations.

This giant's book, the most plastically beautiful that he has written, gives also the impression of a magnificent dream. Is it thus that events passed such as Gustave Flaubert relates? No, undoubtedly no. If the facts are exact, the pomp of poesy which he throws over them show them to us in a kind of apotheosis, the lyric art of which envelops whatever it touches.

But scarcely had he ended that sonorous recitation of a mercenary revolt, when he felt himself called on anew by subjects less superb, and he composed with slowness that great romance of patience, that long, sober, and perfect study which is called the *Sentimental Education*.

This time he took for his personages, no longer types, as in the *Bovary*, but any sort of men, mediocre men, the kind we meet every day. Although this work demanded a superhuman amount of labour in

its composition, so much does it resemble life itself
that it has the air of being executed without plan or
purpose. It is the perfect image of what takes place
each day; it is an exact journal of existence. And
yet, the philosophy in it remains so completely latent,
so completely concealed behind the facts; the psychology is so perfectly enclosed in the action, attitudes
and words of the personages, that the great public,
accustomed to underscored effects, to manifest teaching, did not comprehend the value of this incomparable romance.

Only very keen minds and observers have seized
the purport of this unique book, so artless, so sad, so
simple in appearance, but so profound, so veiled, and
so bitter. The *Sentimental Education,* scorned for the
most part by the critics, accustomed as they are to the
known forms and the immutable in art, has, nevertheless, numerous and enthusiastic admirers who give it
the highest place among Flaubert's works.

But it became necessary for him, in consequence of
one of those inevitable reactions of the mind, to undertake a new subject, something large and poetic;
and he finished a work, sketched some time before,
entitled *The Temptation of Saint Antony.*

This is certainly the most powerful effort of the
mind he ever made. But the very nature of the subject, its extent, its inaccessible height, rendered such a
work almost beyond human strength. Taking up the
old legend, he no longer has him assailed by visions
of nude women and succulent nourishment alone, but
by all the doctrines, all the beliefs and superstitions by
which the disturbed mind of man is bewildered. It
is a colossal defile of religious escort, of all the strange

conceptions, simple and complicated, enclosed in the brain of dreamer, priest, or philosopher who is tortured by a desire to penetrate the unknown.

As soon as this enormous task was finished (a work somewhat painful and confused, a chaos of tottering beliefs), he began again upon nearly the same subject, taking the sciences in place of religion and two narrow-minded citizens instead of the ecstatic saint.

Here are some of the ideas and the development of this encyclopædic book, *Bouvard and Pécuchet*, which might have as a sub-title: "Concerning false methods in the study of human knowledge."

Two copyists employed in Paris met by chance and became bound together in the closest friendship. One of them had a small inheritance, the other his savings. With the combined sum they bought a farm in Normandy, the dream of their existence, and left the capital. Then they began a series of studies and experiences embracing all human knowledge, and thus are developed the philosophic data of the work.

At first, they took to gardening, then to agriculture, to chemistry, astronomy, medicine, archæology, history, literature, politics, hygiene, to magnetism and sorcery; they finally came to philosophy, losing themselves in its abstractions; they fell into religion, which soon disgusted them; they took up the education of two orphans, but finding themselves frustrated again and in despair, they go back to copying as in days gone by.

The book is thus a review of all the sciences, as they appear to two lucid enough minds of the mediocre, simple order. It is at the same time a formidable collection of knowledge, and above all a prodigious criticism on all scientific systems, opposing the one to the other, tearing down both sides by bringing fact to bear upon them, contradicting them by the aid of accepted and undisputed laws. It is a history of the feebleness of human intelligence, a promenade through the labyrinth of erudition with a thread in one's hand. This thread is the grand irony of a thinker who proves, in all things and without ceasing, eternal and universal stupidity.

Beliefs, established for some centuries, are exposed, developed, and dismembered in ten lines by placing in opposition other beliefs so deftly and briskly as to undo and demolish them. From page to page, from line to line, a notion comes up, and immediately another rises in its turn, when the first withdraws or falls, struck down by its neighbor.

What Flaubert did for religions and antique philosophy in *The Temptation of Saint Antony*, he has here accomplished anew for all modern knowledge. It is the Tower-of-Babel of science, where all doctrines, diverse, contrary, and absolute (above all), speaking each its own language, demonstrate the impotence of effort, the vanity of affirmation and always "the eternal misery of all."

The truth of to-day becomes the error of to-morrow; all is uncertain, variable, containing in unknown proportions, some quantity of the true and of the false. At least, what is there is neither true nor false. The moral of the book seems contained in this phrase of Bouvard's: "Knowledge is gained by following the data furnished by an angle in space. Perhaps it will not bring all that we are ignorant of, which would require so much greater space that one can never hope to discover it."

This book touches upon that which is greatest, most curious, most subtle and most interesting in man: it is the history of an idea under all its forms, in all its manifestations, with all its transformations, in its weakness and in its power.

It is curious to notice here in Gustave Flaubert a tendency towards an ideal more and more abstract and elevated. By ideal must not be understood that sentimental kind which seduces the common citizen's imagination. For the ideal, with most men, is nothing other than the unlikely. For the rest, it is simply the domain of the idea.

Flaubert's early romances have been first of all a study of customs, very true and very human; then, a dazzling poem, a procession of images and visions. In *Bouvard and Pécuchet*, the personages themselves belong to systems and not to mankind. The actors serve uniquely for expressing ideas which, as if they were beings, move, unite, combat and destroy each other. And some particularly comic part, or wicked idea, takes its place in the procession of beliefs in the brains of these two poor gentlemen who personify humanity. They are always of good faith, always zealous; and invariably experience contradicts the best established theory, and the most subtle reasoning is demolished by the most simple fact.

This surprising edifice of knowledge, built for demonstrating human impotence, should have a crowning conclusion, a shining justification. After this formidable array, the author has heaped up an irresistible amount of proof, the wrong side of foolishness culled from among great men.

When Bouvard and Pécuchet, disgusted with everything, returned to their copying, they naturally opened the books that they had read, taking them in the natural order of their studies, and transcribed minutely some choice passages from them into the works from which they were drawing. Then begins a series of frightful absurdities, ignorance, flagrant contradictions, monstrous errors, shameful statements, and mistakes inconceivable to high minds and those of more intelligence. Whoever has written upon a subject has sometime said a foolish thing. This foolish statement Flaubert has unfailingly found and set down; and, putting with it another, then another, then another, he has made a formidable array which disconcerts all belief and all statement.

This inner view of human stupidity resulted in a mountain of notes too mixed ever to be published unabridged. He has classed them, however; but this classification should be revised, and half, at least, of this mass of documents suppressed. Nevertheless, here is the order in which he left these notes:

Morality.
Love.
Philosophy.
Mysticism.
Religion.
Prophecy.
Socialism. (Religious and political.)
Criticism.
Estheticism.

Specimens of Style: { Periphrases.
Recantation.
Rococo.

Styles of great writers, journalists and poets.

Style:
- Classic.
- Scientific: (Medical, Agricultural).
- Clerical.
- Revolutionary.
- Romantic.
- Realistic.
- Dramatic.
- Official, of Sovereigns.
- Poetic-official.

HISTORY OF SCIENTIFIC IDEAS.

FINE ARTS.

Beauty:
- On the part of order.
- Of people of letters.
- Of religion.
- Of sovereigns.

Opinions of great men.
The classics corrected.
Whimsicality.— Ferocity.— Eccentricities.— Injuries.— Foolish-
   ness.—Cowardice.
Exaltation of the low.

Official popularity:
- Discourse.
- Circulars.

IMBECILES.

The dictionary of accepted ideas.
The catalogue of *chic* opinions.

This then, is the history of human stupidity in all its forms.

Some quotations to make the purport and nature of these notes comprehended:

PHILOSOPHY, MORALITY, RELIGION.

The Greeks corrupted by their philosophic reasoners.

"This so brilliant people has founded nothing, established nothing lasting, and there remains of them only memories of crimes and disasters, books and statues. They always lacked reason."
—LAMENAIS: *Essay upon Indifference,* vol. 4, p. 171.

MORALITY.

"Sovereigns have the right to make changes in morals."
—DESCARTES: *Discourse on Method,* part 6.

"The study of mathematics, comprising as it does, sensibility and imagination, sometimes causes a terrible explosion of the passions."
—DUPANLOUP: *Intellectual Education,* p. 147.

"Superstition is a production put forth by religion, which there is no need of destroying."
—DE MAISTRE:
Evenings at St. Petersburg, No. 7, p. 234.

"Water is made for sustaining these prodigious floating edifices which we call vessels."
—FÉNELON.

RELIGIOUS AND PHILOSOPHICAL AND MORAL BEAUTIES.

POLITICAL ECONOMY.

"In 1823, the inhabitants of the town of Lille, speaking in the name of rape-seed oil, exposed to the government the fact that a new product, gas, had begun to make itself known; that this mode of lighting, if put into general use, would leave all others behind, inasmuch as it appeared at once the best and the lowest in price, etc. By reason of which, they prayed humbly, but firmly, that his Majesty, the natural protector of their work, would be willing to protect them from all attack upon their rights by absolutely interdicting this perturbing product."

——FREDERIC PASSY: *Discourse upon Free Trade.*
Dec. 5, 1878.

———

"Shakespeare himself, crude as he was, was not without reading or without knowledge."

——LA HARPE: *Introduction to a Literary Course.*

THE ECCLESIASTICAL STYLE.

"Ladies, in the march of Christian society, upon the railway of the world, woman is a drop of water whose magnetic influence, vivified and purified by the fire of the Holy Spirit, communicates movement to the social convoy under her beneficent impulse; it runs along the way of progress and advances towards the eternal doctrines.

"But if, instead of furnishing the drop of water of the divine benediction, woman supplies the pebble of derailment, some frightful catastrophes are the result."

——MGR. MERMILLOD:
On Supernatural Life in the Soul.

PERIPHRASES.

IMBECILE.

"I should consider it bad for a not over-wise girl to live with a man before marriage."

(*Translation of Homer.*) PONSARD.

ROMANTIC STYLE.

"Sibyl, playing on the harp, was generally adorable. The word angel came to the lips in looking at her."

—*Sibylle* (p. 146) O. FEUILLET.

STYLE OF SOVEREIGNS.

"The riches of a country depend upon its general prosperity."

—LOUIS NAPOLEON: Quoted in the *Rive Gauche*, March 12, 1865.

THE CATHOLIC STYLE.

"Philosophic teaching makes youth drink of the rancour of the dragon in the chalice of Babylon."

—PIUS IX: *Manifesto*, 1847.

———

"The inundations of the Loire are due to the excess of pressure and the non-observance of Sunday."

—THE BISHOP OF METZ: *Mandate,* December, 1846.

SCIENTIFIC IDEAS.

NATURAL HISTORY.

"The women in Egypt prostituted themselves publicly to the crocodiles!"

—PROUDHON: (*On the celebration of Sunday*, 1850.)

"Dogs are ordinarily of two opposite tints, the one light and the other dark, so that in whatever part of the house they may be, they can be seen upon the furniture, with the colour of which they might be confounded."

— BERNARDIN DE SAINT-PIERRE:
Harmonies of Nature.

"Fleas throw themselves, wherever they are, upon a white colour. This instinct was given to them that we might catch them more easily."

— BERNARDIN DE SAINT-PIERRE:
Harmonies of Nature.

"The melon is divided by nature into sections so as to be eaten in the family; the pumpkin, being much larger, can be eaten with the neighbours."

— BERNARDIN DE SAINT-PIERRE: *Études de la Nature.*

CARE FOR THE TRUTH.

"All authority, especially that of the church, ought to oppose new things, without letting themselves be frightened at the danger of retarding the discovery of some new truths, which may be inconvenient, fleeting, and wholly useless as compared with the shocking of institutions and accepted opinions."

—P. 283, vol. 2, DE MAISTRE, *Exam. Phil. Bacon.*

"A disease of potatoes was caused by the disaster at Monville. The meteor was most active in the valleys, where it drew off the heat. It had the effect of a sudden coldness."

—RASPAIL: *Hist. Health and Sickness,* p. 246, 247.

FISHES.

"I notice in fishes that it is a marvel they are born and live in the waters of the ocean, which are salt, and that their race was not annihilated long ago."

—GAUME: *Catechism of Perseverance,* 57.

CONCERNING CHEMISTRY.

"Is it necessary to observe that this vast science (Chemistry) is absolutely out of place in general teaching? Of what use is it to the minister, the magistrate, the sailor, or the merchant?"

—DE MAISTRE: *Letters and unedited pamphlets.*

SCORN OF SCIENCE.

"Many persons have thought that science in the hands of man dries up the heart, disenchants nature, leads the minds of the weak to atheism, and from atheism to crime."

—CHATEAUBRIAND: *Genius of Christianity,* p. 335.

ZOÖLOGY.

"It is, as it seems to us, a great pity to find man to-day ranked among the mammiferous (after Linnæus's system) with the monkeys, the bats and the sloths. Is he not worthy to be left at the head of creation where Moses, Aristotle, Buffon, and Nature placed him?"

—CHATEAUBRIAND: *Genius of Christianity,* p. 351.

———

"His movements [of the serpent] differ from those of all animals. One does not know where to say the principle of his locomotion lies, for he has neither fins, nor feet, nor wings; nevertheless he flees like a shadow and vanishes magically."

— CHATEAUBRIAND: *Genius of Christianity,* p. 138.

LINGUISTIC.

"If one had a dictionary of savage tongues, he might find there the remaining evidence of a language spoken before their day by an enlightened people, and, if we did not find it, the only conclusion would be that degradation had arrived at such a point that the last remnants had been effaced."

— DE MAISTRE: *Evenings at St. Petersburg.*

THE NATURAL SCIENCES ARE SECONDARY.

"They belong to prelates, to the nobles, to the great officers of State, to be the depositories and the guardians of conserved truth, to teach nations what is good and what is bad, what is true and what is false, in moral and spiritual order. Others have no right to reason upon this kind of matter. They have the natural sciences to amuse them; of what can they complain?"

— 8th *Conversation,* p. 131. DE MAISTRE.
Evenings at St. Petersburg.

SCIENCE SHOULD BE PUT IN SECOND PLACE.

"If we do not look well to ancient maxims, if education be not given up to the priests, and if science is not put in the second place, the evils which await us are incalculable; we shall be brutalized by science, and that is the last degree of brutality."

— DE MAISTRE: *Essay on generating principles.*

Historic Review.

Opinion on the study of history.

"The teaching of history may have, in my opinion, some inconvenient peril for the professor. It has some also for pupils."   —Dupanloup.

critical history.

"If we consider Napoleon in respect to his moral qualities, it is difficult to estimate him, because it is difficult to discover goodness in a soldier who is ever occupied with strewing the earth with the dead; friendship in a man who never has his equals about him; probity in a potentate who is master of the riches of the universe. At the same time, however outside the ordinary rules this mortal may be, it is not impossible to seize here and there certain traits of his moral physiognomy."

                    —A. Thiers:
History of the Consulate and the Empire, vol. 22, p. 713.

———

"Many times have I heard deplored the blindness of the judgment of Francis I., who thrust away Christopher Columbus when he proposed the Indes."
                    —Montesquieu:
The Mind of Louis XIV., Book 21, Chap. 22.
(Francis I. mounted the throne in 1515. Columbus died in 1506.)

a pipe in the xv. century.

"Some steps from this very lively scene, the Spanish chief sat motionless smoking a long pipe."
                    —Villemain: *Lascaris.*

ON THE EVE OF THE NAPOLEONIC EMPIRE.

"There has never existed a sovereign family whom one could connect with a plebeian origin. If this phenomenon should make its appearance, it would make an epoch in the world."

—DE MAISTRE:
Evenings at St. Petersburg.

PRUSSIA WILL NOT BE RE-ESTABLISHED.

"Nothing can establish the power of Prussia (1807). This famous edifice, constructed of blood, of filth, of false money and the leaves of pamphlets, has crumbled in the twinkling of an eye and gone forever."

—DE MAISTRE: *Letters and Pamphlets,* p. 98.

SAINT JOHN CHRYSOSTOM, THE AFRICAN BOSSUET.

(St. John Chrysostom was born in Antioch, Asia.)

"The town of Cannes, doubly celebrated for the victory gained by Hannibal over the Romans and the landing of Bonaparte."

"He accuses Louis XI. of having persecuted Abélard." (Louis XI. was born in 1423. Abélard was born in 1079.)

"Smyrna is an island."

—J. JANIN, in *G. de Flotte,* 1860.

EXALTATION OF THE LOWLY.

"It requires more genius to be a boatman on the Rhône than to reach the Orient."

3—3 —PROUDHON.

STUPIDITIES OF GREAT MEN.

CORNEILLE.

"His morals [Chimène] are at least scandalous, if, in fact, not depraved. This pernicious example renders the work notably defective and destroys the aim of the poetry which would otherwise be useful."

—*Academy* (*On The Cid*).

"Let one quote me an excerpt from the great Corneille that I would not have undertaken to do better myself than he has done it! Who is to be the judge? I should only do what any man is capable of doing, provided he believed as firmly in Aristotle as in me."

—LESSING: *Dramatists of Hamburg,* p. 462, 463.

"In spite of the reputation which this writter [La Bruyère] enjoyed, there is much negligence in his style."

—CONDILLAC: *Treatise on the Art of Writing.*

"A famous dreamer [Descartes], subject to flights of the imagination, whose name is made for a chimerical country."

—MARAT: *Concerning the Panthéon.*

"Rabelais, filth of humanity."   —LAMARTINE.

LULLI.

"His songs, so often repeated in the world, serve only to suggest passions the most irregular."

—BOSSUET: *Maxims on Comedy.*

MOLIÈRE

"It is a pity that Molière did not know how to write." —FÉNELON.

"Molière is an infamous actor." —BOSSUET.

BYRON.

"Byron's genius seems to me to be at bottom a little stupid."—L. VEUILLOT: *Free Thoughts,* p. 11.

"In my opinion, Byron, after he had been very justly rejected by his family and his country,—that is to say,—put in a convict-prison for being a faithless husband and a scandalous citizen,—if he had been a man of sense, and truly great in mind and heart, he would have made the simplest reparation for the sake of recovering the right to bring up his daughter and serve his country."—L. VEUILLOT: *Free Thoughts,* p. 11.

ABUSE OF GREAT MEN.

"He [Bonaparte] is in fact a great winner of battles; but aside from that the least General is more skilful than he."
—CHATEAUBRIAND: *Napoleon and the Bourbons.*

BONAPARTE.

"It has been believed that he had perfected the art of war, while it is certain that he has retrograded toward the infancy of the art."
—CHATEAUBRIAND: *Bonaparte and the Bourbons.*

BACON.

"Bacon is absolutely devoid of the spirit of analysis; not only does he not know how to resolve questions, but he does not know how to place them."
—DE MAISTRE:
Examination of Bacon's Philosophy, vol. i, p. 37.

"Bacon was a man ignorant of all the sciences, and all his ideas were fundamentally false."
DE MAISTRE:
Examination of Bacon's Philosophy, vol. i, p. 82.

"Bacon had an eminently false mind, of a kind of falseness which never has belonged to any one but him. His absolute incapacity, essential, radical, was seen in all branches of natural science."
—DE MAISTRE:
Examination of Bacon's Philosophy, vol. i, p. 285.

VOLTAIRE.

"Voltaire is nothing as a philosopher, without authority as a critic and an historian, and antiquated as a scholar; daylight has been let in upon his private life, but through pride, the wickedness and little meannesses of his soul and character are discredited."
—DUPANLOUP: *High Intellectual Education.*

GOETHE.

"Posterity, to whom Goethe has left his work to be judged, will do what it has to do. It will write on tablets of bronze:

'Goethe, born at Frankfort in 1749, died at Weimar in 1832; a great writer, a great poet and a great artist.' And then the fanatics, who are for form for the sake of form, and art for the sake of art, for love and materialism, will come and ask to have added: 'Great man!' and Posterity will answer: 'No!'"

—A. DUMAS, fils.

July 23, 1873.

IDEAS OF ART.

IMBECILE.

"There is no doubt that extraordinary men, in whatever way it may be, owe a part of their success to the superior qualities with which they are endowed by organization."

—DAMIRON: Course of Philosophy, vol. 11, p. 35.

"The grocery shop is respectable. It is a branch of commerce. The army is more respectable still, because it is an institution whose aim is order. The grocery is useful, the army is necessary."

—The News: JULES NORIAC.

Oct. 26, 1865.

JOCRISSES.

"As soon as a Frenchman has passed the frontier, he enters upon foreign territory."

—L. HAVIN: Sunday Courier, Dec. 15.

"When the limit is overleaped, there are limits no longer."

—PONSARD.

There are in existence almost enough of these notes to fill three volumes. The aptitude of Gustave Flaubert for discovering this kind of stupidity was surprising. The following example is characteristic.

On reading the discourse of Scribe's reception at the French Academy, he stopped short before this phrase, which he noticed immediately:

"Does Molière's comedy instruct us in the great events of the Louis XIV. century? Does it tell us a word of the weaknesses or faults of the great king? Does it speak of the revoking of the Edict of Nantes?"

He wrote under this quotation:

"Revocation of the Edict of Nantes, 1685."
"Death of Molière, 1673."

How was it that no one of the Academicians, meeting to listen to this discourse before it was delivered, happened upon this very simple comparison of dates?

Gustave Flaubert counted upon forming a volume of these justifying documents. In order to render the collection of stupidity less heavy and fastidious, there were to be at intervals two or three stories, of poetic idealism, also copied in *Bouvard and Pechuchet.*

Among his papers was found the plan of one of these stories, which would have been entitled: *A Night with Don Juan.* This plan, indicated by short phrases, often by single words alone, reveals better than any dissertation his manner of conceiving and preparing his work. From this point of view it is interesting. Here it is:

A Night with Don Juan.

I.

"Make him without accomplishments, of a single trait.

"Begin with tumult of action,—tableau of two cavaliers arriving upon horses out of breath. Glimpse of the landscape, but not too marked, only as seen through the trees,—let the horses graze in the brushwood,—they become entangled in the lines, etc.—In the midst of the dialogue, from time to time, break in with little details of action.

"Don Juan unbuttons and throws down his sword which comes out of the scabbard a little upon the turf.—He comes to kill the brother of Donna Elvira.—He has fled.—The conversation begins in sharp, brusque speeches.

"Landscape.—The convent behind them.—They are seated on a grassplot, on a declivity under some orange trees.—Circle of woods about them.—Slightly rising land before them.—Horizon of mountains, bare at the summit.—Setting sun.

"Don Juan is weary and betakes himself to Leporello.—But is it my fault, the life you lead and make me lead? Ah, well, the life that I lead —is that my fault also? What! It is not your fault.—Leporello believed him, for he had often seen in him the good intention of leading a more regular life,—yes, and the chance of making it otherwise. Examples.—Leporello mentions the examples: desire that he has for knowing all the women he sees, universal jealousy of the human race.— You would wish all to belong

to you.— You would seek occasions.— Yes, a disquiet
urges me. I should wish . . . aspiration. . . .
— Less than ever he knows what he would wish, what
he wishes.— Leporello for a long time has comprehended
little that his master said.— Don Juan wishes to be pure,
to be a virgin youth.— He has never been so because
he is so bold, impudent and positive.— He has often
wished for the emotions of innocence.— In all and
above all, it is the woman he seeks.— But why do
you leave them?— Ah! why?— Don Juan says it is
from weariness of a woman possessed.— Annoyance
which takes his eye, temptation to strike those
who weep.— How you repel them, the poor little
hinds! How you forget!— Don Juan astonishes himself even in forgetting and sounds this idea, finding
it a sad thing.— I have found some tokens of love,
but know not whence they have come to me.— You
complain of life, master; it is unjust.— Leporello wick-
edly enjoys the idea of goodness in Don Juan.— The
young people look at him, Leporello, with envy,
thinking that he participates somewhat in the poesy
of his master.

"Reverie of Don Juan on the idea submitted to
him by Leporello, that he may have a son some-
where. . . .

"And I have seen you in having seen your ancestors.— Desire that Don Juan has to define in his
thoughts the countenances now nearly effaced.—
What would he not give to have once more a clear
idea of these images!

"It is not all the change itself. It is that you
change often for the worse.— Love of plain women.
Have you not been mad during the past year over
that old Neapolitan marchioness?

"Don Juan relates how he lost his virginity (an old duenna, in a shadow, in a castle).—But you did not know then that this was only a desire; poor man (Seized him in her arms), and what it is born of?— Excitation of physical desire—Corruption.—Abyss which separates subject and object, and the appetite of the one for entering the other.—This is what I am always in quest of.—Silence.

"There was in my father's garden the figure of a woman which had been on the prow of a ship.— Desire showed in it. —He clambers up one day and takes hold of her breasts. —Dead spiders in the wood. —First sentiment of woman, a feeling of peril. —And I have always found the heart of wood. And especially so when they are at play! I see you are happy. Atonement for joy (calm before, calm after), this has alway given me the suspicion that there was something concealed. —But no. —Impossibility of a perfect communion, however adherent the kiss may be. — Something constrains and in itself makes a wall. Silence of the pupils of the eye while they devour themselves. The look goes for more than words. From there comes the desire, for a most intimate attachment, always being renewed and deceived. (Note it from different standpoints):

> Jealousy in desire: to know, to have.
> Jealousy in possession: to look at in sleep, to understand at heart.
> Jealousy in remembrance: to see again and remember well.

"It is always the same thing, said Leporello. —Ah, no! it is never the same thing! So many women, so many desires, and the different joys and bitternesses.

"Let the vulgarism of Leporello bring out the superiority of Don Juan and place it objectively in showing the difference, especially that the difference is only in intensity!

"Desire of other men. Willing to be all that the women expect. — How does it affect me? What is this great number of mistresses compared to the rest? How many there are who do not know me and to whom I have never been anything!

"Two kinds of love. That which attracts to itself, which imbibes, where individualism and the senses predominate (not all of the voluptuous kind, however). To this belongs jealousy. The second is the love which draws you outside of itself. It is larger, more rending, more sweet. It has some magnetic influence where the other has recurring sharpnesses. Don Juan has proved the two, sometimes in the case of the same woman. There are some women who bring the first, there are others who provoke the second, some both at the same time. This also depends upon the moment, chance and the disposition.

"Don Juan is weary and finishes with a feeling that his head would split, as one does when he has thought too long, without a solution.—They hear the bell toll for the dead. And this is one for whom all is done! What is it for?

"They raise their heads.

II.

"Don Juan scales the wall and sees Anna Maria asleep. — Tableau. — Long contemplation, — desire, — remembrance. — She awakes. At first, some words cut short, as if following her thought. She has no fear of him (the least clash possible without their being able to distinguish the fantastic from the real).

"It is long that I have awaited you. You did not come.— Relate her illness and death.— As the dialogue proceeds, she awakes more and more.— Sweat upon her head-bands; raises herself slowly, slowly, at first on her elbows, then sits.— Great astonished eyes. Return to the exact. How?

"Then it is you whose steps I was listening for in the wood.— Stifling heat of the nights.— The promenade in the cloister, shade of the columns, which did not move as the trees had. I plunged my hands into the fountain.— Symbolic comparison of the changed stag.— A summer afternoon.

"They prohibit our telling our thoughts — *à propos* of the crucifix which stands over Anna Maria's bed, the Christ who watches over our dreams.— The crucifix is alway immovable while the heart of the young girl is agitated and often grieved.

"This crucifix is a comfort to Anna Maria, but it does not respond to her in her love.— Oh! I have prayed to Him so often! Why will He not, why has He not listened to me? Aspirations of the flesh and love that is true (perfecting the mystic love), in parallel with the shameless aspirations of Don Juan who has had, in his other loves, especially in moments of lassitude, some mystic needs. (Indicate this, as to Don Juan, in his conversation with Leporello.)

"Movement of Anna Maria encircling Don Juan with her arms.— The flesh of the fore-arm borne upon the arteries and the wrists at the end of the stiff hands, too small to reach to him; a lock of Don Juan's hair catches in a button of her chemise, as he lowers his head towards her.

"The night becomes animated,— a few shepherds are heard upon the mountains. There also they speak of love.— It is love which occupies them.— You do not know the simple joy.— The day dawns.

"Aspirations of Anna Maria's life at harvest times. Sunday afternoons the feast days of the church.— The overseers torment her.— I loved the confessional much. She approached it with a sentiment of voluptuous fear, because her heart was open.— Mystery, shade.— But she had no sins to tell, although she could have wished she had. There are, they say, some women of the ardent life,— happy.

"One day she swooned all alone in the church, where she went to place some flowers (the organist was playing all alone), while contemplating a large window penetrated by the sunlight.

"Frequent desires which she has at communion. To have Jesus in the body. God in self!— At each new sacrament it seems to her that the thirst may be appeased.— She multiplies her works, fasts, prayers, etc.— Sensuality of the young.— Feels the stomach pulling, weakness of the head.— She is afraid, and studies how to overcome these fears, etc.— Mortifications.— Is fond of pleasant odours. She smells some disgusting things.— Voluptuousness of bad odours.— She is ashamed before Don Juan, because of her enthusiasm.— Anna Maria is astonished at his desire.— What is it ? How is it that I desire and she desires that which she does not know? Voluptuousness creeps into her, as disgust into Don Juan. I heard you speaking of the world. Speak to me! Speak to me!

"The lamp goes out for want of oil.— The stars shine into the room (not the moon). Then the day dawns.— Anna Maria falls dead.

"The horses are heard browsing and shaking the saddles on their backs. Don Juan escapes.

"Tone of character of Anna Maria: *sweet.*

"*Never lose sight of Don Juan!* The principal object (at least of the second part) is the union, the equality, the duality, each of which terms has been incomplete up to the present time, melting them together, and each showing gradually that it is coming to complete itself by uniting with the neighboring term."

Gustave Flaubert did not write *Bouvard and Pécuchet* at a single stroke. It might be said that half of his life was passed in meditation upon this book, and that he consecrated his last six years to the execution of this *tour de force.* An insatiable reader, indefatigable in research, he heaped up documents without ceasing. Finally, one day, he put himself to work, somewhat terrified before the enormity of the task. "One must be mad," he often said, "to undertake a work like that." And it was indeed necessary to have superhuman patience and an ineradicable will.

Down there at Croisset, in his great study with five windows, he moaned day and night over his work. Without relaxation, without recreation, pleasures or distractions, with mind fearfully intent, he advanced with a desperate slowness, discovering each day some new study to be made, some new research to undertake. And his phrases also tormented him, his phrase, so concise, so precise, so coloured as to enclose in two lines a whole volume, and in a paragraph all the thoughts of a savant. He would take a number of ideas of the same nature, and, as a chemist prepares an elixir, dissolve them and mix them, rejecting the accessories and simplifying the principles, until out of his crucible would come absolute formulas containing in fifty words an entire system of philosophy.

Once it became necessary for him to stop, exhausted and almost discouraged; then, as a recreation, he wrote his delicious volume entitled: *Three Stories*.

It might be said here that he wished to make this a complete and perfect *résumé* of his work. The three novels: *A Simple Soul, The Legend of Saint Julien the Hospitaller* and *Herodias*, show in a short and admirable fashion the three aspects of his talent.

If it were necessary to class these three jewels, perhaps we should put *Saint Julien the Hospitaller* in the first rank. It is an absolute masterpiece in colour and style, a masterpiece in art.

A Simple Soul relates the story of a poor country servant, honest and shallow, whose life goes on until death without a glimmer of true happiness ever shining upon it.

The Legend of Saint Julien the Hospitaller shows us the miraculous adventures of a saint as made by an old, stained-glass church window, with a wise and highly-coloured simplicity.

Herodias tells us of the tragedy of the decapitation of Saint John the Baptist.

Gustave Flaubert still had many subjects for novels and romances. He counted on writing, from the first, the Battle of Thermopylæ, and for this purpose made a voyage to Greece in the beginning of the year 1872 to see the actual country of this superhuman struggle. He wished to make of it a kind of patriotic recitation, simple and terrible, which might be read to the children of the people, to teach them to make them love their country.

He wished to show the valiant souls, the magnanimous hearts and the vigorous bodies of these
symbolic heroes and, without employing a technical
word, or an ancient term, to tell the story of this
immortal battle, which belonged not to the history of
a single nation but of the world. He rejoiced at the
idea of writing the adieux of these warriors to their
wives in sonorous terms, where they recommend
them, in case they fall in the encounter, to marry
again some robust men soon, in order to give new
sons to their country. The very thought of this
heroic story gave Flaubert a powerful enthusiasm.

He had planned, too, a kind of modern *Matron of
Ephesus*, having been carried away by a subject
which Turgenief related to him.

Finally, he meditated a great romance upon the
second Empire, where could be seen the mixture and
contact of Oriental and Occidental civilisations,—the
amalgamation of the Greeks from Constantinople, so
many of whom came to Paris during Napoleon's
reign, playing an important rôle in Parisian society
and the factitious, refined world of Imperial France.

Two personages chiefly attracted him, a man and
a woman, a Parisian household, showing craftiness
with ingenuousness, ambition and corruption. The
man, a superior officer, dreams of a great fortune
which he is slowly amassing, and with a natural,
egotistic profligacy he makes his wife, who is very
pretty and full of intrigue, serve his projects.

In spite of all the efforts, of every nature, of his
companion, his desires are not satisfied to his liking.
Then, after long years of attempts, both realise the
vanity of their hopes and finish their life as honest,
deceived people, resigned and tranquil.

He saw still, in project, another great romance upon the administration, with this title: *The Head of the Department*, and he affirmed that no one has ever yet comprehended what a comic personage, and how important and useless, a Head of the Department is.

Gustave Flaubert was before all, and above all, an artist. The public to-day scarcely distinguishes the signification of this word as applied to a man of letters. The sense of art, that scent so delicate, so subtle, so difficult, so unseizable, so inexpressible, is essentially a gift of the aristocracy of intelligence; it can scarcely belong to the democracy.

Some very great writers have not been artists. The public and even the greater part of the critics make no difference between the one and the other.

In the last century, on the contrary, the public, adjudged difficult and refined, carried to an extreme this artistic sense which has now disappeared. It worked itself into a passion for a phrase, for a verse, for an ingenious or a bold epithet. Twenty lines, a page, a portrait, an episode, sufficed it for judging and classing an author. It sought the underneath, the inner meaning of the words, penetrated the secret reasoning of the author, read slowly without passing over anything, seeking, after digesting the phrase, to find out whether there still remained anything more to penetrate. And minds, slowly prepared for literary sensations, receive readily the secret influence of this mysterious power which puts some soul into a work.

When a man, however richly endowed he may be, concerns himself only with relating something, when he takes no account of the fact that veritable literary power is not in the anecdote but in the manner of preparing, presenting, and expressing it, he has no sense of art.

The profound and delicious joy which leaps to your heart before certain pages, before certain phrases, comes only through those who have said them; they come from an accordance of expression and idea which is absolute, from a sensation of secret beauty and harmony which escapes for the most part the observation of the multitude.

Musset, that great poet, was not an artist. The charming things he said, in an easy, seductive language, left quite indifferent those who are occupied in the pursuit, the research, and the emotions of a higher beauty, more unreachable, more intellectual.

The multitude, on the contrary, found in Musset satisfaction for all their poetic appetites, which are a little gross, and unable to comprehend the trembling, almost the ecstasy, which certain pieces of Baudelaire, Victor Hugo, and Leconte de Lisle can give. Those words have a soul. Most readers, and even writers, ask only a meaning. They find that this soul, which appears in contact with other words, which shines upon and illumines certain books with an unknown light, is very difficult to call forth.

There are, in the joining and combinations of the language written by certain men, the evocation of a whole poetic world, that the people of the mundane world know neither how to perceive nor to surmise. When one speaks to them of it, they are offended, begin to reason, argue, deny, and cry out that they wish you would show it to them. It would be useless to try. Feeling it not, they could never comprehend.

3—4

Some educated, intelligent men, writers even, are astonished when one speaks to them of this mystery of which they are ignorant; and they laugh and shrug their shoulders. What matters it? They do not know. As well talk music to a people who have no ear.

Ten words exchanged are sufficient for two minds endowed with this mysterious sense of art to comprehend each other's meaning, as if they were speaking a language of which others were ignorant.

Flaubert was tortured all his life in the pursuit of this unseizable perfection. He had a conception of style which bestows upon him, in this one word, all the qualities of the thinker and the writer. So, when he declared: "There is nothing but style," one must understand him to mean: There is nothing but sonorousness or harmony of words.

One usually means by "style," the fashion in which each individual writer presents his thought. Style would then be different according as the man, brilliant or sombre, abundant or concise, followed his own temperament. Gustave Flaubert thought that the personality of the author should disappear in the originality of the book, and that the originality of the book should not come from the singularity of style.

For he did not consider "styles" as a series of moulds each of which carries the particular mark of a writer and in which he runs all of his ideas; but he believed in *style*, that is to say, in a unique, absolute manner for expressing a thing in all its colour and all its intensity.

For him it was the work itself. Just as among beings, the blood nourishes the flesh and even determines the contour and external appearance, following its race and family, so, for him, the foundation in a work imposed the expression with a fatality, unique and true; also the measure, rhythm, and all the lines of the form.

He did not understand that foundation could exist without form, nor form without foundation. The style, then, became the being, the impersonal being, so to speak; and imprinted only its qualities upon the quality of the thought and the power of vision.

Possessed by the absolute belief that there existed only one way of expressing a thing, one word to use, one adjective to qualify it and one verb to give it life, he gave himself superhuman labor to discover, in each phrase, that word, that epithet and that verb. Thus, he believed in a mysterious harmony of expression, and, when a correct term did not seem to him euphonious, he would seek another with an invincible patience, certain that he had not found the true, the unique.

Writing, then, was for him a formidable thing, full of torment, peril and fatigue. He would seat himself at his table with a fear of and a desire for this loved but torturing work. He would remain there for hours, immovable, vexed by his frightful labour, fearful of this colossus, patient and careful as one who would build a pyramid of a child's marbles.

Sunk in his oak armchair with its high back, his head drawn down between his shoulders, he would look steadily at his paper with his blue eye, whose small pupil seemed like a black dot always in motion. A light cap of silk, such as ecclesiastics wear, covering the top of his head, allowed long locks of hair to escape, which fell down and spread out upon his back. A large dressing-gown, of brown cloth, enveloped him entirely; and his red face, cut by a heavy moustache, white at the drooping ends, appeared swollen under a furious rush of blood. His eyes, shaded by great, sombre brows, ran along the lines, digging out words, overturning phrases, consulting the physiognomy of the assembled letters, spying the effect as a hunter eyes his game.

Then he would begin to write, slowly, stopping often, beginning again, erasing, writing across words, filling the margins, and intervening spaces, blackening twenty pages to finish one, and, under the heavy effort of his thought, whining meantime like a sawyer.

Sometimes, throwing the quill which he held in his hand into a large Oriental tin plate filled with goose-quills carefully sharpened, he would take up the sheet of paper, raise it to a level with his eyes and, leaning upon his elbow, would declaim in a sharp, high voice. He would listen to the rhythm of his prose, stop as if seizing a passing cadence, place the commas with exact knowledge, like the halting-places in a long journey.

"A phrase is likely to live," he would say, "when it corresponds to all the necessities of respiration. I know that a phrase is good when it can be read very loud."

"Phrases badly written," he writes in a preface to the *Last Songs* of Louis Bouilhet, "will not submit to this test; they oppress the chest, strain the cords of the heart, and are thus found outside the conditions of life."

A thousand occupations besieged him at the same time, taking possession of him; but that certain attitude of desperation always remained fixed in his mind: "Among all expressions, all turns, all forms, there is but one expression, one turn, one form for expressing what I have to say."

And with cheek inflated, neck congested, brow reddened, and muscles stretched like those of an athlete in a struggle, he would fight desperately for an idea, for a word, seizing them and coupling them in spite of themselves, holding them together in an indissoluble fashion by the power of his will, grasping the thought and subjugating it little by little, with fatigue and almost superhuman effort, encaging it like a captive beast, in solid and precise form.

From this formidable labour was born for him an extreme respect for literature and for the phrase. The moment that he had constructed a phrase, with so much difficulty and torture, he would not admit that a word of it could be changed. When he read to his friends the story entitled *A Simple Soul*, they made some remarks and criticisms upon a passage of ten lines, in which the old maid ends by confounding her parrot with the Holy Spirit. The idea would appear too subtle for a peasant's mind. Flaubert listened, reflected, and recognised that the observation was just. But a sudden anguish seized him: "You are right," said he, "only—in that case I must change my phrase."

That same evening, however, he put himself to the task; he passed the night in changing ten words, scratching and erasing twenty sheets of paper and in the end changed nothing, not having been able to construct another phrase whose harmony appeared to satisfy him.

At the beginning of the same story, the last word of a new paragraph, serving for the subject of the next following, could but make place for an ambiguity. This defect was pointed out to him; he recognized it, forced himself to modify the sense, and, not succeeding in producing the cadence that he wished, he cried out discouraged: "So much the worse for the sense; rhythm before everything!"

That question of rhythm in prose sent him forth into passionate dissertations, at times: "In verse," he would say, "the poet has fixed rules. He has measure, cæsura, rhyme, and a quantity of practical indications making a science of the trade. In prose, a profound sentiment of rhythm is necessary, of fugitive rhythm, without rules, without certainty, an inborn quality, and with that a power of reasoning, the artistic sense infinitely more subtle and more keen, in order to change at any instant the movement, the color, the style, to follow the things one wishes to say. When one knows how to handle this fluid thing which is called French prose, when one knows the exact value of words, and when one knows how to modify that value according to the place he gives it, when one knows how to put all the interest of a page to one line, put one idea in relief among a hundred others, and this uniquely by the choice and position of the terms which express it; when one knows how to strike with a word, with a single word placed in a certain fashion, as one strikes with an arm; when one knows how to overturn a soul, to fill it suddenly with joy or fear, enthusiasm, chagrin, or anger, by simply putting an adjective under the eye of the reader, one is truly an artist, the most superior of artists, a true prose-writer."

He had for the great French writers a frantic admiration. Entire chapters of the masters he knew by heart, and would declaim them in a resounding voice, intoxicated by the prose, giving special sounds to the words, scanning, modulating, singing the phrases. Some clauses fascinated him; he would repeat them a hundred times, always astonished at their exactness, and declaring: "One must be a man of genius to find adjectives like that."

No one had a greater respect and love for his art, or sentiment for the literary dignity, than Gustave Flaubert. A single passion, love for literature, filled his life, even to his last day. He loved it furiously, in a unique, absolute fashion.

Nearly always, an artist conceals some secret ambition foreign to his art. It is often glory that he pursues, that radiant glory which places us, while we are yet living, in an apotheosis, which turns heads, brings down applause and captivates the hearts of women.

To please the ladies! This is also the desire of nearly all. To be all-powerful through talent, in Paris, in the world, an exceptional being, admired, praised, loved, who can cull at will, almost, these fruits of the living flesh of which we are ahungered! To enter, especially where one is preceded by renown, respect and adoration, and see all eyes fixed upon him, and all smiles turned towards himself. It is this that they seek who give themselves up to this strange and difficult trade, this trade of reproducing and interpreting nature by artificial means.

Others have sought money, perhaps for itself, perhaps for the satisfaction it gives: the luxury of existence and the delicacies of the table.

Gustave Flaubert loved letters in an absolute fashion, so absolute that in his soul filled with this love, there was no place for any other ambition.

Never had he any other interest, any other desire; it was almost impossible for him to talk of anything else. His mind, possessed by literary occupations, always returned to them, and he declared useless all those things which interest the people of the world.

He lived alone nearly all the year, worked without respite, without interruption. An indefatigable reader, his repose was in his books, and he possessed an entire library of notes taken from the volumes in which he had dug. Besides, his memory was marvellous; he could recall a chapter, page, or paragraph where he had found a little detail in an unknown work, five or ten years before. He also knew an incalculable number of facts.

The greater part of his life he passed on his estate at Croisset, near Rouen. It was a pretty white house, of ancient style, on the bank of the Seine, in the midst of a magnificent garden which extended back and scaled, by steep roads, the great side of Canteleu. From some of the windows of his large study, could be seen the great ships coming up to Rouen, or going down to the sea, passing so near that they almost seemed to touch the walls with their yards. He loved to watch this mute movement of the vessels gliding along on the great river, going out to all the countries of which one dreams.

Often, leaving his table, he would go and frame his giant chest and his head, which was like one of an ancient Gaul, in one of the windows. On the left, the thousand steeples of Rouen outlined upon space their silhouettes and their carved profiles of stone; a little more to the right, the thousand chimneys of the Saint-Sever manufactories, vomited into the sky their festoons of smoke. The water-tower, as high as the highest of the pyramids of Egypt, looks from the other side of the water at the spire of the cathedral, the highest clock-tower in the world.

Opposite extended green fields where red and white cows were lying down or feeding and, still more to the right, a great forest upon the coast shuts off the horizon where flows the large, calm river, full of tree-covered islands, on its way to the sea, disappearing in the distance in the curve of an immense valley.

He loved this superb, tranquil landscape, which his eyes had looked upon since his infancy. He almost never descended to the garden, having a distaste for moving about. Sometimes, however, when a friend came to see him, he would walk with him along the great avenue of willows planted on the terrace, which seemed made for serious or tender conferences.

He pretended that Pascal had already been in that house, and that he had walked and talked and dreamed with him under those trees.

Three windows of his study opened on the garden and two on the river. The room was large, having no ornaments except books, a few portraits of friends and some souvenirs of his travels. There were the bodies of some little alligators, dried, the foot of a mummy (which a simple-minded domestic had blackened and polished like a boot), some amber beads from the Orient, a gilt Buddha dominating his great work-table and looking both divine and secular out of his motionless, long, yellow eyes; an admirable bust of Caroline Flaubert, Gustave's sister, who died as a young woman, and on the floor beside a Turkish divan covered with cushions, a magnificent white bear skin.

He would set himself to work at nine or ten o'clock in the morning, stop long enough for breakfast, and immediately take up his labour again. He often slept an hour or two in the afternoon; but he was awake until three or four o'clock in the morning, accomplishing the best part of his task in the calm silence of the night, in the tranquillity of that great apartment, scarcely lighted by the two lamps with green shades. Mariners upon the river made use of "Monsieur Gustave's" windows for a lighthouse.

There was in the country-side a sort of legend about him. They looked upon him as a brave man, a little queer, whose singular costumes astonished their eyes and their minds.

He was always clothed for work in large trousers, held by a silk cord, à la girdle, and an immense dressing-gown which reached the floor. This garment, which he adopted not for pose, but because of its ample comfort, was made of brown cloth in winter, and in summer of some light stuff having a white ground with bright-colored design. The citizens of Rouen, going to breakfast at the *Bouille*, on Sunday, returned cheated in their hopes when they could not see from the bridge of the steamboat the original of M. Flaubert's portrait standing in his high window.

He took pleasure also in looking at the boats full of people. He would put up to his eyes an opera-glass that always lay on the edge of his table or the corner of the chimney-piece, and watch curiously all the faces turned towards him. Their ugliness amused him, their astonishment made him expand; he read the character, temperament, and stupidity of each one from his face.

Much has been said of his hatred of the common citizen, the *bourgeois*. He made this word *bourgeois* a synonym for stupidity and defined it thus: "I call anybody who thinks sordidly a *bourgeois*." He had, then, nothing against the *bourgeois* class, but against a particular kind of stupidity that he met most often in that class. He had also perfect scorn for "good people." But, finding himself less often in contact with the workman than with the people of the world, he suffered less from popular foolishness than from the worldly sort. That ignorance whence comes absolute beliefs, so-called immortal principles, all the conventions, all prejudice, the whole arsenal of commonplace, elegant opinions exasperated him. Instead of smiling, as very many do, at the universal silliness, at the intellectual inferiority of the greater number, he suffered horribly from it. When he went away from a drawing-room where mediocrity of talk had continued for an evening, he was cast down, weakened, as if he had been beaten unmercifully — was half-idiot himself, he affirmed — so much did he possess the faculty of penetrating another's thoughts. Always vibrating and very impressionable, he likened himself to one flayed, who leaped from pain at the least contact; and human stupidity assuredly wounded him during his whole life, as great misfortunes of the intimate, secret kind, wound.

He considered stupidity a little in the light of a personal enemy, tormenting him to the point of martyrdom; and he pursued it with fury, as a hunter follows his prey, attacking it from the lowest to the greatest brains. He had the subtle sense of a bloodhound for discovering it, and his rapid eye would fall upon it as it was concealing itself in the columns of a journal or even in the lines of a beautiful book. He would sometimes arrive at such a degree of exasperation from it that he wished to destroy the whole human race.

The misanthropy of his works comes from no other thing. The bitter savour found in them is only that continual discovery of mediocrity, of common-placeness, of foolishness in all its forms. He makes a note of it on every page, in every paragraph, by a word, a simple design, by accenting a scene or a dia-logue. He fills the intelligent reader with melancholy and makes him desolate by proving the folly of human life. The unexplained uneasiness that many people have had on opening the *Sentimental Education,* was only the unreasoned sensation of that eternal stupidity of thought shown openly in skulls.

He said sometimes that he ought to have called that book *Dried Fruits*, in order to make its mean-ing better comprehended. Each man reading it asked himself with uneasiness whether he were not one of those sad personages of that gloomy romance, so much that was intimate and rending did one find in each of the personal statements.

After an enumeration of his grim studies, he wrote one day: "And all this in the unique aim of sputter-ing upon my contemporaries the disgust they inspire in me! I shall finally tell my manner of thought, ex-hale my resentment, vomit my hatred, expectorate my gall, purge my indignation."

This scorn of the exalted idealist for the current stupidity and the customary commonplaceness was accompanied by a vehement admiration for superior people, whatever was their talent or their erudition. Never having loved anything but Thought, he respected it in all its manifestations; and his reading extended into books that would ordinarily seem most foreign to literary art. He became angry with a friendly journal when some one criticised M. Renan adversely in it: the name of Victor Hugo filled him with enthusiasm; his friends were such men as MM. Georges Pouchet and Berthelot; his *salon* in Paris was very curious.

He received there Sundays, from one o'clock until seven, in a very simple bachelor's apartment on the fifth story. The walls were bare and the furniture modest, for he had a horror of the playthings of art.

As soon as a touch of the bell announced the first visitor, he would throw over his work-table (which was covered with scattered leaves of paper black with writing) a light cover of red silk that enveloped and concealed all the implements of his work, which were as sacred to him as the objects of divine service are to a priest. Then, as his domestic nearly always went out on Sunday, he would open the door himself.

The first comer was often Ivan Turgenief, whom he embraced as he would a brother. Larger still than Flaubert, the Russian romance writer loved the French romancer with an affection profound and rare. Affinity in talent, philosophy, and mind, similarity in tastes, in life and in dreams, a conformity in literary tendencies, in exalted idealism, in admiration and erudition, put so many points of contact between these two that on seeing each other they experienced perhaps a still greater joy of heart than joy of intelligence.

Turgenief would sink into an armchair and speak slowly, in a sweet voice, a little feeble and hesitating, which gave to anything he said a charm and an extreme interest. Flaubert would listen religiously, fixing upon the great white face of his friend his large blue eyes with their moving pupils, and respond in his sonorous voice, which came out like the sound of a clarion from under the moustache of an old Gallic warrior. Their conversation rarely touched upon current affairs and scarcely ever got far from literary history. Often Turgenief was laden with foreign books, and would make running translations of Goethe's, Poushkin's, or Swinburne's poems.

Others would arrive, from time to time; M. Taine, his eyes concealed behind his spectacles, of timid gait, carrying historical documents containing unknown facts, all with the odor and savor of stirred-up archives, a vision of ancient life perceived by the piercing eye of philosophy.

Here were MM. Frederic Baudry, a member of the institute and director of the Mazarine Library; Georges Pouchet, professor of comparative anatomy in the Museum of Natural History; Claudius Popelin, the master enameler; Philippe Burty, writer, collector, art critic, of subtle and charming mind.

Then there was Alphonse Daudet, who brought the air of Paris, the living Paris, a lover of pleasure, brisk and gay. He would trace in a few words some infinitely droll silhouettes, walk over each and all with his charming irony, Southern and personal, accentuating the fine points of his lively mind with his attractiveness of face and gesture, as well as with the skill of his recitals, always composed like his written stories. His head, shapely and very fine, was covered with a mass of black hair falling to his shoulders, mingling with his curly beard, the pointed ends of which he often rolled between his fingers. His eye, long in cut but little open, sent forth a look as black as ink, vague sometimes, by reason of excessive short-sightedness. His voice sang a little; his gesture was lively, manner active; in short, he had all the signs of a son of the South.

Émile Zola enters in his turn, breathless from climbing the five stories, and always followed by his faithful son, Paul Alexis. He throws himself into an armchair and seeks, with a glance of his eye over the faces, the state of mind, the tone and nature of the talk. Seated a little at one side, one leg under him, holding his ankle in his hand, and speaking little, he listens attentively. Sometimes when literary enthusiasm, an artists' muddle, carries them away, throwing them into excessive theories and paradoxes so dear to men of lively imagination, he becomes restless, removes the leg, utters, from time to time, a "But—" suppressed in the great uproar; then, when Flaubert's lyric is over, he takes up the discussion tranquilly, in a calm voice and peaceable words. He is of medium height, a little stout, of gentlemanly and obstinate aspect. His head, much like those seen in old Italian paintings, without being beautiful shows a great character of power and intelligence. His short hair springs from a very well developed brow, and the straight nose stops as if cut short by a blow of the shears, too abruptly, above the lip shaded by a rather heavy black moustache. The lower part of the face is full but energetic, and is covered with a trimmed beard almost beautiful. His black, short-sighted, penetrating eye smiles often ironically, while a peculiar fold draws back the upper lip in a droll and mocking fashion.

Some others still arrive; here is the editor, Charpentier. Except for some white hairs among the long black locks, one might take him for a youth. He is a slender and handsome bachelor, with a thin pointed chin shaded blue from the closely shaved beard. He wears only a moustache. He laughs easily with a young and sceptical laugh, listens, and promises all that each writer asks of him, as they seize him and push him into a corner, recommending to him a thousand things. Here is the charming poet, Catulle Mendès, with the face of a sensual, seductive saint, whose silken beard and light hair surround, in a blonde cloud, a fine, pale face. An incomparable talker, a refined artist, subtle, seizing upon all the most fugitive literary sensations, he especially pleases Flaubert by the charm of his words and the delicacy of his mind. Here is Émile Bergerat, his brother-in-law, who married the second daughter of Théophile Gautier. Here is José-Maria Hérédia, that marvellous maker of sonnets, who will live as one of the most perfect poets of his time. Here are Huysmans, Hennique, Céard, and others still, Léon Cladel, the difficult and refined stylist, and Gustave Toudouze.

Then enters, almost always the last, a man of tall, thin figure, whose serious face, although often laughing, shows a great character of a high and noble order. He has long, grayish hair that has a faded appearance, a moustache a little lighter, still, and singular eyes whose pupils are strangely dilated. He has the aspect of a gentleman, that fine, nervous air of people of blood. He is (one can feel it) of the world, and of the best of it. It is Edmond de Goncourt. He advances holding in his hand a package of tobacco which he carefully guards while he extends to his friends his free hand.

The little drawing-room is overflowing. Some groups pass into the dining-room. It is then that one sees Gustave Flaubert.

With large gestures, by which he appears to fly, going about from one to another, crossing the apartment with a single step, his long robe swelling out behind him in his brusque movements like the brown sail of a fishing barque, full of exaltations, indignations, of vehement flames, of resounding eloquence, he amuses with his rage, his good nature, stupefies with his prodigious erudition, to which his surprising memory is an aid, terminates a discussion by a clear, profound word, runs through the centuries at a bound of thought to bring together two facts of the same order, two men of the same race, two lessons of the same nature, whence light would leap out as if flint struck flint.

Then the friends depart, one after another. He accompanies them into the anteroom where they chat a moment, each alone with him, shaking hands vigorously, tapping each other on the shoulder with a good, affectionate laugh. And when Zola, who was the last to leave, was gone, always followed by Paul Alexis, Flaubert slept an hour under a large canopy before changing his coat to call upon his friend, the Princess Mathilde, who received every Sunday.

He loved the world, although he grew indignant over some of the conversation in it; and he had for

3—5

women a tender and paternal friendship, although he judged them severely at a distance and often repeated that phrase of Proudhon's: "Woman is the desolation of the just"; he loved great luxury and sumptuous elegance; it was apparent, although he lived in the most simple manner possible.

Among his intimates he was gay and good. His powerful gayety seemed to have descended directly from the joviality of Rabelais. He loved farces and amusements throughout the whole year. He laughed often, with a contented, frank, deep laugh; and this laugh seemed even more natural to him, and more normal than his exasperation against humanity. He loved to receive his friends and to dine with them. When one went to see him at Croisset it was a great happiness for him, and he prepared the reception beforehand with a cordial and visible pleasure. He was a great eater and loved fine, delicate things for the table.

This sad misanthropy which has been so much spoken of was not innate with him, but came little by little from a permanent realization of human stupidity. His soul was naturally joyous and his heart full of generous impulses. In short, he loved to live and he lived fully, sincerely, as one can live with the French temperament, with which melancholy never takes the same desolating way that it does among certain Germans and certain Englishmen.

And now, is it not sufficient to have loved life with a long and powerful passion? He had it, this passion, until his death. He had given, from his youth up, all his life to letters, and he never took it away. He used his existence in this immoderate, exalted tenderness, passing feverish nights, like a lover, trembling with ardour, falling from fatigue after hours of taxing and violent love, and beginning again each morning from the time of his waking to give his thought to the well-beloved.

Finally, one day he fell, stricken, against the foot of his work-table, killed by HER, by LITERATURE; killed as are all great passionate souls by the passion that fires them.   GUY DE MAUPASSANT.

PREFACE

In 1849 Flaubert, accompanied by his close friend
and ardent admirer, Maxime Ducamp, set out for a
lengthened tour in the East. That they might enjoy
every facility for their expedition, Ducamp succeeded
in obtaining governmental missions of a nominal nature for himself and his companion, Flaubert's charge
being the collection of any information that might be
thought suitable for communication to the Chambers
of Commerce. The two friends journeyed through
Egypt, Nubia, Palestine, Syria, and Rhodes, and so
home through Asia Minor, Turkey in Europe, and
Greece. During all the earlier portions of their travels,
and in spite of the eagerness with which he had
anticipated them, Flaubert displayed only listlessness
and lack of curiosity, though, strange to say, the
scenes which at that time impressed him so slightly
came back to him afterwards with great vividness,
and were of infinite service to him when writing
Salammbô. On arriving in Greece, however, and
finding himself surrounded by those historic scenes
with which books had made him so familiar, a change
came. His enthusiasm was kindled; he began to make
notes; he resolved to write the tale of Thermopylæ;

he laughed at difficulty and hardship, and flung himself, with all the ardour of which his nature was capable, into the enjoyment of the hour. It was a time which dwelt long in his memory; a gleam of light falling across his darkened life, to which in after days he was wont to look back with lingering regret.

On his return to France in 1851 Flaubert resumed his former life at Croisset, a house which had belonged to his father, near Rouen. Here for the most part he lived, working, feeling, remembering, distrusting, until 1857, when his first published work, *Madame Bovary,* made its appearance in the columns of the *Revue de Paris,* a journal established a few years before by some of his own friends. The story of the publication of this pitiless book, the hubbub it created, and the prosecution to which it gave rise, can only be alluded to in passing. A fact, however, to be noted, is that it struck loudly the keynote of a new literary school. Flaubert may be called the creator of realism in modern French literature. For its subsequent development away from and down from himself he is, of course, in no way responsible. Indeed, seeing, as he did, much writing that he despised characterized as "realistic," he shrank from the application of the epithet to his own books. Yet he was wrong. Realism in art is simply minute and impersonal presentation. Part of Flaubert's work was anticipated by his predecessors. Scrupulosity of description is to be found in Balzac. Flaubert, taking up the work where Balzac laid it down, added impersonality and perfected the new literary creed.

It was a cardinal principle with him that to the reader the author should be altogether non-existent, that of his private views and feeling there should be absolutely no trace. Not a phrase, not an epithet must betray him. What he preached was the pure objectivity of literature. He conceived it to be the duty of an author to hold the mirror up to nature, but to be no less his duty sedulously to refrain from adding any comment on the reflections that he obtained. It was no part of art, as art, to teach. Any didactic face that it possessed, whether for good or evil, could inhere only in the facts themselves. And these facts must be scrupulously and faithfully portrayed. Flaubert, then, was undoubtedly a realist, and if we find him at times impatiently repudiating the title, it is because it had come to be frequently applied to men who were clever copyists — unimaginative though faithful presenters of fact — and little if anything more. But Flaubert himself was much more. He was a realist, it is true, but he was a great artist as well, — how great only those possessed of the literary sense and of some poetical feeling can fully know.

There is the same distinction between Flaubert's work and that of many imitators of his method as there is between a waxen figure at Madame Tussaud's and a masterpiece of portraiture by Millais. Both are truthful, both are real, but the one possesses what the other lacks — that power, namely, of stimulating the imagination which differences a picture from a design, or a description from a catalogue. Flaubert was no mere depicter of crude facts. A fact in itself was nothing to him. He held it valuable only in so far as it was capable, in combination with other facts, of assisting to set forth a picture that should be artistic as well as true. His works are constructions, not compilations.

Flaubert's literary ideals were therefore two — Truth and Art — and his devotion to them guided and leavened his whole career. To attain to the first he shrank from no toil, and the subjects of most of his works were such as to render the most arduous toil necessary. His appetite for knowledge was Gargantuan. His researches were extraordinary and were sometimes so recondite as to be superfluous. He would ransack volumes to furnish forth the detail of a phrase, and his books bear testimony to his extraordinary capacity for assimilating and utilising the information that he acquired. Yet his writings are not the products of a pedant. Truth stood high in his estimation, but Art held a higher place still. Indeed he frequently dwelt upon its claims with an almost extravagantly enthusiastic insistence. "What is said is nothing; the manner in which it is said is everything. A work of art which seeks to prove anything fails from that very reason. A fine verse with no meaning is superior to one which is less fine and which has a meaning." And in phrases such as these he frequently and passionately emphasised the necessity of perfection in form.

It is not surprising to find that to Flaubert, with his lofty ideas concerning art, writing was literally an anguish. His distress was no doubt partly the sad effect of nervous disease, and partly the outcome of that natural anxiety felt by many great writers respecting their work, and of the existence of which George Eliot's experience affords a recent proof. To a very large extent, however, it proceeded from a peculiarly eager restlessness after an ideal perfection of form and phrase. "Style" was to him something lofty and almost sacred. As commonly employed the term denotes a manner of writing characteristic of an individual. Flaubert understood it differently. Art, he believed, was impersonal. "Style," accordingly, denoted not one method, but the only method, of expressing a given idea, and it was to the discovery of this intimate relationship between thought and speech that his mighty energies were directed. "Amid all these expressions," he says, "all these forms and all these terms, there is but one expression, one turn, and one form to describe what I wish to say."

The labour bestowed by Flaubert upon the execution of his work, was, therefore, as prodigious as that devoted to the accumulation of material for them. His letters to George Sand are studded with allusions to the "terrors of style," and to his "literary agonies." He considers the writing of twenty pages within a month as an extraordinary feat. He describes his work as being both a pleasure and a torture. He was harassed by an intense longing after an ideal perfection of style. His language must be at once the exact and the harmonious expression of his thought.

Immediately after the publication of *Madame Bovary*, Flaubert set about the writing of *Salammbô*, which appeared in 1862. It is interesting to learn that he had intended his second book to be a reply to those critics who accused him of merely copying what he had seen and of being altogether incapable of invention. "No one," he said, speaking of what he would put into his projected work, "shall accuse me of realism." His purpose, however, was not fulfilled. *Salammbô* is to the full as realistic as *Madame Bovary,* the difference between the two consisting simply in the fact that whereas the author had actually seen the life depicted in the latter, that in the former had to be framed by his imagination out of the materials afforded him by long and painful study.

Salammbô must be regarded as Flaubert's masterpiece. It is the book in which his powers found the freest scope, and in which he is at his best. It was, further, the book for which he himself entertained most affection, and so much was this the case that he would grow angry when people spoke of him as "the author of *Madame Bovary*."

In 1858 he had visited Tunis and the ruins of Carthage in order to prosecute his researches amid the very scenes in which the action of his story was to proceed, while the studies which he undertook to enable him to conjure up so vividly before us the events of a most obscure historical period were, to use a favourite expression of his own, "enormous." His replies to Sainte-Beuve and Frœhner, contained in the appendix in Volume II. of this edition of *Salammbô*, will give some idea of the conscientious care with which he executed his work, and which on this occasion was all the more honourable to him, seeing that the obscurity of his subject and the absence of general information about it, almost invited to a lax exercise of the imagination. He was true to his principles, nevertheless, and was in a position to adduce authorities for every detail in his book, from the name of a god to the epithet given to a precious stone, and from the costume of Salammbô to the ingredients of a medicament. His critics certainly experienced *le quart d'heure de Rabelais* when he took up his pen to reply to them. Had some of them known the man with whom they had to deal, their strictures would have been less sweeping, and they would have regarded him with a feeling of awe similar to that with which the accomplishments of our own Ben Jonson inspired the critics of his day.

It is no small merit in *Salammbô* that all its wealth of detail is rarely oppressive, and that the human interest distinctly dominates throughout.

Of the characters in the book the highest praise has generally been given to Hamilcar. He is certainly a grand creation. There is infinite art displayed in the manner in which his various qualities are contrasted with one another, and at the same time harmonised into a single living whole. His tender affection for his little son, his brutal treatment of his slaves, his generosity to the poor, his commercial dishonesty, his lofty scorn of the Ancients, and his faithless cruelty towards his vanquished foes, are all combined to form a portrait that is both congruous and real. Nevertheless I should, for my own part, be inclined to award the palm to Matho. Nothing could be more excellent than the delineation of this African Hercules. The savage simplicity of his nature is wrought out with marvellous skill. His utter lack of self-consciousness or self-restraint, his passionate tears and groans, his stupefaction at the sight of Salammbô, the fitful play of his moods in the tent scene, his dogged submission to his fate when he realizes that he can never again see the woman that he loves,— all his actions and feelings, from his first appearance in Hamilcar's gardens down to the climax of his great agony in the presence of assembled Carthage, are depicted with a vividness so startling that the man seems to be living before our eyes. Such a character as this finds an excellent foil in the wily Greek,

Spendius. Subtle, keen-witted, audacious, cowardly, he contrasts in every way with the simple, one-idead, brutally-brave Libyan, who, save on the one occasion when the ardour of his passion bears down all attempts at opposition, is as wax in his hands. Some of Flaubert's most artistic touches are to be found in the contrasts suggested between these two widely different natures.

Salammbô herself is the only unsatisfactory character in the book. She is an enigma. Flaubert himself recognised this, but the plea which he urged in excuse can scarcely be admitted. It may be true that we can have no intimate knowledge of the Eastern woman, but nevertheless if the actions of one are to be described at all, there should surely be some attempt to indicate their motives. Respecting Salammbô's motives, however, we are left altogether in the dark. Her earlier conduct, indeed, is not wholly unintelligible. Her secluded life and burning religious enthusiasm might perhaps have induced that semi-ecstatic state which apparently is hers, a condition which almost defies analysis, and in which actions seem to be the creatures of wholly unaccountable impulses. But the description of her behaviour subsequent to her disillusion is disappointing. There are incidents that seem to denote the dull, purposeless atony of despair, and others that point to a loss of religious faith. The gradual growth of a tender feeling towards Matho is also hinted at, but all is left in provoking uncertainty, and if her conduct is not inexplicable it is certainly not explained. Yet, in spite of all its defects, the portrait of Salammbô is a striking one. In the gardens among the soldiers, on the terrace invoking Tanith, with Matho in the tent, or bending down in the last scene towards the tortured man whose life she would now gladly save, she is very real to us. She may perplex us but she certainly lives. She is at once as vivid and as incomprehensible as a dream.

The world in which these characters move is brought before us with a realism that is a triumph of art. We feel indeed as if we had been transported bodily into a new region. We are given no vague description of what once has been. We are placed in the centre of what, for the time being, actually is. The surroundings are by no means pleasant ones, it is true, and it is very possible to sympathise with the feeling which prompted Sainte-Beuve to declare that the atmosphere irritated him, and to deplore the absence of some character who might have bridged over the gulf lying between the ideas of Modern Europe and those of Ancient Carthage. Yet the existence of this very feeling is a testimony to Flaubert's artistic skill. The people whom we are called upon to contemplate revolt us at every turn, but there is that in them, nevertheless, which compels us to recognise that they are our own flesh and blood. The inhuman humanity of the book tries us often as we read, but the pain that it causes us is in itself a proof of the author's realistic power.

Nothing can in fact exceed the vividness of the scenes described. Flaubert excels himself in this work as a *metteur en scène*. The bustling, selfish, immoral, superstitious town seems to live before us. The brutal, unsophisticated, credulous Mercenaries stare us in the face. We reel with the Barbarians at their feast; we hold our breath in agony as Matho makes his wondrous escape; we can see every incident in the siege; we shudder at the horrors of the Pass, and we are harrowed almost beyond endurance by the spectacle of Matho's terrible end.

It would be a graceless task to dwell upon the faults in such a book as this. Faults, of course, there are, for the greatest artist cannot command complete success. There are some improbabilities in the story, the most notable of which is, perhaps, Hanno's escape from the camp at Sicca. Occasionally, too, insufficient regard is paid to the necessity of perspective, and the elaboration of detail for the purpose of producing a realistic effect is carried to an extreme which defeats its own object. Instances are the disaster to the woman and child in Chapter XIII., and the contest for the rat in Chapter IX. But, after all, the scratches at the base of a cathedral do not detract from the grandeur of the pile, and in spite of such relatively microscopic blemishes, *Salammbô* is a work which will always be noted for its grand simplicity and purity of diction, its artistic construction, its dramatic force, and its truth to humanity.

SALAMMBÔ

I.

THE FEAST.

IT WAS at Megara, a suburb of Carthage, in the gardens of Hamilcar. The soldiers whom he had commanded in Sicily were having a great feast to celebrate the anniversary of the battle of Eryx, and as the master was away, and they were numerous, they ate and drank with perfect freedom.

The captains, who wore bronze cothurni, had placed themselves in the central path, beneath a gold-fringed purple awning, which reached from the wall of the stables to the first terrace of the palace; the common soldiers were scattered beneath the trees, where numerous flat-roofed buildings might be seen, wine-presses, cellars, storehouses, bakeries, and arsenals, with a court for elephants, dens for wild beasts, and a prison for slaves.

Fig-trees surrounded the kitchens; a wood of sycamores stretched away to meet masses of verdure, where the pomegranate shone amid the white tufts of the cotton-plant; vines, grape-laden, grew up into the branches of the pines; a field of roses bloomed beneath the plane-trees; here and there lilies rocked upon the turf; the paths were strewn with black sand mingled with powdered coral, and in the centre the avenue of cypress formed, as it were, a double colonnade of green obelisks from one extremity to the other.

Far in the background stood the palace, built of yellow mottled Numidian marble, broad courses supporting its four terraced stories. With its large, straight, ebony staircase, bearing the prow of a vanquished galley at the corners of every step, its red doors quartered with black crosses, its brass gratings protecting it from scorpions below, and its trellises of gilded rods closing the apertures above, it seemed to the soldiers in its haughty opulence as solemn and impenetrable as the face of Hamilcar.

The Council had appointed his house for the holding of this feast; the convalescents lying in the temple of Eschmoun had set out at daybreak and dragged themselves thither on their crutches. Every minute others were arriving. They poured in ceaselessly by every path like torrents rushing into a lake; through the trees the slaves of the kitchens might be seen running scared and half-naked; the gazelles fled bleating on the lawns; the sun was setting, and the perfume of citron trees rendered the exhalation from the perspiring crowd heavier still.

Men of all nations were there, Ligurians, Lusitanians, Balearians, Negroes, and fugitives from Rome. Beside the heavy Dorian dialect were audible the resonant Celtic syllables rattling like chariots of war, while Ionian terminations conflicted with consonants reflections with amazement, and grimacing to make themselves laugh. They tossed the ivory stools and golden spatulas to one another across the tables. They gulped down all the Greek wines in their leathern bottles, the Campanian wines enclosed in amphoras, the Cantabrian wines brought in casks, with the wines of the jujube, cinnamomum and lotus. There were pools of these on the ground that made the foot slip. The smoke of the meats ascended into the foliage with the vapour of the breath. Simultaneously were heard the snapping of jaws, the noise of speech, songs, and cups, the crash of Campanian vases shivering into a thousand pieces, or the limpid sound of a large silver dish.

In proportion as their intoxication increased they more and more recalled the injustice of Carthage. The Republic, in fact, exhausted by the war, had allowed all the returning bands to accumulate in the town. Gisco, their general, had however been prudent enough to send them back severally in order to facilitate the liquidation of their pay, and the Council had believed that they would in the end consent to some reduction. But at present ill-will was caused by the inability to pay them. This debt was confused in the minds of the people with the 3200 Euboic talents exacted by Lutatius, and equally with Rome they were regarded as enemies to Carthage. The Mercenaries understood this, and their indignation found vent in threats and outbreaks. At last they demanded permission to assemble to celebrate one of their victories, and the peace party yielded, at the same time revenging themselves on Hamilcar who had so strongly upheld the war. It had been terminated notwithstanding all his efforts, so that, despairing of Carthage, he had entrusted the government of the Mercenaries to Gisco. To appoint his palace for their reception was to draw upon him something of the hatred that was borne to them. Moreover, the expense must be excessive, and he would incur nearly the whole.

Proud of having brought the Republic to submit, the Mercenaries thought that they were at last about to return to their homes with the payment for their blood in the hoods of their cloaks. But as seen through the mists of intoxication, their fatigues seemed to them prodigious and but ill-rewarded. They showed one another their wounds, they told of their combats, their travels and the hunting in their native lands. They imitated the cries and the leaps of wild beasts. Then came unclean wagers; they buried their heads in the amphoras and drank on without interruption, like thirsty dromedaries. A Lusitanian of gigantic stature ran over the tables, carrying a man in each hand at arm's length, and spitting out fire through his nostrils. Some Lacedæmonians, who had not taken off their cuirasses, were leaping with a heavy step. Some advanced like women, making obscene gestures; others stripped naked to fight amid the cups after the fashion of gladiators, and a company of Greeks danced around a vase whereon nymphs were to be seen, while a negro tapped with an ox-bone on a brazen buckler.

Suddenly they heard a plaintive song, a song loud and soft, rising and falling in the air like the wing-beating of a wounded bird.

It was the voice of the slaves in the ergastulum. Some soldiers rose at a bound to release them and disappeared.

They returned, driving forward through the dust amid shouts, twenty men, distinguished by their greater paleness of face. Small black felt caps of conical shape covered their shaven heads; they all wore wooden shoes, and yet made a noise as of old iron like driving chariots.

They reached the avenue of cypress, where they were lost among the crowd of those questioning them. One of them had remained apart, standing. Through the rents in his tunic his shoulders could be seen striped with long scars. Drooping his chin, he looked round him with distrust, closing his eyelids somewhat against the dazzling light of the torches, but when he saw that none of the armed men were unfriendly to him, a great sigh escaped from his breast; he stammered, he sneered through the bright tears that bathed his face. At last he seized a brimming cantharus by its rings, raised it straight up into the air with his outstretched arms, from which his chains hung down, and then looking to heaven, and still holding the cup he said:

"Hail first to thee, Baal-Eschmoun, the deliverer, whom the people of my country call Æsculapius! and to you, genii of the fountains, light, and woods! and to you, ye gods hidden beneath the mountains and in the caverns of the earth! and to you, strong men in shining armour who have set me free!"

Then he let fall the cup and related his history. He was called Spendius. The Carthaginians had taken him in the battle of Æginusæ, and he thanked the Mercenaries once more in Greek, Ligurian and Punic; he kissed their hands; finally he congratulated them on the banquet, while expressing his surprise at not perceiving the cups of the Sacred Legion.

These cups, which bore an emerald vine on each of
their six golden faces, belonged to a corps composed
exclusively of young patricians of the tallest stature.
They were a privilege, almost a sacerdotal distinction,
and accordingly nothing among the treasures of the
Republic was more coveted by the Mercenaries.
They detested the Legion on this account, and some
of them had been known to risk their lives for the
inconceivable pleasure of drinking out of these cups.

Accordingly they commanded that the cups should
be brought. They were in the keeping of the Syssitia, companies of traders, who had a common table.
The slaves returned. At that hour all the members
of the Syssitia were asleep.

"Let them be awakened!" responded the Mercenaries.

After a second excursion it was explained to them
that the cups were shut up in a temple.

"Let it be opened!" they replied.

And when the slaves confessed with trembling
that they were in the possession of Gisco, the general, they cried out:

"Let him bring them!"

Gisco soon appeared at the far end of the garden
with an escort of the Sacred Legion. His full, black
cloak, which was fastened on his head to a golden
mitre starred with precious stones, and which hung
all about him down to his horse's hoofs, blended in
the distance with the colour of the night. His white
beard, the radiancy of his head-dress, and his triple
necklace of broad blue plates beating against his
breast, were alone visible.

When he entered, the soldiers greeted him with
loud shouts, all crying:

"The cups! The cups!"

He began by declaring that if reference were had to their courage, they were worthy of them.

The crowd applauded and howled with joy.

He knew it, he who had commanded them over yonder, and had returned with the last cohort in the last galley!

"True! True!" said they.

Nevertheless, Gisco continued, the Republic had respected their national divisions, their customs, and their modes of worship; in Carthage they were free! As to the cups of the Sacred Legion, they were private property. Suddenly a Gaul, who was close to Spendius, sprang over the tables and ran straight up to Gisco, gesticulating and threatening him with two naked swords.

Without interrupting his speech, the General struck him on the head with his heavy ivory staff, and the Barbarian fell. The Gauls howled, and their frenzy, which was spreading to the others, would soon have swept away the legionaries. Gisco shrugged his shoulders as he saw them growing pale. He thought that his courage would be useless against these exasperated brute beasts. It would be better to revenge himself upon them by some artifice later; accordingly, he signed to his soldiers and slowly withdrew. Then, turning in the gateway towards the Mercenaries, he cried to them that they would repent of it.

The feast recommenced. But Gisco might return, and by surrounding the suburb, which was beside the last ramparts, might crush them against the walls. Then they felt themselves alone in spite of their crowd, and the great town sleeping beneath them in the shade suddenly made them afraid, with its piles

of staircases, its lofty black houses, and its vague
gods fiercer even than its people. In the distance a
few ships'-lanterns were gliding across the harbour,
and there were lights in the temple of Khamon.
They thought of Hamilcar. Where was he? Why
had he forsaken them when peace was concluded?
His differences with the Council were doubtless but a
pretence in order to destroy them. Their unsatisfied
hate recoiled upon him, and they cursed him, exasperating one another with their own anger. At this
juncture they collected together beneath the plane-
trees to see a slave who, with eyeballs fixed, neck
contorted, and lips covered with foam, was rolling on
the ground, and beating the soil with his limbs.
Some one cried out that he was poisoned. All then
believed themselves poisoned. They fell upon the
slaves, a terrible clamour was raised, and a vertigo
of destruction came like a whirlwind upon the drunken
army. They struck about them at random, they
smashed, they slew; some hurled torches into the
foliage; others, leaning over the lions' balustrade,
massacred the animals with arrows; the most daring
ran to the elephants, desiring to cut down their
trunks and eat ivory.

Some Balearic slingers, however, who had gone
round the corner of the palace, in order to pillage
more conveniently, were checked by a lofty barrier,
made of Indian cane. They cut the lock-straps with
their daggers, and then found themselves beneath the
front that faced Carthage, in another garden full of
trimmed vegetation. Lines of white flowers all following one another in regular succession formed long
parabolas like star-rockets on the azure-coloured earth.
The gloomy bushes exhaled warm and honied odours.

There were trunks of trees smeared with cinnabar, which resembled columns covered with blood. In the centre were twelve pedestals, each supporting a great glass ball, and these hollow globes were indistinctly filled with reddish lights, like enormous and still palpitating eyeballs. The soldiers lighted themselves with torches as they stumbled on the slope of the deeply laboured soil.

But they perceived a little lake divided into several basins by walls of blue stones. So limpid was the wave that the flames of the torches quivered in it at the very bottom, on a bed of white pebbles and golden dust. It began to bubble, luminous spangles glided past, and great fish with gems about their mouths, appeared near the surface.

With much laughter the soldiers slipped their fingers into the gills, and brought them to the tables. They were the fish of the Barca family, and were all descended from those primordial lotes which had hatched the mystic egg wherein the goddess was concealed. The idea of committing a sacrilege revived the greediness of the Mercenaries; they speedily placed fire beneath some brazen vases, and amused themselves by watching the beautiful fish struggling in the boiling water.

The surge of soldiers pressed on. They were no longer afraid. They commenced to drink again. Their ragged tunics were wet with the perfumes that flowed in large drops from their foreheads, and resting both fists on the tables, which seemed to them to be rocking like ships, they rolled their great drunken eyes around to devour by sight what they could not take. Others walked amid the dishes on the purple table covers, breaking ivory stools, and phials of

Tyrian glass to pieces with their feet. Songs mingled with the death-rattle of the slaves expiring amid the broken cups. They demanded wine, meat, gold. They cried out for women. They raved in a hundred languages. Some thought that they were at the vapour baths on account of the steam which floated around them, or else, catching sight of the foliage, imagined that they were at the chase, and rushed upon their companions as upon wild beasts. The conflagration spread to all the trees, one after another, and the lofty mosses of verdure, emitting long white spirals, looked like volcanoes beginning to smoke. The clamour redoubled; the wounded lions roared in the shade.

In an instant the highest terrace of the palace was illuminated, the central door opened, and a woman, Hamilcar's daughter herself, clothed in black garments, appeared on the threshold. She descended the first staircase, which ran obliquely along the first story, then the second, and the third, and stopped on the last terrace at the head of the galley staircase. Motionless and with head bent, she gazed upon the soldiers.

Behind her, on each side, were two long shadows of pale men, clad in white, red-fringed robes, which fell straight to their feet. They had no beard, no hair, no eyebrows. In their hands, which sparkled with rings, they carried enormous lyres, and with shrill voice they all sang a hymn to the divinity of Carthage. They were the eunuch priests of the temple of Tanith, who were often summoned by Salammbô to her house.

At last she descended the galley staircase. The priests followed her. She advanced into the avenue of cypress, and walked slowly through the tables of the captains, who drew back somewhat as they watched her pass.

Her hair, which was powdered with violet sand, and combined into the form of a tower, after the fashion of the Chanaanite maidens, added to her height. Tresses of pearls were fastened to her temples, and fell to the corners of her mouth, which was as rosy as a half-open pomegranate. On her breast was a collection of luminous stones, their variegation imitating the scales of the murena. Her arms were adorned with diamonds, and issued naked from her sleeveless tunic, which was starred with red flowers on a perfectly black ground. Between her ankles she wore a golden chainlet to regulate her steps, and her large dark purple mantle, cut of an unknown material, trailed behind her, making, as it were, at each step, a broad wave which followed her.

The priests played nearly stifled chords on their lyres from time to time, and in the intervals of the music might be heard the tinkling of the little golden chain, and the regular patter of her papyrus sandals.

No one as yet was acquainted with her. It was only known that she led a retired life, engaged in pious practices. Some soldiers had seen her in the night on the summit of her palace kneeling before the stars amid the eddyings from kindled perfuming-pans. It was the moon that had made her so pale, and there was something from the gods that enveloped her like a subtle vapour. Her eyes seemed to gaze far beyond terrestrial space. She bent her head as she walked, and in her right hand she carried a little ebony lyre.

They heard her murmur:

"Dead! All dead! No more will you come obedient to my voice as when, seated on the edge of the lake, I used to throw seeds of the watermelon into your mouths! The mystery of Tanith ranged in the depths of your eyes that were more limpid than the globules of rivers." And she called them by their names, which were those of the months — "Siv! Sivan! Tammouz, Eloul, Tischri, Schebar! Ah! have pity on me, goddess!"

The soldiers thronged about her without understanding what she said. They wondered at her attire, but she turned a long frightened look upon them all, then sinking her head beneath her shoulders, and waving her arms, she repeated several times:

"What have you done? what have you done?"

"Yet you had bread, and meats and oil, and all the malobathrum of the granaries for your enjoyment! I had brought oxen from Hecatompylos; I had sent hunters into the desert!" Her voice swelled; her cheeks purpled. She added, "Where, pray, are you now? In a conquered town, or in the palace of a master? And what master? Hamilcar the Suffet, my father, the servant of the Baals! It was he who withheld from Lutatius those arms of yours, red now with the blood of his slaves! Know you of any in your own lands more skilled in the conduct of battles? Look! our palace steps are encumbered with our victories! Ah! desist not! burn it! I will carry away with me the genius of my house, my black serpent slumbering up yonder on lotus leaves! I will whistle and he will follow me, and if I embark in a galley he will speed in the wake of my ship over the foam of the waves."

Her delicate nostrils were quivering. She crushed her nails against the gems on her bosom. Her eyes drooped, and she resumed:

"Ah! poor Carthage! lamentable city! No longer hast thou for thy protection the strong men of former days who went beyond the oceans to build temples on their shores. All the lands laboured about thee, and the sea-plains, ploughed by thine oars, rocked with thy harvests." Then she began to sing the adventures of Melkarth, the god of the Sidonians, and the father of her family.

She told of the ascent of the mountains of Ersiphonia, the journey to Tartessus, and the war against Masisabal to avenge the queen of the serpents:

"He pursued the female monster, whose tail undulated over the dead leaves like a silver brook, into the forest, and came to a plain where women with dragon-croups were round a great fire, standing erect on the points of their tails. The blood-coloured moon was shining within a pale circle, and their scarlet tongues, cloven like the harpoons of fishermen, reached curling forth to the very edge of the flame."

Then Salammbô, without pausing, related how Melkarth, after vanquishing Masisabal, placed her severed head on the prow of his ship. "At each throb of the waves it sank beneath the foam, but the sun embalmed it; it became harder than gold; nevertheless the eyes ceased not to weep, and the tears fell into the water continually."

She sang all this in an old Chanaanite idiom, which the Barbarians did not understand. They asked one another what she could be saying to them with those frightful gestures which accompanied her speech, and mounted round about her on the tables, beds, and sycamore boughs, they strove with open mouths and craned necks to grasp the vague stories hovering before their imaginations, through the dimness of the theogonies, like phantoms wrapped in cloud.

Only the beardless priests understood Salammbô; their wrinkled hands, which hung over the strings of their lyres, quivered, and from time to time they would draw forth a mournful chord; for, feebler than old women, they trembled at once with mystic emotion, and with the fear inspired by men. The Barbarians heeded them not, but listened continually to the maiden's song.

None gazed at her like a young Numidian chief, who was placed at the captains' tables among soldiers of his own nation. His girdle so bristled with darts that it formed a swelling in his ample cloak, which was fastened on his temples with a leather lace. The cloth parted asunder as it fell upon his shoulders, and enveloped his countenance in shadow, so that only the fires of his two fixed eyes could be seen. It was by chance that he was at the feast, his father having domiciled him with the Barca family, according to the custom by which kings used to send their children into the households of the great in order to pave the way for alliances; but Narr' Havas had lodged there for six months without having hitherto seen Salammbô, and now, seated on his heels, with his head brushing the handles of his javelins, he was watching her with dilated nostrils, like a leopard crouching among the bamboos.

On the other side of the tables was a Libyan of colossal stature, and with short black curly hair. He had retained only his military jacket, the brass plates of which were tearing the purple of the couch. A necklace of silver moons was tangled in his hairy breast. His face was stained with splashes of blood; he was leaning on his left elbow with a smile on his large, open mouth.

Salammbô had abandoned the sacred rhythm. With a woman's subtlety she was simultaneously employing all the dialects of the Barbarians in order to appease their anger. To the Greeks she spoke Greek; then she turned to the Ligurians, the Campanians, the Negroes, and listening to her each one found again in her voice the sweetness of his native land. She now, carried away by the memories of Carthage, sang of the ancient battles against Rome; they applauded. She kindled at the gleaming of the naked swords, and cried aloud with outstretched arms. Her lyre fell, she was silent; and, pressing both hands upon her heart, she remained for some minutes with closed eyelids enjoying the agitation of all these men.

Matho, the Libyan, leaned over towards her. Involuntarily she approached him, and impelled by grateful pride, poured him a long stream of wine into a golden cup in order to conciliate the army.

"Drink!" she said.

He took the cup, and was carrying it to his lips when a Gaul, the same that had been hurt by Gisco, struck him on the shoulder, while in a jovial manner he gave utterance to pleasantries in his native tongue. Spendius was not far off, and he volunteered to interpret them.

"Speak!" said Matho.

"The gods protect you; you are going to become rich. When will the nuptials be?"

"What nuptials?"

"Yours! for with us," said the Gaul, "when a woman gives drink to a soldier, it means that she offers him her couch."

He had not finished when Narr' Havas, with a bound, drew a javelin from his girdle, and, leaning his right foot upon the edge of the table, hurled it against Matho.

The javelin whistled among the cups, and piercing the Libyan's arm, pinned it so firmly to the cloth, that the shaft quivered in the air.

Matho quickly plucked it out; but he was weaponless and naked; at last he lifted the over-laden table with both arms, and flung it against Narr' Havas into the very centre of the crowd that rushed between them. The soldiers and Numidians pressed together so closely that they were unable to draw their swords. Matho advanced dealing great blows with his head. When he raised it, Narr' Havas had disappeared. He sought for him with his eyes. Salammbô also was gone.

Then directing his looks to the palace he perceived the red door with the black cross closing far above, and he darted away.

They saw him run between the prows of the galleys, and then reappear along the three staircases until he reached the red door against which he dashed his whole body. Panting, he leaned against the wall to keep himself from falling.

But a man had followed him, and through the darkness, for the lights of the feast were hidden by the corner of the palace, he recognised Spendius.

"Begone!" said he.

The slave without replying began to tear his tunic with his teeth; then kneeling beside Matho he ten-

derly took his arm, and felt it in the shadow to discover the wound.

By a ray of the moon which was then gliding
between the clouds, Spendius perceived a gaping
wound in the middle of the arm. He rolled the
piece of stuff all around it, but the other said irri-
tably, "Leave me! leave me!"

"Oh no!" replied the slave. "You released me
from the ergastulum. I am yours! you are my master! command me!"

Matho walked round the terrace brushing against
the walls. He strained his ears at every step,
glancing down into the silent apartments through the
spaces between the gilded reeds. At last he stopped
with a look of despair.

"Listen!" said the slave to him. "Oh! do not
despise me for my feebleness! I have lived in the
palace. I can wind like a viper through the walls.
Come! in the Ancestors' Chamber there is an ingot
of gold beneath every flagstone; an underground path
leads to their tombs."

"Well! what matters it?" said Matho.

Spendius was silent.

They were on the terrace. A huge mass of shadow
stretched before them, appearing as if it contained
vague accumulations, like the gigantic billows of a
black and petrified ocean.

But a luminous bar rose towards the East; far
below, on the left, the canals of Megara were beginning to stripe the verdure of the gardens with their
windings of white. The conical roofs of the heptag-
onal temples, the staircases, terraces, and ramparts
were being carved by degrees upon the paleness of
the dawn; and a girdle of white foam rocked around

the Carthaginian peninsula, while the emerald sea appeared as if it were curdled in the freshness of the morning. Then as the rosy sky grew larger, the lofty houses, bending over the sloping soil, reared and massed themselves like a herd of black goats coming down from the mountains. The deserted streets lengthened; the palm-trees that topped the walls here and there were motionless; the brimming cisterns seemed like silver bucklers lost in the courts; the beacon on the promontory of Hermæum was beginning to grow pale. The horses of Eschmoun, on the very summit of the Acropolis in the cypress wood, feeling that the light was coming, placed their hoofs on the marble parapet, and neighed towards the sun.

It appeared, and Spendius raised his arms with a cry.

Everything stirred in a diffusion of red, for the god, as if he were rending himself, now poured full-rayed upon Carthage the golden rain of his veins. The beaks of the galleys sparkled, the roof of Khamon appeared to be all in flames, while far within the temples, whose doors were opening, glimmerings of light could be seen. Large chariots, arriving from the country, rolled their wheels over the flagstones in the streets. Dromedaries, baggage-laden, came down the ramps. Money-changers raised the pent-houses of their shops at the cross ways, storks took to flight, white sails fluttered. In the wood of Tanith might be heard the tambourines of the sacred courtesans, and the furnaces for baking the clay coffins were beginning to smoke on the Mappalian point.

Spendius leaned over the terrace; his teeth chattered and he repeated:

"Ah! yes — yes — master! I understand why you scorned the pillage of the house just now."

Matho was as if he had just been awaked by the hissing of his voice, and did not seem to understand. Spendius resumed:

"Ah! what riches! and the men who possess them have not even the steel to defend them!"

Then, pointing with his right arm outstretched to some of the populace who were crawling on the sand outside the mole to look for gold dust:

"See!" he said to him, "the Republic is like these wretches: bending on the brink of the ocean, she buries her greedy arms in every shore, and the noise of the billows so fills her ear that she cannot hear behind her the tread of a master's heel!"

He drew Matho to quite the other end of the terrace, and showed him the garden, wherein the soldiers' swords, hanging on the trees, were like mirrors in the sun:

"But here there are strong men whose hatred is roused! and nothing binds them to Carthage, neither families, oaths nor gods!"

Matho remained leaning against the wall; Spendius came close, and continued in a low voice:

"Do you understand me, soldier? We should walk purple-clad like satraps. We should bathe in perfumes; and I should in turn have slaves! Are you not weary of sleeping on the hard ground, of drinking the vinegar of the camps, and of continually hearing the trumpet? But you will rest later, will you not? When they pull off your cuirass to cast your corpse to the vultures! or perhaps blind, lame, and weak you will go, leaning on a stick, from door to door to tell of your youth to pickle-sellers and little children. Remember all the injustice of your chiefs, the campings in the snow, the marchings in the sun, the tyrannies of discipline, and the everlasting menace of the cross! And after all this misery they have given you a necklace of honour, as they hang a girdle of bells round the breast of an ass to deafen it on its journey, and prevent it from feeling fatigue. A man like you, braver than Pyrrhus! If only you had wished it! Ah! how happy will you be in large cool halls, with the sound of lyres, lying on flowers, with women and buffoons! Do not tell me that the enterprise is impossible. Have not the Mercenaries already possessed Rhegium and other fortified places in Italy? Who is to prevent you? Hamilcar is away; the people execrate the rich; Gisco can do nothing with the cowards who surround him. But you are brave! and they will obey you. Command them! Carthage is ours; let us fall upon it!"

"No!" said Matho, "the curse of Moloch weighs upon me. I felt it in her eyes, and just now I saw a black ram retreating in a temple." Looking around him he added: "But where is she?"

Then Spendius understood that a great disquiet possessed him, and did not venture to speak again.

The trees behind them were still smoking; half-burned carcasses of apes dropped from their blackened boughs from time to time into the midst of the dishes. Drunken soldiers snored open-mouthed by the side of the corpses, and those who were not asleep lowered their heads dazzled by the light of day. The trampled soil was hidden beneath splashes of red. The elephants poised their bleeding trunks between the stakes of their pens. In the open granaries might be seen sacks of spilled wheat, below the gate was a thick line of chariots which had been heaped up by the Barbarians, and the peacocks perched in the cedars were spreading their tails and beginning to utter their cry.

Matho's immobility, however, astonished Spendius; he was even paler than he had recently been, and he was following something on the horizon with fixed eyeballs, and with both fists resting on the edge of the terrace. Spendius couched down, and so at last discovered at what he was gazing. In the distance a golden speck was turning in the dust on the road to Utica; it was the nave of a chariot drawn by two mules; a slave was running at the end of the pole, and holding them by the bridle. Two women were seated in the chariot. The manes of the animals were puffed between their ears after the Persian fashion, beneath a network of blue pearls. Spendius recognised them, and restrained a cry.

A large veil floated behind in the wind.

II.

AT SICCA.

TWO days afterwards the Mercenaries left Carthage.

They had each received a piece of gold on the condition that they should go into camp at Sicca, and they had been told with all sorts of caresses:

"You are the saviours of Carthage! But you would starve it if you remained there; it would become insolvent. Withdraw! The Republic will be grateful to you later for all this condescension. We are going to levy taxes immediately; your pay shall be in full, and galleys shall be equipped to take you back to your native lands."

They did not know how to reply to all this talk. These men, accustomed as they were to war, were wearied by residence in a town; there was no difficulty in convincing them, and the people mounted the walls to see them go away.

They defiled through the street of Khamon, and the Cirta gate, pell-mell, archers with hoplites, captains with soldiers, Lusitanians with Greeks. They marched with a bold step, rattling their heavy cothurni

on the paving stones. Their armour was dinted by
the catapult, and their faces blackened by the sun-
burn of battles. Hoarse cries issued from their thick
beards, their tattered coats of mail flapped upon
the pommels of their swords, and through the holes
in the brass might be seen their naked limbs, as
frightful as engines of war. Sarissæ, axes, spears, felt
caps and bronze helmets, all swung together with a
single motion. They filled the street thickly enough
to have made the walls crack, and the long mass of
armed soldiers overflowed between the lofty bitumen-
smeared houses six storys high. Behind their gratings
of iron or reed the women, with veiled heads, silently
watched the Barbarians pass.

The terraces, fortifications, and walls were hidden
beneath the crowd of Carthaginians, who were dressed
in garments of black. The sailors' tunics showed
like drops of blood among the dark multitude, and
nearly naked children, whose skin shone beneath
their copper bracelets, gesticulated in the foliage of
the columns, or amid the branches of a palm tree.
Some of the Ancients were posted on the platform of
the towers, and people did not know why a personage with a long beard stood thus in a dreamy attitude here and there. He appeared in the distance
against the background of the sky, vague as a
phantom and motionless as stone.

All, however, were oppressed with the same anxiety; it was feared that the Barbarians, seeing themselves so strong, might take a fancy to stay. But
they were leaving with so much good faith that the
Carthaginians grew bold and mingled with the soldiers. They overwhelmed them with protestations
and embraces. Some with exaggerated politeness

and audacious hypocrisy even sought to induce them
not to leave the city. They threw perfumes, flowers,
and pieces of silver to them. They gave them amu-
lets to avert sickness; but they had spit upon them
three times to attract death, or had enclosed jackal's
hair within them to put cowardice into their hearts.
Aloud, they invoked Melkarth's favour, and in a
whisper, his curse.

Then came the mob of baggage, beasts of burden,
and stragglers. The sick groaned on the backs of
dromedaries, while others limped along leaning on
broken pikes. The drunkards carried leathern bottles,
and the greedy quarters of meat, cakes, fruits, butter
wrapped in fig leaves, and snow in linen bags.
Some were to be seen with parasols in their hands,
and parrots on their shoulders. They had mastiffs,
gazelles, and panthers following behind them. Women
of Libyan race, mounted on asses, inveighed against
the Negresses who had forsaken the lupanaria of
Malqua for the soldiers; many of them were suckling
children suspended on their bosoms by leathern
thongs. The mules were goaded on at the point of
the sword, their backs bending beneath the load of
tents, while there were numbers of serving-men and
water-carriers, emaciated, jaundiced with fever, and
filthy with vermin, the scum of the Carthaginian
populace, who had attached themselves to the Barbarians.

When they had passed, the gates were shut behind them, but the people did not descend from the
walls. The army soon spread over the breadth of
the isthmus.

It parted into unequal masses. Then the lances
appeared like tall blades of grass, and finally all was

lost in a train of dust; those of the soldiers who looked back towards Carthage could now only see its long walls with their vacant battlements cut out against the edge of the sky.

Then the Barbarians heard a great shout. They thought that some from among them (for they did not know their own number) had remained in the town, and were amusing themselves by pillaging a temple. They laughed a great deal at the idea of this, and then continued their journey.

They were rejoiced to find themselves, as in former days, marching all together in the open country; and some of the Greeks sang the old song of the Mamertines:

"With my lance and sword I plough and reap; I am master of the house! The disarmed man falls at my feet and calls me Lord and Great King."

They shouted, they leaped, the merriest began to tell stories; the time of their miseries was past. As they arrived at Tunis, some of them remarked that a troop of Balearic slingers was missing. They were doubtless not far off; and no further heed was paid to them.

Some went to lodge in the houses, others camped at the foot of the walls, and the townspeople came out to chat with the soldiers.

During the whole night fires were seen burning on the horizon in the direction of Carthage; the light stretched like giant torches across the motionless lake. No one in the army could tell what festival was being celebrated.

On the following day the Barbarians passed through a region that was covered with cultivation. The domains of the patricians succeeded one another along the border of the route; channels of water flowed through woods of palm; there were long, green lines of olive-trees; rose-coloured vapours floated in the gorges of the hills, while blue mountains reared themselves behind. A warm wind was blowing. Chameleons were crawling on the broad leaves of the cactus.

The Barbarians slackened their speed.

They marched on in isolated detachments, or lagged behind one another at long intervals. They ate grapes along the margin of the vines. They lay on the grass and gazed with stupefaction upon the large, artificially twisted horns of the oxen, the sheep clothed with skins to protect their wool, the furrows crossing one another so as to form lozenges, and the ploughshares like ships' anchors, with the pomegranate trees that were watered with silphium. Such wealth of the soil and such inventions of wisdom dazzled them.

In the evening they stretched themselves on the tents without unfolding them; and thought with regret of Hamilcar's feast, as they fell asleep with their faces towards the stars.

In the middle of the following day they halted on the bank of a river, amid clumps of rose-bays. Then they quickly threw aside lances, bucklers and belts. They bathed with shouts, and drew water in their helmets, while others drank lying flat on their stomachs, and all in the midst of the beasts of burden whose baggage was slipping from them.

Spendius, who was seated on a dromedary stolen in Hamilcar's parks, perceived Matho at a distance, with his arm hanging against his breast, his head bare, and his face bent down, giving his mule drink, and watching the water flow. Spendius immediately ran through the crowd calling him, "Master! master!"

Matho gave him but scant thanks for his blessings, but Spendius paid no heed to this, and began to march behind him, from time to time turning restless glances in the direction of Carthage.

He was the son of a Greek rhetor and a Campanian prostitute. He had at first grown rich by dealing in women; then, ruined by a shipwreck, he had made war against the Romans with the herdsmen of Samnium. He had been taken and had escaped; he had been retaken, and had worked in the quarries, panted in the vapour-baths, shrieked under torture, passed through the hands of many masters, and experienced every frenzy. At last, one day, in despair, he had flung himself into the sea from the top of a trireme where he was working at the oar. Some of Hamilcar's sailors had picked him up when at the point of death, and had brought him to the ergastulum of Megara, at Carthage. But, as fugitives were to be given back to the Romans, he had taken advantage of the confusion to fly with the soldiers.

During the whole of the march he remained near Matho; he brought him food, assisted him to dismount, and spread a carpet in the evening beneath his head. Matho at last was touched by these attentions, and by degrees unlocked his lips.

He had been born in the gulf of Syrtis. His father had taken him on a pilgrimage to the temple of Ammon. Then he had hunted elephants in the forests of the Garamantes. Afterwards he had entered the service of Carthage. He had been appointed tetrarch at the capture of Drepanum. The Republic owed him four horses, twenty-three medimni of wheat, and a winter's pay. He feared the gods, and wished to die in his native land.

Spendius spoke to him of his travels, and of the peoples and temples that he had visited. He knew many things: he could make sandals, boar-spears and nets; he could tame wild beasts and could cook fish.

Sometimes he would interrupt himself, and utter a hoarse cry from the depths of his throat; Matho's mule would quicken his pace, the others would hasten after them, and then Spendius would begin again though still torn with agony. This subsided at last on the evening of the fourth day.

They were marching side by side to the right of the army on the side of a hill; below them stretched the plain lost in the vapours of the night. The lines of soldiers also were defiling below, making undulations in the shade. From time to time these passed over eminences lit up by the moon; then stars would tremble on the points of the pikes, the helmets would glimmer for an instant, all would disappear, and others would come on continually. Startled flocks bleated in the distance, and a something of infinite sweetness seemed to sink upon the earth.

Spendius, with his head thrown back and his eyes half-closed, inhaled the freshness of the wind with great sighs; he spread out his arms, moving his fingers that he might the better feel the caress that streamed over his body. Hopes of vengeance came back to him and transported him. He pressed his hand upon his mouth to check his sobs, and half-swooning with intoxication, let go the halter of his dromedary, which was proceeding with long, regular steps. Matho had relapsed into his former melancholy;

his legs hung down to the ground, and the grass made a continuous rustling as it beat against his cothurni.

The journey, however, spread itself out without ever coming to an end. At the extremity of a plain they would always reach a round-shaped plateau; then they would descend again into a valley, and the mountains which seemed to block up the horizon would, in proportion as they were approached, glide as it were from their positions. From time to time a river would appear amid the verdure of tamarisks to lose itself at the turning of the hills. Sometimes a huge rock would tower aloft like the prow of a vessel or the pedestal of some vanished colossus.

At regular intervals they met with little quadrangular temples, which served as stations for the pilgrims who repaired to Sicca. They were closed like tombs. The Libyans struck great blows upon the doors to have them opened. But no one inside responded.

Then the cultivation become more rare. They suddenly entered upon belts of sand bristling with thorny thickets. Flocks of sheep were browsing among the stones; a woman with a blue fleece about her waist was watching them. She fled screaming when she saw the soldiers' pikes among the rocks.

They were marching through a kind of large passage bordered by two chains of reddish coloured hillocks, when their nostrils were greeted with a nauseous odour, and they thought that they could see something extraordinary on the top of a carob tree: a lion's head reared itself above the leaves.

They ran thither. It was a lion with his four limbs fastened to a cross like a criminal. His huge muzzle fell upon his breast, and his two fore-paws, half-hidden beneath the abundance of his mane, were spread out wide like the wings of a bird. His ribs stood severally out beneath his distended skin; his hind legs, which were nailed against each other, were raised somewhat, and the black blood, flowing through his hair, had collected in stalactites at the end of his tail, which hung down perfectly straight along the cross. The soldiers made merry around; they called him consul, and Roman citizen, and threw pebbles into his eyes to drive away the gnats.

But a hundred paces further on they saw two more, and then there suddenly appeared a long file of crosses bearing lions. Some had been so long dead that nothing was left against the wood but the remains of their skeletons; others which were half eaten away had their jaws twisted into horrible grimaces; there were some enormous ones; the shafts of the crosses bent beneath them, and they swayed in the wind, while bands of crows wheeled ceaselessly in the air above their heads. It was thus that the Carthaginian peasants avenged themselves when they captured a wild beast; they hoped to terrify the others by such an example. The Barbarians ceased their laughter and were long lost in amazement. "What people is this," they thought, "that amuses itself by crucifying lions!"

They were, besides, especially the men of the North, vaguely uneasy, troubled, and already sick. They tore their hands with the darts of the aloes; great mosquitoes buzzed in their ears, and dysentery was breaking out in the army. They were weary at not yet seeing Sicca. They were afraid of losing themselves and of reaching the desert, the country of sands and terrors. Many even were unwilling to advance further. Others started back to Carthage.

At last on the seventh day, after following the base of a mountain for a long time, they turned abruptly to the right, and there then appeared a line of walls resting on white rocks and blending with them. Suddenly the entire city rose; blue, yellow, and white veils moved on the walls in the redness of the evening. These were the priestesses of Tanith, who had hastened thither to receive the men. They stood ranged along the rampart, striking tambourines, playing lyres, and shaking crotala, while the rays of the sun, setting behind them in the mountains of Numidia, shot between the strings of their lyres over which their naked arms were stretched. At intervals their instruments would become suddenly still, and a cry would break forth strident, precipitate, frenzied, continuous, a sort of barking which they made by striking both corners of the mouth with the tongue. Others, more motionless than the Sphynx, rested on their elbows with their chins on their hands, and darted their great black eyes upon the army as it ascended.

Although Sicca was a sacred town it could not hold such a multitude; the temple alone, with its appurtenances, occupied half of it. Accordingly the Barbarians established themselves at their ease on the plain; those who were disciplined in regular troops, and the rest according to nationality or their own fancy.

The Greeks ranged their tents of skin in parallel lines; the Iberians placed their canvas pavilions in a circle; the Gauls made themselves huts of planks; the Libyans cabins of dry stones, while the Negroes with their nails hollowed out trenches in the sand to sleep in. Many, not knowing where to go, wandered about among the baggage, and at nightfall lay down in their ragged mantles on the ground.

The plain, which was wholly bounded by mountains, expanded around them. Here and there a palm tree leaned over a sand hill, and pines and oaks flecked the sides of the precipices: sometimes the rain of a storm would hang from the sky like a long scarf, while the country everywhere was still covered with azure and serenity; then a warm wind would drive before it tornadoes of dust, and a stream would descend in cascades from the heights of Sicca, where, with its roofing of gold on its columns of brass, rose the temple of the Carthaginian Venus, the mistress of the land. She seemed to fill it with her soul. In such convulsions of the soil, such alternations of temperature, and such plays of light would she manifest the extravagance of her might with the beauty of her eternal smile. The mountains at their summits were crescent-shaped; others were like women's bosoms presenting their swelling breasts, and the Barbarians felt a heaviness that was full of delight weighing down their fatigues.

Spendius had bought a slave with the money brought him by his dromedary. The whole day long he lay asleep stretched before Matho's tent. Often he would awake, thinking in his dreams that he heard the whistling of the thongs; with a smile he would pass his hands over the scars on his legs at the place where the fetters had long been worn, and then he would fall asleep again.

Matʰ accepted his companionship, and when he went ⸺ Spendius would escort him like a lictor

with a long sword on his thigh; or perhaps Matho
would rest his arm carelessly on the other's shoulder,
for Spendius was small.

One evening when they were passing together
through the streets in the camp they perceived some
men covered with white cloaks; among them was
Narr' Havas, the prince of the Numidians. Matho
started.

"Your sword!" he cried; "I will kill him!"

"Not yet!" said Spendius, restraining him. Narr'
Havas was already advancing towards him.

He kissed both his thumbs in token of alliance,
showing nothing of the anger which he had experienced at the drunkenness of the feast; then he spoke
at length against Carthage, but did not say what
brought him among the Barbarians.

"Was it to betray them, or else the Republic?"
Spendius asked himself; and as he expected to profit
by every disorder, he felt grateful to Narr' Havas for
the future perfidies of which he suspected him.

The chief of the Numidians remained amongst the
Mercenaries. He appeared desirous of attaching Matho
to himself. He sent him fat goats, gold dust, and
ostrich feathers. The Libyan, who was amazed at
such caresses, was in doubt whether to respond to
them or to become exasperated at them. But Spendius pacified him, and Matho allowed himself to be
ruled by the slave, remaining ever irresolute and in
an unconquerable torpor, like those who have once
taken a draught of which they are to die.

One morning when all three went out lion-hunting,
Narr' Havas concealed a dagger in his cloak. Spendius
kept continually behind him, and when they returned
the dagger had not been drawn.

3—8

Another time Narr' Havas took them a long way off, as far as the boundaries of his kingdom. They came to a narrow gorge, and Narr' Havas smiled as he declared that he had forgotten the way. Spendius found it again.

But most frequently Matho would go off at sunrise, as melancholy as an augur, to wander about the country. He would stretch himself on the sand, and remain there motionless until the evening.

He consulted all the soothsayers in the army one after the other,—those who watch the trail of serpents, those who read the stars, and those who breathe upon the ashes of the dead. He swallowed galbanum, seseli, and viper's venom which freezes the heart; Negro women, singing barbarous words in the moonlight, pricked the skin of his forehead with golden stylets; he loaded himself with necklaces and charms; he invoked in turn Baal-Khamon, Moloch, the seven Kabiri, Tanith, and the Venus of the Greeks. He engraved a name upon a copper plate, and buried it in the sand at the threshold of his tent. Spendius used to hear him groaning and talking to himself.

One night he went in.

Matho, as naked as a corpse, was lying on a lion's skin flat on his stomach, with his face in both his hands; a hanging lamp lit up his armour, which was hooked on to the tent-pole above his head.

"You are suffering?" said the slave to him. "What is the matter with you? Answer me?" And he shook him by the shoulder calling him several times, "Master! master!"

At last Matho lifted large troubled eyes towards him.

"Listen!" he said in a low voice, and with a finger on his lips. "It is the wrath of the Gods!

Hamilcar's daughter pursues me! I am afraid of her, Spendius!" He pressed himself close against his breast like a child terrified by a phantom. "Speak to me! I am sick! I want to get well! I have tried everything! But you, you perhaps know some stronger gods, or some resistless invocation?"

"For what purpose?" asked Spendius.

Striking his head with both his fists, he replied:

"To rid me of her!"

Then speaking to himself with long pauses he said:

"I am no doubt the victim of some holocaust which she has promised to the gods?—She holds me fast by a chain which people cannot see. If I walk, it is she that is advancing; when I stop, she is resting! Her eyes burn me, I hear her voice. She encompasses me, she penetrates me. It seems to me that she has become my soul!

"And yet between us there are, as it were, the invisible billows of a boundless ocean! She is far away and quite inaccessible! The splendour of her beauty forms a cloud of light around her, and at times I think that I have never seen her—that she does not exist—and that it is all a dream!"

Matho wept thus in the darkness; the Barbarians were sleeping. Spendius, as he looked at him, recalled the young men who once used to entreat him with golden vases in their hands, when he led his herd of courtesans through the towns; a feeling of pity moved him, and he said—

"Be strong, my master! Summon your will, and beseech the gods no more, for they turn not aside at the cries of men! Weeping like a coward! And you are not humiliated that a woman can cause you so much suffering?"

"Am I a child?" said Matho. "Do you think that I am moved by their faces and songs? We kept them at Drepanum to sweep out our stables. I have embraced them amid assaults, beneath failing ceilings, and while the catapult was still vibrating!—But she, Spendius, she!——"

The slave interrupted him:

"If she were not Hamilcar's daughter——"

"No!" cried Matho. "She has nothing in common with other daughters of men! Have you seen her great eyes beneath her great eyebrows, like suns beneath triumphal arches? Think: when she appeared all the torches grew pale. Her naked breast shone here and there through the diamonds of her necklace; behind her you perceived as it were the odour of a temple, and her whole being emitted something that was sweeter than wine and more terrible than death. She walked, however, and then she stopped."

He remained gaping with his head cast down and his eyeballs fixed.

"But I want her! I need her! I am dying for her! I am transported with frenzied joy at the thought of clasping her in my arms, and yet I hate her, Spendius! I should like to beat her! What is to be done? I have a mind to sell myself and become her slave! *You* have been that! You were able to get sight of her; speak to me of her! Every night she ascends to the terrace of her palace, does she not? Ah! the stones must quiver beneath her sandals, and the stars bend down to see her!"

He fell back in a perfect frenzy, with a rattling in his throat like a wounded bull.

Then Matho sang: "He pursued into the forest the female monster, whose tail undulated over the

strides; they went at random to right or left, being embarrassed by the tent-ropes, the animals that were straying about, or the tripods where food was being cooked. Sometimes a fat hand, laden with rings, would partially open the litter, and a hoarse voice would utter loud reproaches; then the bearers would stop and take a different direction through the camp.

But the purple curtains were raised, and a human head, impassible and bloated, was seen resting on a large pillow; the eyebrows, which were like arches of ebony, met each other at the points; golden dust sparkled in the frizzled hair, and the face was so wan that it looked as if it had been powdered with marble raspings. The rest of the body was concealed beneath the fleeces which filled the litter.

In the man so reclining the soldiers recognised the Suffet Hanno, he whose slackness had assisted to lose the battle of the Ægatian islands; and as to his victory at Hecatompylos over the Libyans, even if he did behave with clemency, thought the Barbarians, it was owing to cupidity, for he had sold all the captives on his own account, although he had reported their deaths to the Republic.

After seeking for some time for a convenient place from which to harangue the soldiers, he made a sign; the litter stopped, and Hanno, supported by two slaves, put his tottering feet to the ground.

He wore boots of black felt strewn with silver moons. His legs were swathed in bands like those wrapped about a mummy, and the flesh crept through the crossings of the linen; his stomach came out beyond the scarlet jacket which covered his thighs; the folds of his neck fell down to his breast like the dewlaps of an ox; his tunic, which was painted with flowers, was bursting at the arm-pits; he wore a scarf, a girdle, and an ample black cloak with laced double sleeves. But the abundance of his garments, his great necklace of blue stones, his golden clasps, and heavy earrings only rendered his deformity still more hideous. He might have been taken for some big idol rough-hewn in a block of stone; for a pale leprosy, which was spread over his whole body, gave him the appearance of an inert thing. His nose, however, which was hooked like a vulture's beak, was violently dilated to breathe in the air, and his little eyes, with their gummed lashes, shone with a hard and metallic lustre. He held a spatula of aloe-wood in his hand wherewith to scratch his skin.

At last two heralds sounded their silver horns; the tumult subsided, and Hanno commenced to speak.

He began with an eulogy of the gods and the Republic; the Barbarians ought to congratulate themselves on having served it. But they must show themselves more reasonable; times were hard, "and if a master has only three olives, is it not right that he should keep two for himself?"

The old Suffet mingled his speech in this way with proverbs and apologues, nodding his head the while to solicit some approval.

He spoke in Punic, and those surrounding him (the most alert, who had hastened thither without their arms), were Campanians, Gauls, and Greeks, so that no one in the crowd understood him. Hanno, perceiving this, stopped and reflected, swaying himself heavily from one leg to the other.

It occurred to him to call the captains together; then his heralds shouted the order in Greek, the language which, from the time of Xanthippus, had been used for commands in the Carthaginian armies.

The guards dispersed the mob of soldiers with strokes of the whip; and the captains of the Spartan phalanxes and the chiefs of the Barbarian cohorts soon arrived with the insignia of their rank, and in the armour of their nation. Night had fallen, a great tumult was spreading through the plain; fires were burning here and there; and the soldiers kept going from one to another asking what the matter was, and why the Suffet did not distribute the money?

He was setting the infinite burdens of the Republic before the captains. Her treasury was empty. The tribute to Rome was crushing her. "We are quite at a loss what to do! She is much to be pitied!"

From time to time he would rub his limbs with his aloe-wood spatula, or perhaps he would break off to drink a ptisan made of the ashes of a weasel and asparagus boiled in vinegar from a silver cup handed to him by a slave; then he would wipe his lips with a scarlet napkin and resume:

"What used to be worth a shekel of silver is now worth three shekels of gold, while the cultivated lands which were abandoned during the war bring in nothing! Our purpura fisheries are nearly gone, and even pearls are becoming exorbitant; we have scarcely unguents enough for the service of the gods! As for the things of the table, I shall say nothing about them; it is a calamity! For want of galleys we are without spices, and it is a matter of great difficulty to procure silphium on account of the rebellions on the Cyrenian frontier. Sicily, where so many slaves used to be had, is now closed to us!

Only yesterday I gave more money for a bather and four scullions than I used at one time to give for a pair of elephants!"

He unrolled a long piece of papyrus; and, without omitting a single figure, read all the expenses that the government had incurred; so much for repairing the temples, for paving the streets, for the construction of vessels, for the coral-fisheries, for the enlargement of the Syssitia, and for engines in the mines in the country of the Cantabrians.

But the captains understood Punic as little as the soldiers, although the Mercenaries saluted one another in that language. It was usual to place a few Carthaginian officers in the Barbarian armies to act as interpreters; after the war they had concealed themselves through fear of vengeance, and Hanno had not thought of taking them with him; his hollow voice, too, was lost in the wind.

The Greeks, girthed in their iron waist-belts, strained their ears as they strove to guess at his words, while the mountaineers, covered with furs like bears, looked at him with distrust, or yawned as they leaned on their brass-nailed clubs. The heedless Gauls sneered as they shook their lofty heads of hair, and the men of the desert listened motionless, cowled in their garments of grey wool; others kept coming up behind; the guards, crushed by the mob, staggered on their horses; the Negroes held out burning fir branches at arm's length; and the big Carthaginian, mounted on a grassy hillock, continued his harangue.

The Barbarians, however, were growing impatient; murmuring arose, and every one apostrophized him. Hanno gesticulated with his spatula; and those who wished the others to be quiet shouted still more loudly, thereby adding to the din.

Suddenly a man of mean appearance bounded to Hanno's feet, snatched up a herald's trumpet, blew it, and Spendius (for it was he) announced that he was going to say something of importance. At this declaration, which was rapidly uttered in five different languages, Greek, Latin, Gallic, Libyan and Balearic, the captains, half laughing and half surprised, replied: "Speak! Speak!"

Spendius hesitated; he trembled; at last, addressing the Libyans who were the most numerous, he said to them:

"You have all heard this man's horrible threats!"

Hanno made no exclamation, therefore he did not understand Libyan; and, to carry on the experiment, Spendius repeated the same phrase in the other Barbarian dialects.

They looked at one another in astonishment; then, as by a tacit agreement, and believing perhaps that they had understood, they bent their heads in token of assent.

Then Spendius began in vehement tones:

"He said first that all the Gods of the other nations were but dreams beside the Gods of Carthage! He called you cowards, thieves, liars, dogs, and the sons of dogs! But for you (he said that!) the Republic would not be forced to pay tribute to the Romans; and through your excesses you have drained it of perfumes, aromatics, slaves, and silphium, for you are in league with the nomads on the Cyrenian frontier! But the guilty shall be punished! He read the enumeration of their torments; they shall be made to work at the paving of the streets, at the equipment of the vessels, at the adornment of the Syssitia, while the rest shall be sent to scrape the earth in the mines in the country of the Cantabrians."

Spendius repeated the same statements to the Gauls, Greeks, Campanians and Balearians. The Mercenaries, recognising several of the proper names which had met their ears, were convinced that he was accurately reporting the Suffet's speech. A few cried out to him, "You lie!" but their voices were drowned in the tumult of the rest; Spendius added:

"Have you not seen that he has left a reserve of his horse-soldiers outside the camp? At a given signal they will hasten hither to slay you all."

The Barbarians turned in that direction, and as the crowd was then scattering, there appeared in the midst of them, and advancing with the slowness of a phantom, a human being, bent, lean, entirely naked, and covered down to his flanks with long hair bristling with dried leaves, dust and thorns. About his loins and his knees he had wisps of straw and linen rags; his soft and earthy skin hung on his emaciated limbs like tatters on dried boughs; his hands trembled with a continuous quivering, and as he walked he leaned on a staff of olive-wood.

He reached the Negroes who were bearing the torches. His pale gums were displayed in a sort of idiotic titter; his large, scared eyes gazed upon the crowd of Barbarians around him.

But uttering a cry of terror he threw himself behind them, shielding himself with their bodies. "There they are! There they are!" he stammered out, pointing to the Suffet's guards, who were motionless in their glittering armour. Their horses, dazzled by the light of the torches which crackled in the

darkness, were pawing the ground; the human spectre
struggled and howled:

"They have killed them!"

At these words, which were screamed in Balearic, some Balearians came up and recognised him;
without answering them he repeated:

"Yes, all killed, all! crushed like grapes! The
fine young men! the slingers! my companions and
yours!"

They gave him wine to drink, and he wept; then
he launched forth into speech.

Spendius could scarcely repress his joy, as he explained the horrors related by Zarxas to the Greeks
and Libyans; he could not believe them, so appro-
priately did they come in. The Balearians grew pale
as they learned how their companions had perished.

It was a troop of three hundred slingers who had
disembarked the evening before, and had on that day
slept too late. When they reached the square of Khamon the Barbarians were gone, and they found themselves defenceless, their clay bullets having been put
on the camels with the rest of the baggage. They
were allowed to advance into the street of Satheb as
far as the brass sheathed oaken gate; then the people
with a single impulse had sprung upon them.

Indeed, the soldiers remembered a great shout;
Spendius, who was flying at the head of the columns,
had not heard it.

Then the corpses were placed in the arms of the
Patæc gods that fringed the temple of Khamon. They
were upbraided with all the crimes of the Mercenaries; their gluttony, their thefts, their impiety, their
disdain, and the murder of the fishes in Salammbô's
garden. Their bodies were subjected to infamous

mutilations; the priests burned their hair in order to torture their souls; they were hung up in pieces in the meat-shops; some even buried their teeth in them, and in the evening funeral-piles were kindled at the cross-ways to finish them.

These were the flames that had gleamed from a distance across the lake. But some houses having taken fire, any dead or dying that remained were speedily thrown over the walls; Zarxas had remained among the reeds on the edge of the lake until the following day; then he had wandered about through the country, seeking for the army by the footprints in the dust. In the morning he hid himself in caves; in the evening he resumed his march with his bleeding wounds, famished, sick, living on roots and carrion; at last one day he perceived lances on the horizon, and he had followed them, for his reason was disturbed through his terrors and miseries.

The indignation of the soldiers, restrained so long as he was speaking, broke forth like a tempest; they were going to massacre the guards together with the Suffet. A few interposed, saying that they ought to hear him and know at least whether they should be paid. Then they all cried: "Our money!" Hanno replied that he had brought it.

They ran to the outposts, and the Suffet's baggage arrived in the midst of the tents, pressed forward by the Barbarians. Without waiting for the slaves, they very quickly unfastened the baskets; in them they found hyacinth robes, sponges, scrapers, brushes, perfumes, and antimony pencils for painting the eyes — all belonging to the guards, who were rich men and accustomed to such refinements. Next they uncovered a large bronze tub on a camel: it belonged to the Suffet who had it for bathing in during his journey; for he had taken all manner of precautions, even going so far as to bring caged weasels from Hecatompylos, which were burnt alive to make his ptisan. But, as his malady gave him a great appetite, there were also many comestibles and many wines, pickle, meats and fishes preserved in honey, with little pots of Commagene, or melted goose-fat covered with snow and chopped straw. There was a considerable supply of it; the more they opened the baskets the more they found, and laughter arose like conflicting waves.

As to the pay of the Mercenaries it nearly filled two esparto-grass baskets; there were even visible in one of them some of the leathern discs which the Republic used to economise its specie; and as the Barbarians appeared greatly surprised, Hanno told them that, their accounts being very difficult, the Ancients had not had leisure to examine them. Meanwhile they sent them this.

Then everything was in disorder and confusion: mules, serving men, litter, provisions, and baggage. The soldiers took the coin in the bags to stone Hanno. With great difficulty he was able to mount an ass; and he fled, clinging to its hair, howling, weeping, shaken, bruised, and calling down the curse of all the gods upon the army. His broad necklace of precious stones rebounded up to his ears. His cloak which was too long, and which trailed behind him, he kept on with his teeth, and from afar the Barbarians shouted at him, "Begone coward! pig! sink of Moloch! sweat your gold and your plague! quicker! quicker!" The routed escort galloped beside him.

But the fury of the Barbarians did not abate. They remembered that several of them who had set out for Carthage had not returned; no doubt they had been killed. So much injustice exasperated them, and they began to pull up the stakes of their tents, to roll up their cloaks, and to bridle their horses; every one took his helmet and sword, and instantly all was ready. Those who had no arms rushed into the woods to cut staves.

Day dawned; the people of Sicca were roused, and stirring in the streets. "They are going to Carthage," said they, and the rumour of this soon spread through the country.

From every path and every ravine men arose. Shepherds were seen running down from the mountains.

Then, when the Barbarians had set out, Spendius circled the plain, riding on a Punic stallion, and attended by his slave, who led a third horse.

A single tent remained. Spendius entered it.

"Up, master! rise! we are departing!"

"And where are you going?" asked Matho.

"To Carthage!" cried Spendius.

Matho bounded upon the horse which the slave held at the door.

III.

SALAMMBÔ.

THE moon was rising just above the waves, and on the town which was still wrapped in darkness there glittered white a n d luminous specks:—the pole of a chariot, a dangling rag of linen, the corner of a wall, or a golden necklace on the bosom of a god. The glass balls on the roofs of the temples beamed like great diamonds here and there. But ill-defined ruins, piles of black earth, and gardens formed deeper masses in the gloom, and below Malqua fishermen's nets stretched from one house to another like gigantic bats spreading their wings. The grinding of the hydraulic wheels which conveyed water to the highest storys of the palaces, was no longer heard; and the camels, lying ostrich fashion on their stomachs, rested peacefully in the middle of the terraces. The porters were asleep in the streets on the thresholds of the houses; the shadows of the colossuses stretched across the deserted squares; occasionally in the distance the smoke of a still burning sacrifice would escape through the bronze tiling, and the heavy breeze would waft the odours of aromatics blended with the scent of the

3—9

sea and the exhalation from the sun-heated walls. The motionless waves shone around Carthage, for the moon was spreading her light at once upon the mountain-circled gulf and upon the lake of Tunis, where flamingoes formed long rose-coloured lines amid the banks of sand, while further on beneath the catacombs the great salt lagoon shimmered like a piece of silver. The blue vault of heaven sank on the horizon in one direction into the dustiness of the plains, and in the other into the mists of the sea, and on the summit of the Acropolis, the pyramidal cypress trees, fringing the temple of Eschmoun, swayed murmuring like the regular waves that beat slowly along the mole beneath the ramparts.

Salammbô ascended to the terrace of her palace, supported by a female slave who carried an iron dish filled with live coals.

In the middle of the terrace there was a small ivory bed covered with lynx skins, and cushions made with the feathers of the parrot, a fatidical animal consecrated to the gods; and at the four corners rose four long perfuming-pans filled with nard, incense, cinnamomum, and myrrh. The slave lit the perfumes. Salammbô looked at the polar star; she slowly saluted the four points of heaven, and knelt down on the ground in the azure dust which was strewn with golden stars in imitation of the firmament. Then with both elbows against her sides, her fore-arms straight and her hands open, she threw back her head beneath the rays of the moon, and said:

"O Rabetna!—Baalet!—Tanith!" and her voice was lengthened in a plaintive fashion as if calling to some one. "Anaïtis! Astarte! Derceto! Astoreth! Mylitta! Athara! Elissa! Tiratha!—By the hidden sym-

bols, — by the resounding sistra, — by the furrows of
the earth, — by the eternal silence and by the eternal
fruitfulness, — mistress of the gloomy sea and of the
azure shores, O Queen of the watery world, all
hail!"

She swayed her whole body twice or thrice, and
then cast herself face downwards in the dust with
both arms outstretched.

But the slave nimbly raised her, for according to
the rites some one must catch the suppliant at the
moment of his prostration; this told him that the
gods accepted him, and Salammbô's nurse never
failed in this pious duty.

Some merchants from Darytian Gætulia had brought
her to Carthage when quite young, and after her en-
franchisement she would not forsake her old masters,
as was shown by her right ear, which was pierced
with a large hole. A petticoat of many-coloured
stripes fitted closely on her hips, and fell to her ankles,
where two tin rings clashed together. Her somewhat
flat face was yellow like her tunic. Silver bodkins of
great length formed a sun behind her head. She
wore a coral button on the nostril, and she stood beside the bed more erect than a Hermes, and with her
eyelids cast down.

Salammbô walked to the edge of the terrace; her
eyes swept the horizon for an instant, and then were
lowered upon the sleeping town, while the sigh that
she heaved swelled her bosom, and gave an undulating movement to the whole length of the long white
simar which hung without clasp or girdle about her.
Her curved and painted sandals were hidden beneath
a heap of emeralds, and a net of purple thread was
filled with her disordered hair.

But she raised her head to gaze upon the moon, and murmured, mingling her speech with fragments of hymns:

"How lightly turnest thou, supported by the impalpable ether! It brightens about thee, and 'tis the stir of thine agitation that distributes the winds and fruitful dews. According as thou dost wax and wane the eyes of cats and spots of panthers lengthen or grow short. Wives shriek thy name in the pangs of childbirth! Thou makest the shells to swell, the wine to bubble, and the corpse to putrefy! Thou formest the pearls at the bottom of the sea!

"And every germ, O goddess! ferments in the dark depths of thy moisture.

"When thou appearest, quietness is spread abroad upon the earth; the flowers close, the waves are soothed, wearied man stretches his breast toward thee, and the world with its oceans and mountains looks at itself in thy face as in a mirror. Thou art white, gentle, luminous, immaculate, helping, purifying, serene!"

The crescent of the moon was then over the mountain of the Hot Springs, in the hollow formed by its two summits, on the other side of the gulf. Below it there was a little star, and all around it a pale circle. Salammbô went on:

"But thou art a terrible mistress!—Monsters, terrifying phantoms, and lying dreams come from thee; thine eyes devour the stones of buildings, and the apes are ever ill each time thou growest young again.

"Whither goest thou? Why dost thou change thy forms continually? Now, slender and curved thou glidest through space like a mastless galley; and then, amid the stars, thou art like a shepherd keeping his flock. Shining and round, thou dost graze the mountain-tops like the wheel of a chariot.

"O Tanith! thou dost love me? I have looked so much on thee! But no! thou sailest through thine azure, and I—I remain on the motionless earth.

"Taanach, take your nebal and play softly on the silver string, for my heart is sad!"

The slave lifted a sort of harp of ebony wood, taller than herself, and triangular in shape like a delta; she fixed the point in a crystal globe, and with both hands began to play.

The sounds followed one another hurried and deep, like the buzzing of bees, and with increasing sonorousness floated away into the night with the complaining of the waves, and the rustling of the great trees on the summit of the Acropolis.

"Hush!" cried Salammbô.

"What ails you, mistress? The blowing of the breeze, the passing of a cloud, everything disquiets you just now!"

"I do not know," she said.

"You are wearied with too long prayers!"

"Oh! Taanach, I would fain be dissolved in them like a flower in wine!"

"Perhaps it is the smoke of your perfumes?"

"No!" said Salammbô; "the spirit of the gods dwells in fragrant odours."

Then the slave spoke to her of her father. It was thought that he had gone towards the amber country, behind the pillars of Melkarth. "But if he does not return," she said, "you must nevertheless, since it was his will, choose a husband among the sons of the Ancients, and then your grief will pass away in a man's arms."

"Why?" asked the young girl. All those that she had seen had horrified her with their fallow-deer laughter and their coarse limbs.

"Sometimes, Taanach, from the depths of my being there exhale as it were hot fumes heavier than the vapours from a volcano. Voices call me, a globe of fire rolls and mounts within my bosom, it stifles me, I am at the point of death; and then, something sweet, flowing from my brow to my feet, passes through my flesh—it is a caress enfolding me, and I feel myself crushed as if some god were stretched upon me. Oh! would that I could lose myself in the mists of the night, the waters of the fountains, the sap of the trees, that I could issue from my body, and be but a breath, or a ray, and glide, mount up to thee, O Mother!"

She raised her arms to their full length, arching her form, which in its long garment was as pale and light as the moon. Then she fell back, panting, on the ivory couch; but Taanach passed an amber necklace with dolphin's teeth about her neck to banish terrors, and Salammbô said in an almost stifled voice: "Go and bring me Schahabarim."

Her father had not wished her to enter the college of priestesses, nor even to be made at all acquainted with the popular Tanith. He was reserving her for some alliance that might serve his political ends; so that Salammbô lived alone in the midst of the palace. Her mother was long since dead.

She had grown up with abstinences, fastings and purifications, always surrounded by grave and exquisite things, her body saturated with perfumes, and her soul filled with prayers. She had never tasted wine, nor eaten meat, nor touched an unclean animal, nor set her heels in the house of death.

She knew nothing of obscene images, for as each god was manifested in different forms, the same principle often received the witness of contradictory cults, and Salammbô worshipped the goddess in her sidereal presentation. An influence had descended upon the maiden from the moon; when the planet passed diminishing away, Salammbô grew weak. She languished the whole day long, and revived at evening. During an eclipse she had nearly died.

But Rabetna, in jealousy, revenged herself for the virginity withdrawn from her sacrifices, and she tormented Salammbô with possessions, all the stronger for being vague, which were spread through this belief and excited by it.

Unceasingly was Hamilcar's daughter disquieted about Tanith. She had learned her adventures, her travels, and all her names, which she would repeat without their having any distinct signification for her. In order to penetrate into the depths of her dogma, she wished to become acquainted, in the most secret part of the temple, with the old idol in the magnificent mantle, whereon depended the destinies of Carthage, for the idea of a god did not stand out clearly from his representation, and to hold, or even see the image of one, was to take away part of his virtue, and in a measure to rule him.

But Salammbô turned around. She had recognised the sound of the golden bells which Schahabarim wore at the hem of his garment.

He ascended the staircases; then at the threshold of the terrace he stopped and folded his arms.

His sunken eyes shone like the lamps of a sepulchre; his long thin body floated in its linen robe which was weighted by the bells, the latter alternating with balls of emeralds at his heels. He had feeble limbs, an oblique skull and a pointed chin; his skin seemed cold to the touch, and his yellow face, which was deeply furrowed with wrinkles, was as if it contracted in a longing, in an everlasting grief.

He was the high priest of Tanith, and it was he who had educated Salammbô.

"Speak!" he said. "What will you?"

"I hoped—you had almost promised me—" She stammered and was confused; then suddenly: "Why do you despise me? what have I forgotten in the rites? You are my master, and you told me that no one was so accomplished in the things pertaining to the goddess as I; but there are some of which you will not speak. Is it so, O father?"

Schahabarim remembered Hamilcar's orders, and replied:

"No, I have nothing more to teach you!"

"A genius" she resumed, "impels me to this love. I have climbed the steps of Eschmoun, god of the planets and intelligences; I have slept beneath the golden olive of Melkarth, patron of the Tyrian colonies; I have pushed open the doors of Baal-Khamon, the enlightener and fertiliser; I have sacrificed to the subterranean Kabiri, to the gods of woods, winds, rivers and mountains; but, can you understand? they are all too far away, too high, too insensible, while she—I feel her mingled in my life; she fills my soul, and I quiver with inward startings, as though she were leaping in order to escape. Methinks I am about to hear her voice, and see her face, lightnings dazzle me and then I sink back again into the darkness."

Schahabarim was silent. She entreated him with suppliant looks. At last he made a sign for the dismissal of the slave, who was not of Chanaanitish race. Taanach disappeared, and Schahabarim, raising one arm in the air, began:

"Before the gods darkness alone was, and a breathing stirred dull and indistinct as the conscience of a man in a dream. It contracted, creating Desire and Cloud, and from Desire and Cloud there issued primitive Matter. This was a water, muddy, black, icy and deep. It contained senseless monsters, incoherent portions of the forms to be born, which are painted on the walls of the sanctuaries.

"Then Matter condensed. It became an egg. It burst. One half formed the earth and the other the firmament. Sun, moon, winds and clouds appeared, and at the crash of the thunder intelligent creatures awoke. Then Eschmoun spread himself in the starry sphere; Khamon beamed in the sun; Melkarth thrust him with his arms behind Gades; the Kabiri descended beneath the volcanoes, and Rabetna like a nurse bent over the world pouring out her light like milk, and her night like a mantle."

"And then?" she said.

He had related the secret of the origins to her, to divert her from sublimer prospects; but the maiden's desire kindled again at his last words, and Schahabarim, half yielding resumed:

"She inspires and governs the loves of men."

"The loves of men!" repeated Salammbô dreamily.

"She is the soul of Carthage," continued the priest; "and although she is everywhere diffused, it is here the she dwells, beneath the sacred veil."

"O father!" cried Salammbô, "I shall see her, shall I not? you will bring me to her! I had long been hesitating; I am devoured with curiosity to see her form. Pity! help me! let us go?"

He repulsed her with a vehement gesture that was full of pride.

"Never! Do you not know that it means death? The hermaphrodite Baals are unveiled to us alone who are men in understanding and women in weakness. Your desire is sacrilege; be satisfied with the knowledge that you possess!"

She fell upon her knees placing two fingers against her ears in token of repentance; and crushed by the priest's words, and filled at once with anger against him, with terror and with humiliation, she burst into sobs. Schahabarim remained erect, and more insensible than the stones of the terrace. He looked down upon her quivering at his feet, and felt a kind of joy on seeing her suffer for his divinity whom he himself could not wholly embrace. The birds were already singing, a cold wind was blowing, and little clouds were drifting in the paling sky.

Suddenly he perceived on the horizon, behind Tunis, what looked like slight mists trailing along the ground; then these became a great curtain of dust extending perpendicularly, and, amid the whirlwinds of the thronging mass, dromedaries' heads, lances and shields appeared. It was the army of the Barbarians advancing upon Carthage.

IV.

BENEATH THE WALLS OF CARTHAGE.

SOME country people, riding on asses or running on foot, arrived in the town, pale, breathless, and mad with fear. They were flying before the army. It had accomplished the journey from Sicca in three days, in order to reach Carthage and wholly exterminate it.

The gates were shut. The Barbarians appeared almost immediately; but they stopped in the middle of the isthmus, on the edge of the lake.

At first they made no hostile announcement. Several approached with palm branches in their hands. They were driven back with arrows, so great was the terror.

In the morning and at nightfall prowlers would sometimes wander along the walls. A little man carefully wrapped in a cloak, and with his face concealed beneath a very low visor, was especially noticed. He would remain whole hours gazing at the aqueduct, and so persistently that he doubtless wished to mislead the Carthaginians as to his real designs. Another man, a sort of giant who walked bareheaded, used to accompany him.

But Carthage was defended throughout the whole breadth of the isthmus: first by a trench, then by a grassy rampart, and lastly by a wall thirty cubits high, built of freestone, and in two storys. It contained stables for three hundred elephants with stores for their caparisons, shackles, and food; other stables again for four thousand horses with supplies of barley and harness, and barracks for twenty thousand soldiers with armour and all materials for war. Towers rose from the second story, all provided with battlements, and having bronze bucklers hung on cramps on the outside.

This first line of wall gave immediate shelter to Malqua, the sailors' and dyers' quarter. Masts might be seen whereon purple sails were drying, and on the highest terraces clay furnaces for heating the pickle were visible.

Behind, the lofty houses of the city rose in an amphitheatre of cubical form. They were built of stone, planks, shingle, reeds, shells, and beaten earth. The woods belonging to the temples were like lakes of verdure in this mountain of diversely-coloured blocks. It was levelled at unequal distances by the public squares, and was cut from top to bottom by countless intersecting lanes. The enclosures of the three old quarters which are now lost might be distinguished; they rose here and there like great reefs, or extended in enormous fronts, blackened, half-covered with flowers, and broadly striped by the casting of filth, while streets passed through their yawning apertures like rivers beneath bridges.

The hill of the Acropolis, in the centre of Byrsa, was hidden beneath a disordered array of monuments. There were temples with wreathed columns bearing bronze capitals and metal chains, cones of dry stones with bands of azure, copper cupolas, marble architraves, Babylonian buttresses, obelisks poised on their points like inverted torches. Peristyles reached to pediments; volutes were displayed through colonnades; granite walls supported tile partitions; the whole mounting, half-hidden, the one above the other in a marvellous and incomprehensible fashion. In it might be felt the succession of the ages, and, as it were, the memorials of forgotten fatherlands.

Behind the Acropolis the Mappalian road, which was lined with tombs, extended through red lands in a straight line from the shore to the catacombs; then spacious dwellings occurred at intervals in the gardens, and this third quarter, Megara, which was the new town, reached as far as the edge of the cliff, where rose a giant pharos that blazed forth every night.

In this fashion was Carthage displayed before the soldiers quartered in the plain.

They could recognize the markets and crossways in the distance, and disputed with one another as to the sites of the temples. Khamon's, fronting the Syssitia, had golden tiles; Melkarth, to the left of Eschmoun, had branches of coral on its roofing; beyond, Tanith's copper cupola swelled among the palm trees; the dark Moloch was below the cisterns, in the direction of the pharos. At the angles of the pediments, on the tops of the walls, at the corners of the squares, everywhere, divinities with hideous heads might be seen, colossal or squat, with enormous bellies, or immoderately flattened, opening their jaws, extending their arms, and holding forks, chains or javelins in their hands; while the blue of the sea stretched away behind the streets which were rendered still steeper by the perspective.

They were filled from morning till evening with a tumultuous people; young boys shaking little bells, shouted at the doors of the baths; the shops for hot drinks smoked, the air resounded with the noise of anvils, the white cocks, sacred to the Sun, crowed on the terraces, the oxen that were being slaughtered bellowed in the temples, slaves ran about with baskets on their heads; and in the depths of the porticoes a priest would sometimes appear, draped in a dark cloak, barefooted, and wearing a pointed cap.

The spectacle afforded by Carthage irritated the Barbarians; they admired it and execrated it, and would have liked both to annihilate it and to dwell in it. But what was there in the Military Harbour defended by a triple wall? Then behind the town, at the back of Megara, and higher than the Acropolis, appeared Hamilcar's palace.

Matho's eyes were directed thither every moment. He would ascend the olive trees and lean over with his hand spread out above his eyebrows. The gardens were empty, and the red door with its black cross remained constantly shut.

More than twenty times he walked round the ramparts, seeking some breach by which he might enter. One night he threw himself into the gulf and swam for three hours at a stretch. He reached the foot of the Mappalian quarter and tried to climb up the face of the cliff. He covered his knees with blood, broke his nails, and then fell back into the waves and returned.

His impotence exasperated him. He was jealous of this Carthage which contained Salammbô, as

if of some one who had possessed her. His nerve-
lessness left him to be replaced by a mad and continual eagerness for action. With flaming cheek,
angry eyes, and hoarse voice, he would walk with
rapid strides through the camp; or seated on the
shore he would scour his great sword with sand.
He shot arrows at the passing vultures. His heart
overflowed into frenzied speech.

"Give free course to your wrath like a runaway
chariot," said Spendius. "Shout, blaspheme, ravage
and slay. Grief is allayed with blood, and since you
cannot sate your love, gorge your hate; it will sustain you!"

Matho resumed the command of his soldiers. He
drilled them pitilessly. He was respected for his
courage and especially for his strength. Moreover he
inspired a sort of mystic dread, and it was believed
that he conversed at night with phantoms. The
other captains were animated by his example. The
army soon grew disciplined. From their houses the Carthaginians could hear the bugle-flourishes that reg-
ulated their exercises. At last the Barbarians drew
near.

To crush them in the isthmus it would have been
necessary for two armies to take them simultaneously
in the rear, one disembarking at the end of the gulf
of Utica, and the second at the mountain of the Hot
Springs. But what could be done with the single
sacred Legion, mustering at most six thousand men?
If the enemy bent towards the east they would join
the nomads and intercept the commerce of the desert.
If they fell back to the west, Numidia would rise.
Finally, lack of provisions would sooner or later lead
them to devastate the surrounding country like grass-

hoppers, and the rich trembled for their fine country-houses, their vineyards and their cultivated lands.

Hanno proposed atrocious and impracticable measures, such as promising a heavy sum for every Barbarian's head, or setting fire to their camp with ships and machines. His colleague Gisco, on the other hand, wished them to be paid. But the Ancients detested him owing to his popularity; for they dreaded the risk of a master, and through terror of monarchy strove to weaken whatever contributed to it or might re-establish it.

Outside the fortifications there were people of another race and of unknown origin, all hunters of the porcupine, and eaters of shell-fish and serpents. They used to go into caves to catch hyenas alive, and amuse themselves by making them run in the evening on the sands of Megara between the stelæ of the tombs. Their huts, which were made of mud and wrack, hung on the cliff like swallows' nests. There they lived, without government and without gods, pell-mell, completely naked, at once feeble and fierce, and execrated by the people of all time on account of their unclean food. One morning the sentries perceived that they were all gone.

At last some members of the Great Council arrived at a decision. They came to the camp without necklaces or girdles, and in open sandals like neighbours. They walked at a quiet pace, waving salutations to the captains, or stopped to speak to the soldiers, saying that all was finished and that justice was about to be done to their claims.

Many of them saw a camp of Mercenaries for the first time. Instead of the confusion which they had pictured to themselves, there prevailed everywhere

terrible silence and order. A grassy rampart formed
a lofty wall round the army immovable by the shock
of catapults. The ground in the streets was sprinkled
with fresh water; through the holes in the tents
they could perceive tawny eyeballs gleaming in the
shade. The piles of pikes and hanging panoplies dazzled them like mirrors. They conversed in low tones.
They were afraid of upsetting something with their
long robes.

The soldiers requested provisions, undertaking to
pay for them out of the money that was due.

Oxen, sheep, guinea fowl, fruit and lupins were
sent to them, with smoked scombri, that excellent
scombri which Carthage dispatched to every port.
But they walked scornfully around the magnificent cattle, and disparaging what they coveted, offered the
worth of a pigeon for a ram, or the price of a pomegranate for three goats. The Eaters of Uncleanness
came forward as arbitrators, and declared that they
were being duped. Then they drew their swords
with threats to slay.

Commissaries of the Great Council wrote down the
number of years for which pay was due to each soldier. But it was no longer possible to know how
many Mercenaries had been engaged, and the Ancients
were dismayed at the enormous sum which they
would have to pay. The reserve of silphium must be
sold, and the trading towns taxed; the Mercenaries
would grow impatient; Tunis was already with them;
and the rich, stunned by Hanno's ragings and his
colleague's reproaches, urged any citizens who might
know a Barbarian to go to see him immediately in
order to win back his friendship, and to speak him
fair. Such a show of confidence would soothe them.

3—10

Traders, scribes, workers in the arsenal, and whole families visited the Barbarians.

The soldiers allowed all the Carthaginians to come in, but by a single passage so narrow that four men abreast jostled one another in it. Spendius, standing against the barrier, had them carefully searched; facing him Matho was examining the multitude, trying to recognize some one whom he might have seen at Salammbô's palace.

The camp was like a town, so full of people and of movement was it. The two distinct crowds mingled without blending, one dressed in linen or wool, with felt caps like fir-cones, and the other clad in iron and wearing helmets. Amid serving men and itinerant vendors there moved women of all nations, as brown as ripe dates, as greenish as olives, as yellow as oranges, sold by sailors, picked out of dens, stolen from caravans, taken in the sacking of towns, women that were jaded with love so long as they were young, and plied with blows when they were old, and that died in routs on the roadsides among the baggage and the abandoned beasts of burden. The wives of the nomads had square, tawny robes of dromedary's hair swinging at their heels; musicians from Cyrenaïca, wrapped in violet gauze and with painted eyebrows, sang, squatting on mats; old Negresses with hanging breasts gathered the animals' dung that was drying in the sun to light their fires; the Syracusan women had golden plates in their hair; the Lusitanians had necklaces of shells; the Gauls wore wolf skins upon their white bosoms; and sturdy children, vermin-covered, naked and uncircumcised, butted with their heads against passers-by, or came behind them like young tigers to bite their hands.

The Carthaginians walked through the camp, surprised at the quantities of things with which it was
running over. The most miserable were melancholy,
and the rest dissembled their anxiety.

The soldiers struck them on the shoulder, and exhorted them to be gay. As soon as they saw any
one, they invited him to their amusements. If they
were playing at discus, they would manage to crush
his feet, or if at boxing to fracture his jaw with the
very first blow. The slingers terrified the Carthaginians with their slings, the Psylli with their vipers, and
the horsemen with their horses, while their victims,
addicted as they were to peaceful occupations, bent
their heads and tried to smile at all these outrages.
Some, in order to show themselves brave, made signs
that they should like to become soldiers. They were
set to split wood and to curry mules. They were
buckled up in armour, and rolled like casks through
the streets of the camp. Then, when they were
about to leave, the Mercenaries plucked out their hair
with grotesque contortions.

But many, from foolishness or prejudice, innocently
believed that all the Carthaginians were very rich, and
they walked behind them entreating them to grant
them something. They requested everything that they
thought fine: a ring, a girdle, sandals, the fringe of a
robe, and when the despoiled Carthaginian cried —
"But I have nothing left. What do you want?"
they would reply, "Your wife!" Others even said,
"Your life!"

The military accounts were handed to the captains, read to the soldiers, and definitively approved.
Then they claimed tents; they received them. Next
the polemarchs of the Greeks demanded some of the

handsome suits of armour that were manufactured **at**
Carthage; the Great Council voted sums of money for
their purchase. But it was only fair, so the horsemen
pretended, that the Republic should indemnify them
for their horses; one had lost three at such a siege,
another, five during such a march, another, fourteen
in the precipices. Stallions from Hecatompylos were
offered to them, but they preferred money.

Next they demanded that they should be paid in
money (in pieces of money, and not in leathern coins)
for all the corn that was owing to them, and at the
highest price that it had fetched during the war; so
that they exacted four hundred times as much for a
measure of meal as they had given for a sack of
wheat. Such injustice was exasperating; but it was
necessary, nevertheless, to submit.

Then the delegates from the soldiers and from the
Great Council swore renewed friendship by the Genius
of Carthage and the gods of the Barbarians. They
exchanged excuses and caresses with oriental demon-
strativeness and verbosity. Then the soldiers claimed,
as a proof of friendship, the punishment of those who
had estranged them from the Republic.

Their meaning, it was pretended, was not understood, and they explained themselves more clearly by
saying that they must have Hanno's head.

Several times in the day, they left their camp, and
walked along the foot of the walls, shouting a demand
that the Suffet's head should be thrown to them, and
holding out their robes to receive it.

The Great Council would perhaps have given way
but for a last exaction, more outrageous than the rest;
they demanded maidens, chosen from illustrious families, in marriage for their chiefs. It was an idea

which had emanated from Spendius, and which many
thought most simple and practicable. But the as-
sumption of their desire to mingle with Punic blood
made the people indignant; and they were bluntly
told that they were to receive no more. Then they
exclaimed that they had been deceived, and that if
their pay did not arrive within three days, they would
themselves go and take it in Carthage.

The bad faith of the Mercenaries was not so complete as their enemies thought. Hamilcar had made
them extravagant promises, vague, it is true, but at
the same time solemn and reiterated. They might
have believed that when they disembarked at Carthage the town would be abandoned to them, and that
they should have treasures divided among them; and
when they saw that scarcely their wages would be
paid, the disillusion touched their pride no less than
their greed.

Had not Dionysius, Pyrrhus, Agathocles, and the
generals of Alexander furnished examples of marvellous good fortune? Hercules, whom the Chanaanites
confounded with the sun, was the ideal which shone
on the horizon of armies. They knew that simple
soldiers had worn diadems, and the echoes of crum-
bling empires would furnish dreams to the Gaul in
his oak forest, to the Ethiopian amid his sands. But
there was a nation always ready to turn courage to
account; and the robber driven from his tribe, the
parricide wandering on the roads, the perpetrator of
sacrilege pursued by the gods, all who were starving
or in despair strove to reach the port where the
Carthaginian broker was recruiting soldiers. Usually
the Republic kept its promises. This time, however,
the eagerness of its avarice had brought it into peril-

ous disgrace. Numidians, Libyans, the whole of
Africa was about to fall upon Carthage. Only the
sea was open to it, and there it met with the
Romans; so that, like a man assailed by murderers, it
felt death all around it.

It was quite necessary to have recourse to Gisco,
and the Barbarians accepted his intervention. One
morning they saw the chains of the harbour lowered,
and three flat-bottomed boats passing through the
canal of the Tænia entered the lake.

Gisco was visible on the first at the prow. Behind him rose an enormous chest, higher than a cata-
falque, and furnished with rings like hanging crowns.
Then appeared the legion of interpreters, with their
hair dressed like sphinxes, and with parrots tattooed
on their breasts. Friends and slaves followed, all
without arms, and in such numbers that they shoul-
dered one another. The three long, dangerously-loaded
barges advanced amid the shouts of the onlooking
army.

As soon as Gisco disembarked, the soldiers ran to
meet him. He had a sort of tribune erected with
knapsacks, and declared that he should not depart before he had paid them all in full.

There was an outburst of applause, and it was a
long time before he was able to speak.

Then he censured the wrongs done to the Republic, and to the Barbarians; the fault lay with a few
mutineers who had alarmed Carthage by their violence.
The best proof of good intention on the part of the
latter was that it was he, the eternal adversary of the
Suffet Hanno, who was sent to them. They must
not credit the people with the folly of desiring to provoke brave men, nor with ingratitude enough not to

recognise their services; and Gisco began to pay the
soldiers, commencing with the Libyans. As they had
declared that the lists were untruthful, he made no
use of them.

They defiled before him according to nationality,
opening their fingers to show the number of their
years of service; they were marked in succession with
green paint on the left arm; the scribes dipped into
the yawning coffer, while others made holes with a
style on a sheet of lead.

A man passed walking heavily like an ox.

"Come up beside me," said the Suffet, suspecting
some fraud; "how many years have you served?"

"Twelve," replied the Libyan.

Gisco slipped his fingers under his chin, for the
chin-piece of the helmet used in course of time to occasion two callosities there; these were called carobs,
and "to have the carobs" was an expression used to
denote a veteran.

"Thief!" exclaimed the Suffet, "your shoulders
ought to have what your face lacks!" and tearing off
his tunic he laid bare his back which was covered
with a bleeding scab; he was a labourer from Hippo-
Zarytus. Hootings were raised, and he was decapitated.

As soon as night fell, Spendius went and roused
the Libyans, and said to them:

"When the Ligurians, Greeks, Balearians, and men
of Italy are paid, they will return. But as for you,
you will remain in Africa, scattered through your
tribes, and without any means of defence! It will be
then that the Republic will take its revenge! Mistrust
the journey! Are you going to believe everything
that is said? Both the Suffets are agreed, and this
one is imposing on you! Remember the Island of

Bones, and Xanthippus, whom they sent back to
Sparta in a rotten galley!"

"How are we to proceed?" they asked.

"Reflect!" said Spendius.

The two following days were spent in paying the
men of Magdala, Leptis, and Hecatompylos; Spendius
went about among the Gauls.

"They are paying off the Libyans, and then they
will discharge the Greeks, the Balearians, the Asiatics
and all the rest! But you, who are few in number,
will receive nothing! You will see your native lands
no more! You will have no ships, and they will kill
you to save your food!"

The Gauls came to the Suffet. Autaritus, he whom
he had wounded at Hamilcar's palace, put questions
to him, but was repelled by the slaves, and disappeared swearing that he would be revenged.

The demands and complaints multiplied. The
most obstinate penetrated at night into the Suffet's
tent; they took his hands and sought to move him
by making him feel their toothless mouths, their
wasted arms, and the scars of their wounds. Those
who had not yet been paid were growing angry,
those who had received the money demanded more
for their horses; and vagabonds and outlaws assumed
soldiers' arms and declared that they were being forgotten. Every minute there arrived whirlwinds of men,
as it were; the tents strained and fell; the multitude,
thick pressed between the ramparts of the camp,
swayed with loud shouts from the gates to the centre.
When the tumult grew excessively violent Gisco
would rest one elbow on his ivory sceptre and stand
motionless looking at the sea with his fingers buried
in his beard.

Matho frequently went off to speak with Spendius; then he would again place himself in front of the Suffet, and Gisco could feel his eyes continually like two flaming phalaricas darted against him. Several times they hurled reproaches at each other over the heads of the crowd, but without making themselves heard. The distribution, meanwhile, continued, and the Suffet found expedients to remove every obstacle.

The Greeks tried to quibble about differences in currency, but he furnished them with such explanations that they retired without a murmur. The Negroes demanded white shells such as are used for trading in the interior of Africa, but when he offered to send to Carthage for them they accepted money like the rest.

But the Balearians had been promised something better, namely, women. The Suffet replied that a whole caravan of maidens was expected for them, but the journey was long and would require six moons more. When they were fat and well rubbed with benjamin they should be sent in ships to the ports of the Balearians.

Suddenly Zarxas, now handsome and vigorous, leaped like a mountebank upon the shoulders of his friends and cried:

"Have you reserved any of them for the corpses?" at the same time pointing to the gate of Khamon in Carthage.

The brass plates with which it was furnished from top to bottom shone in the sun's latest fires, and the Barbarians believed that they could discern on it a trail of blood. Every time that Gisco wished to speak their shouts began again. At last he descended with measured steps, and shut himself up in his tent.

When he left it at sunrise his interpreters, who used to sleep outside, did not stir; they lay on their backs with their eyes fixed, their tongues between their teeth, and their faces of a bluish colour. White mucus flowed from their nostrils, and their limbs were stiff, as if they had all been frozen by the cold during the night. Each had a little noose of rushes round his neck.

From that time onward the rebellion was unchecked. The murder of the Balearians which had been recalled by Zarxas strengthened the distrust inspired by Spendius. They imagined that the Republic was always trying to deceive them. An end must be put to it! The interpreters should be dispensed with! Zarxas sang war-songs with a sling around his head; Autaritus brandished his great sword; Spendius whispered a word to one or gave a dagger to another. The boldest endeavoured to pay themselves, while those who were less frenzied wished to have the distribution continued. No one now relinquished his arms, and the anger of all combined into a tumultuous hatred of Gisco.

Some got up beside him. So long as they vociferated abuse they were listened to with patience; but if they tried to utter the least word in his behalf they were immediately stoned, or their heads were cut off by a sabre-stroke from behind. The heap of knapsacks was redder than an altar.

They became terrible after their meal and when they had drunk wine! This was an enjoyment forbidden in the Punic armies under pain of death, and they raised their cups in the direction of Carthage in derision of its discipline. Then they returned to the slaves of the exchequer and again began to kill. The

word *strike,* though different in each language, was
understood by all.

Gisco was well aware that he was being abandoned by his country; but in spite of its ingratitude
he would not dishonour it. When they reminded him
that they had been promised ships, he swore by Moloch
to provide them himself at his own expense, and pulling off his necklace of blue stones he threw it into
the crowd as the pledge of his oath.

Then the Africans claimed the corn in accordance
with the engagements made by the Great Council.
Gisco spread out the accounts of the Syssitia traced
in violet pigment on sheep skins; and read out all
that had entered Carthage month by month and day
by day.

Suddenly he stopped with gaping eyes, as if he
had just discovered his sentence of death among the
figures.

The Ancients had, in fact, fraudulently reduced
them, and the corn sold during the most calamitous
period of the war was set down at so low a rate that,
blindness apart, it was impossible to believe it.

"Speak!" they shouted. "Louder! Ah! he is trying to lie, the coward! Don't trust him."

For some time he hesitated. At last he resumed
his task.

The soldiers, without suspecting that they were
being deceived, accepted the accounts of the Syssitia
as true. But the abundance that had prevailed at
Carthage made them furiously jealous. They broke
open the sycamore chest; it was three parts empty.
They had seen such sums coming out of it, that they
thought it inexhaustible; Gisco must have buried
some in his tent. They scaled the knapsacks. Matho

led them, and as they shouted "The money! the money!" Gisco at last replied:

"Let your general give it to you!"

He looked them in the face without speaking, with his great yellow eyes, and his long face that was paler than his beard. An arrow, held by its feathers, hung from the large gold ring in his ear, and a stream of blood was trickling from his tiara upon his shoulder.

At a gesture from Matho all advanced. Gisco held out his arms; Spendius tied his wrists with a slip knot; another knocked him down, and he disappeared amid the disorder of the crowd which was stumbling over the knapsacks.

They sacked his tent. Nothing was found in it except things indispensable to life; and, on a closer search, three images of Tanith, and, wrapped up in an ape's skin, a black stone which had fallen from the moon. Many Carthaginians had chosen to accompany him; they were eminent men, and all belonged to the war party.

They were dragged outside the tents and thrown into the pit used for the reception of filth. They were tied with iron chains around the body to solid stakes, and were offered food at the point of the javelin.

Autaritus overwhelmed them with invectives as he inspected them, but being quite ignorant of his language they made no reply; and the Gaul from time to time threw pebbles at their faces to make them cry out.

The next day a sort of languor took possession of the army. Now that their anger was over they were seized with anxiety. Matho was suffering from vague melancholy. It seemed to him that Salammbô had indirectly been insulted. These rich men were a kind of appendage to her person. He sat down in the night on the edge of the pit, and recognised in their groanings something of the voice of which his heart was full.

All, however, upbraided the Libyans, who alone had been paid. But while national antipathies revived, together with personal hatreds, it was felt that it would be perilous to give way to them. Reprisals after such an outrage would be formidable. It was necessary, therefore, to anticipate the vengeance of Carthage. Conventions and harangues never ceased. Every one spoke, no one was listened to; Spendius, usually so loquacious, shook his head at every proposal.

One evening he asked Matho carelessly whether there were not springs in the interior of the town.

"Not one!" replied Matho.

The next day Spendius drew him to the bank of the lake.

"Master!" said the former slave, "If your heart is dauntless, I will bring you into Carthage."

"How?" repeated the other, panting.

"Swear to execute all my commands and to follow me like a shadow!"

Then Matho, raising his arm towards the planet of Chabar, exclaimed:

"By Tanith, I swear!"

Spendius resumed:

"To-morrow after sunset you will wait for me at the foot of the aqueduct between the ninth and tenth arcades. Bring with you an iron pick, a crestless helmet, and leathern sandals."

The aqueduct of which he spoke crossed the entire isthmus obliquely, — a considerable work, afterwards enlarged by the Romans. In spite of her disdain of other nations, Carthage had awkwardly borrowed this novel invention from them, just as Rome herself had built Punic galleys; and five rows of superposed arches, of a dumpy kind of architecture, with buttresses at their foot and lions' heads at the top, reached to the western part of the Acropolis, where they sank beneath the town to incline what was nearly a river into the cisterns of Megara.

Spendius met Matho here at the hour agreed upon. He fastened a sort of harpoon to the end of a cord and whirled it rapidly like a sling; the iron instrument caught fast, and they began to climb up the wall, the one after the other.

But when they had ascended to the first story the cramp fell back every time that they threw it, and in order to discover some fissure they had to walk along the edge of the cornice. At every row of arches they found that it became narrower. Then the cord relaxed. Several times it nearly broke.

At last they reached the upper platform. Spendius stooped down from time to time to feel the stones with his hand.

"Here it is," he said; "let us begin!" And leaning on the pick which Matho had brought they succeeded in disengaging one of the flagstones.

In the distance they perceived a troop of horsemen galloping on horses without bridles. Their golden bracelets leaped in the vague drapings of their cloaks. A man could be seen in front crowned with ostrich feathers, and galloping with a lance in each hand.

"Narr' Havas!" exclaimed Matho.

"What matter?" returned Spendius, and he leaped into the hole which they had just made by removing the flagstone.

Matho at his command tried to thrust out one of the blocks. But he could not move his elbows for want of room.

"We shall return," said Spendius; "go on in front." Then they ventured into the channel of water.

It reached to their waists. Soon they staggered, and were obliged to swim. Their limbs knocked against the walls of the narrow duct. The water flowed almost immediately beneath the stones above, and their faces were torn by them. Then the current carried them away. Their breasts were crushed with air heavier than that of a sepulchre, and stretching themselves out as much as possible with their heads between their arms and their knees close together, they passed like arrows into the darkness, choking, gurgling, and almost dead. Suddenly all became black before them, and the speed of the waters redoubled. They fell.

When they came to the surface again, they remained for a few minutes extended on their backs, inhaling the air delightfully. Arcades, one behind another, opened up amid large walls separating the various basins. All were filled, and the water stretched in a single sheet throughout the length of the cisterns. Through the air-holes in the cupolas on the ceiling there fell a pale brightness which spread upon the waves discs, as it were, of light, while the darkness round about thickened towards the walls and threw them back to an indefinite distance. The slightest noise made a great echo.

Spendius and Matho commenced to swim again, and passing through the opening of the arches, traversed several chambers in succession. Two other rows of smaller basins extended in a parallel direction on each side. They lost themselves; they turned, and came back again. At last something offered a resistance to their heels. It was the pavement of the gallery that ran along the cisterns.

Then, advancing with great precautions, they felt along the wall to find an outlet. But their feet slipped, and they fell into the great centre-basins. They had to climb up again, and there they fell again. They experienced terrible fatigue, which made them feel as if all their limbs had been dissolved in the water while swimming. Their eyes closed; they were in the agonies of death.

Spendius struck his hand against the bars of a grating. They shook it, it gave way, and they found themselves on the steps of a staircase. A door of bronze closed it above. With the point of a dagger they moved the bar, which was opened from without, and suddenly the pure open air surrounded them.

The night was filled with silence, and the sky seemed at an extraordinary height. Clusters of trees projected over the long lines of walls. The whole town was asleep. The fires of the outposts shone like lost stars.

Spendius, who had spent three years in the ergastulum, was but imperfectly acquainted with the different quarters. Matho conjectured that to reach Hamilcar's palace they ought to strike to the left and cross the Mappalian district.

"No," said Spendius," take me to the temple of Tanith."

Matho wished to speak.

"Remember!" said the former slave, and raising his arm he showed him the glittering planet of Chabar.

Then Matho turned in silence towards the Acropolis.

They crept along the nopal hedges which bordered the paths. The water trickled from their limbs upon the dust. Their damp sandals made no noise; Spendius, with eyes that flamed more than torches, searched the bushes at every step;—and he walked behind Matho with his hands resting on the two daggers which he carried on his arms, and which hung from below the armpit by a leathern band.

V.

TANITH.

AFTER leaving the gardens Matho and Spendius found themselves checked by the rampart of Megara. But they discovered a breach in the great wall and passed through.

The ground sloped downwards, forming a kind of very broad valley. It was an exposed place.

"Listen," said Spendius, "and first of all fear nothing! I shall fulfil my promise——"

He stopped abruptly, and seemed to reflect as though searching for his words,—"Do you remember that time at sunrise when I showed Carthage to you on Salammbô's terrace? We were strong that day, but you would listen to nothing!" Then in a grave voice: "Master, in the sanctuary of Tanith there is a mysterious veil, which fell from heaven and which covers the goddess."

"I know," said Matho.

Spendius resumed: "It is itself divine, for it forms part of her. The gods reside where their images are. It is because Carthage possesses it that Carthage is powerful." Then leaning over to his ear: "I have brought you with me to carry it off!"

Matho recoiled in horror. "Begone! look for some one else! I will not help you in this execrable crime!"

"But Tanith is your enemy," retorted Spendius; "she is persecuting you and you are dying through her wrath. You will be revenged upon her. She will obey you, and you will become almost immortal and invincible."

Matho bent his head. Spendius continued:

"We should succumb; the army would be annihilated of itself. We have neither flight, nor succor, nor pardon to hope for! What chastisement from the gods can you be afraid of since you will have their power in your own hands? Would you rather die on the evening of a defeat, in misery beneath the shelter of a bush, or amid the outrages of the populace and the flames of funeral piles? Master, one day you will enter Carthage among the colleges of the pontiffs, who will kiss your sandals; and if the veil of Tanith weighs upon you still, you will reinstate it in its temple. Follow me! come and take it."

Matho was consumed by a terrible longing. He would have liked to possess the veil while refraining from the sacrilege. He said to himself that perhaps it would not be necessary to take it in order to monopolise its virtue. He did not go to the bottom of his thought but stopped at the boundary, where it terrified him.

"Come on!" he said; and they went off with rapid strides, side by side, and without speaking.

The ground rose again, and the dwellings were near. They turned into the narrow streets amid the darkness. The strips of esparto-grass with which the doors were closed, beat against the walls. Some camels were ruminating in a square before heaps of

cut grass. Then they passed beneath a gallery covered with foliage. A pack of dogs were barking.
But suddenly the space grew wider and they recognised the western face of the Acropolis. At the foot
of Byrsa there stretched a long black mass: it was
the temple of Tanith, a whole made up of monuments and galleries, courts and fore-courts, and
bounded by a low wall of dry stones. Spendius and
Matho leaped over it.

This first barrier enclosed a wood of plane-trees as
a precaution against plague and infection in the air.
Tents were scattered here and there, in which, during
the daytime, depilatory pastes, perfumes, garments,
moon-shaped cakes, and images of the goddess with
representations of the temple hollowed out in blocks
of alabaster, were on sale.

They had nothing to fear, for on nights when the
planet did not appear, all rites were suspended; nevertheless Matho slackened his speed, and stopped before the three ebony steps leading to the second
enclosure.

"Forward!" said Spendius.

Pomegranates, almond trees, cypresses and myrtles alternated in regular succession; the path, which
was paved with blue pebbles, creaked beneath their
footsteps, and full-blown roses formed a hanging
bower over the whole length of the avenue. They
arrived before an oval hole protected by a grating.
Then Matho, who was frightened by the silence, said
to Spendius:

"It is here that they mix the fresh water and the
bitter."

"I have seen all that," returned the former slave,
"in Syria, in the town of Maphug;" and they as-

cended into the third enclosure by a staircase of six silver steps.

A huge cedar occupied the centre. Its lowest branches were hidden beneath scraps of material and necklaces hung upon them by the faithful. They walked a few steps further on, and the front of the temple was displayed before them.

Two long porticoes, with their architraves resting on dumpy pillars, flanked a quadrangular tower, the platform of which was adorned with the crescent of a moon. On the angles of the porticoes and at the four corners of the tower stood vases filled with kindled aromatics. The capitals were laden with pomegranates and coloquintidas. Twining knots, lozenges, and rows of pearls alternated on the walls, and a hedge of silver filigree formed a wide semicircle in front of the brass staircase which led down from the vestibule.

There was a cone of stone at the entrance between a stela of gold and one of emerald, and Matho kissed his right hand as he passed beside it.

The first room was very lofty; its vaulted roof was pierced by numberless apertures, and if the head were raised the stars might be seen. All round the wall rush baskets were heaped up with the firstfruits of adolescence in the shape of beards and curls of hair; and in the centre of the circular apartment the body of a woman issued from a sheath which was covered with breasts. Fat, bearded, and with eyelids downcast, she looked as though she were smiling, while her hands were crossed upon the lower part of her big body, which was polished by the kisses of the crowd.

Then they found themselves again in the open air

in a transverse corridor, wherein there was an altar of small dimensions leaning against an ivory door. There was no further passage; the priests alone could open it; for the temple was not a place of meeting for the multitude, but the private abode of a divinity.

"The enterprise is impossible," said Matho. "You had not thought of this! Let us go back!" Spendius was examining the walls.

He wanted the veil, not because he had confidence in its virtue (Spendius believed only in the Oracle), but because he was persuaded that the Carthaginians would be greatly dismayed on seeing themselves deprived of it. They walked all round behind in order to find some outlet.

Aedicules of different shapes were visible beneath clusters of turpentine trees. Here and there rose a stone phallus, and large stags roamed peacefully about, spurning the fallen fir-cones with their cloven hoofs.

But they retraced their steps between two long galleries which ran parallel to each other. There were small open cells along their sides, and tambourines and cymbals hung against their cedar columns from top to bottom. Women were sleeping stretched on mats outside the cells. Their bodies were greasy with unguents, and exhaled an odour of spices and extinguished perfuming-pans; while they were so covered with tattooings, necklaces, rings, vermilion, and antimony that, but for the motion of their breasts, they might have been taken for idols as they lay thus on the ground. There were lotus-trees encircling a fountain in which fish like Salammbô's were swimming; and then in the background, against the wall of the temple, spread a vine, the branches of which were of glass and the grape-bunches of emerald, the rays from the precious stones making a play of light through the painted columns upon the sleeping faces.

Matho felt suffocated in the warm atmosphere pressed down upon him by the cedar partitions. All these symbols of fecundation, these perfumes, radiations, and breathings overwhelmed him. Through all the mystic dazzling he kept thinking of Salammbô. She became confused with the goddess herself, and his love unfolded itself all the more, like the great lotus-plants blooming upon the depths of the waters.

Spendius was calculating how much money he would have made in former days by the sale of these women; and with a rapid glance he estimated the weight of the golden necklaces as he passed by.

The temple was impenetrable on this side as on the other, and they returned behind the first chamber. While Spendius was searching and ferreting, Matho was prostrate before the door supplicating Tanith. He besought her not to permit the sacrilege, and strove to soften her with caressing words, such as are used to an angry person.

Spendius noticed a narrow aperture above the door.

"Rise!" he said to Matho, and he made him stand erect with his back against the wall. Placing one foot in his hands, and then the other upon his head, he reached up to the air-hole, made his way into it and disappeared. Then Matho felt a knotted cord — that one which Spendius had rolled around his body before entering the cisterns — fall upon his shoulders, and bearing upon it with both hands he soon found himself by the side of the other in a large hall filled with shadow.

Such an attempt was something extraordinary. The inadequacy of the means for preventing it was a sufficient proof that it was considered impossible. The sanctuaries were protected by terror more than by their walls. Matho expected to die at every step.

However a light was flickering far back in the darkness, and they went up to it. It was a lamp burning in a shell on the pedestal of a statue which wore the cap of the Kabiri. Its long blue robe was strewn with diamond discs, and its heels were fastened to the ground by chains which sank beneath the pavement. Matho suppressed a cry. "Ah! there she is! there she is!" he stammered out. Spendius took up the lamp in order to light himself.

"What an impious man you are!" murmured Matho, following him nevertheless.

The apartment which they entered had nothing in it but a black painting representing another woman. Her legs reached to the top of the wall, and her body filled the entire ceiling; a huge egg hung by a thread from her navel, and she fell head downwards upon the other wall, reaching as far as the level of the pavement, which was touched by her pointed fingers.

They drew a hanging aside, in order to go on further; but the wind blew and the light went out.

Then they wandered about, lost in the complications of the architecture. Suddenly they felt something strangely soft beneath their feet. Sparks crackled and leaped; they were walking in fire. Spendius touched the ground and perceived that it was carefully carpeted with lynx skins; then it seemed to them that a big cord, wet, cold, and viscous, was gliding between their legs. Through some fissures cut in the wall there fell thin white rays, and they advanced by this uncertain light. At last they distinguished a large black serpent. It darted quickly away and disappeared.

"Let us fly!" exclaimed Matho. "It is she! I feel her; she is coming."

"No, no," replied Spendius, "the temple is empty."

Then a dazzling light made them lower their eyes. Next they perceived all around them an infinite number of beasts, lean, panting, with bristling claws, and mingled together one above another in a mysterious and terrifying confusion. There were serpents with feet, and bulls with wings, fishes with human heads were devouring fruit, flowers were blooming in the jaws of crocodiles, and elephants with uplifted trunks were sailing proudly through the azure like eagles. Their incomplete or multiplied limbs were distended with terrible exertion. As they thrust out their tongues they looked as though they would fain give forth their souls; and every shape was to be found among them as if the germ-receptacle had been suddenly hatched and had burst, emptying itself upon the walls of the hall.

Round the latter were twelve globes of blue crystal, supported by monsters resembling tigers. Their eyeballs were starting out of their heads like those of snails, with their dumpy loins bent they were turning round toward the background where the supreme Rabbet, the Omnifecund, the last invented, shone splendid in a chariot of ivory.

She was covered with scales, feathers, flowers, and birds as high as the waist. For earrings she had silver cymbals, which flapped against her cheeks. Her large fixed eyes gazed upon you, and a luminous stone, set in an obscene symbol on her brow, lighted the whole hall by its reflection in red copper mirrors above the door.

Mantho took a step forward; but a flag stone yielded beneath his heels and immediately the spheres began to revolve and the monsters to roar; music rose melodious and pealing, like the harmony of the planets; the tumultuous soul of Tanith was poured streaming forth. She was about to arise, as lofty as the hall and with open arms. Suddenly the monsters closed their jaws and the crystal globes revolved no longer.

Then a mournful modulation lingered for a time through the air and at last died away.

"And the veil?" said Spendius.

Nowhere could it be seen. Where was it to be found? How could it be discovered? What if the priests had hidden it? Matho experienced anguish of heart and felt as though he had been deceived in his belief.

"This way!" whispered Spendius. An inspiration guided him. He drew Matho behind Tanith's chariot, where a cleft a cubit wide ran down the wall from top to bottom.

Then they penetrated into a small and completely circular room, so lofty that it was like the interior of a pillar. In the centre there was a big black stone, of semispherical shape like a tambourine; flames were burning upon it; an ebony cone, bearing a head and two arms, rose behind.

But beyond it seemed as though there were a cloud wherein were twinkling stars; faces appeared in the depths of its folds — Eschmoun with the Ka-biri, some of the monsters that had already been seen, the sacred beasts of the Babylonians, and others with

which they were not acquainted. It passed beneath
the idol's face like a mantle, and spread fully out was
drawn up on the wall, to which it was fastened by
the corners, appearing at once bluish as the night,
yellow as the dawn, purple as the sun, multitudinous,
diaphanous, sparkling, light. It was the mantle of
the goddess, the holy zaïmph which might not be
seen.

Both turned pale.

"Take it!" said Matho at last.

Spendius did not hesitate, and leaning upon the
idol he unfastened the veil, which sank to the ground.
Matho laid his hand upon it; then he put his head
through the opening, then he wrapped it about his
body, and he spread out his arms the better to view it.

"Let us go!" said Spendius.

Matho stood panting with his eyes fixed upon the
pavement. Suddenly he exclaimed:

"But what if I went to her? I fear her beauty
no longer! What could she do against me? I am
now more than a man. I could pass through flames
or walk upon the sea! I am transported! Salammbô!
Salammbô! I am your master!"

His voice was like thunder. He seemed to Spendius to have grown taller and transformed.

A sound of footsteps drew near, a door opened,
and a man appeared, a priest with lofty cap and
staring eyes. Before he could make a gesture Spendius had rushed upon him, and clasping him in his
arms had buried both his daggers in his sides. His
head rang upon the pavement.

Then they stood for a while, as motionless as the
corpse, listening. Nothing could be heard but the
murmuring of the wind through the half-opened door.

The latter led into a narrow passage. Spendius advanced along it, Matho followed him, and they found themselves almost immediately in the third enclosure, between the lateral porticoes, in which were the dwellings of the priests.

Behind the cells there must be a shorter way out. They hastened along.

Spendius squatted down at the edge of the fountain and washed his bloodstained hands. The women slept. The emerald vine shone. They resumed their advance.

But something was running behind them under the trees; and Matho, who bore the veil, several times felt that it was being pulled very gently from below. It was a large cynocephalus, one of those which dwelt at liberty within the enclosure of the goddess. It clung to the mantle as though it had been conscious of the theft. They did not dare to strike it, however, fearing that it might redouble its cries; suddenly its anger subsided, and it trotted close beside them swinging its body with its long hanging arms. Then at the barrier it leaped at a bound into a palm tree.

When they had left the last enclosure they directed their steps towards Hamilcar's palace, Spendius understanding that it would be useless to try to dissuade Matho.

They went by the street of the Tanners, the square of Muthumbal, the green market and the cross-ways of Cynasyn. At the angle of a wall a man drew back frightened by the sparkling thing which pierced the darkness.

"Hide the zaïmph!" said Spendius.

Other people passed them, but without perceiving them.

At last they recognised the houses of Megara.

The pharos, which was built behind them on the summit of the cliff, lit up the heavens with a great red brightness, and the shadow of the palace, with its rising terraces, projected a monstrous pyramid, as it were, upon the gardens. They entered through the hedge of jujube-trees, beating down the branches with blows of the dagger.

The traces of the feast of the Mercenaries were everywhere still manifest. The parks were broken up, the trenches drained, the doors of the ergastulum open. No one was to be seen about the kitchens or cellars. They wondered at the silence, which was occasionally broken by the hoarse breathing of the elephants moving in their shackles, and the crepitation of the pharos, in which a pile of aloes was burning.

Matho, however, kept repeating:

"But where is she? I wish to see her! Lead me!"

"It is a piece of insanity!" Spendius kept saying. "She will call, her slaves will run up, and in spite of your strength you will die!"

They reached thus the galley staircase. Matho raised his head, and thought that he could perceive far above a vague brightness, radiant and soft. Spendius sought to restrain him, but he dashed up the steps.

As he found himself again in places where he had already seen her, the interval of the days that had passed was obliterated from his memory. But now had she been singing among the tables; she had disappeared, and he had since been continually ascending this staircase. The sky above his head was covered with fires; the sea filled the horizon; at each step he was surrounded by a still greater immensity, and he continued to climb upward with that strange facility which we experience in dreams.

The rustling of the veil as it brushed against the stones recalled his new power to him; but in the excess of his hope he could no longer tell what he was to do; this uncertainty alarmed him.

From time to time he would press his face against the quadrangular openings in the closed apartments, and he thought that in several of the latter he could see persons asleep.

The last story, which was narrower, formed a sort of dado on the summit of the terraces. Matho walked round it slowly.

A milky light filled the sheets of talc which closed the little apertures in the wall, and in their symmetrical arrangement they looked in the darkness like rows of delicate pearls. He recognised the red door with the black cross. The throbbing of his heart increased. He would fain have fled. He pushed the door and it opened.

A galley-shaped lamp hung burning in the back part of the room, and three rays, emitted from its silver keel, trembled on the lofty wainscots, which were painted red with black bands. The ceiling was an assemblage of small beams, with amethysts and topazes amid their gilding in the knots of the wood. On both the great sides of the apartment there stretched a very low bed made with white leathern straps; while above, semi-circles like shells, opened in the thickness of the wall, suffered a garment to come out and hang down to the ground.

There was an oval basin with a step of onyx round it; delicate slippers of serpent skin were stand-

ing on the edge, together with an alabaster flagon.
The trace of a wet footstep might be seen beyond.
Exquisite scents were evaporating.

Matho glided over the pavement, which was en-
crusted with gold, mother-of-pearl, and glass; and, in
spite of the polished smoothness of the ground, it
seemed to him that his feet sank as though he were
walking on sand.

Behind the silver lamp he had perceived a large
square of azure held in the air by four cords from
above, and he advanced with loins bent and mouth
open.

Flamingoes' wings, fitted on branches of black
coral, lay about among purple cushions, tortoiseshell
strigils, cedar boxes, and ivory spatulas. There were
antelopes' horns with rings and bracelets strung upon
them; and clay vases were cooling in the wind in the
cleft of the wall on a lattice-work of reeds. Several
times he struck his foot, for the ground had various
levels of unequal height, which formed a succession of
apartments, as it were, in the room. In the background there were silver balustrades surrounding a
carpet strewn with painted flowers. At last he came
to the hanging bed beside an ebony stool serving to
get into it.

But the light ceased at the edge;—and the shadow,
like a great curtain, revealed only a corner of the red
mattress with the extremity of a little naked foot
lying upon its ankle. Then Matho took up the lamp
very gently.

She was sleeping with her cheek in one hand and
with the other arm extended. Her ringlets were
spread about her in such abundance that she appeared
to be lying on black feathers, and her ample white

tunic wound in soft draperies to her feet following the curves of her person. Her eyes were just visible beneath her half-closed eyelids. The curtains, which stretched perpendicularly, enveloped her in a bluish atmosphere, and the motion of her breathing, communicating itself to the cords, seemed to rock her in the air. A long mosquito was buzzing.

Matho stood motionless holding the silver lamp at arm's length; but on a sudden the mosquito-net caught fire and disappeared, and Salammbô awoke.

The fire had gone out of itself. She did not speak. The lamp caused great luminous moires to flicker on the wainscots.

"What is it?" she said.

He replied:

"'Tis the veil of the goddess!"

"The veil of the goddess!" cried Salammbô, and supporting herself on both clenched hands she leaned shuddering out. He resumed:

"I have been in the depths of the sanctuary to seek it for you! Look!" The zaïmph shone a mass of rays.

"Do you remember it?" said Matho. "You appeared at night in my dreams, but I did not guess the mute command of your eyes!" She put out one foot upon the ebony stool. "Had I understood I should have hastened hither, I should have forsaken the army, I should not have left Carthage. To obey you I would go down through the caverns of Hadrumetum into the kingdom of the shades!—Forgive me! it was as though mountains were weighing upon my days; and yet something drew me on! I tried to come to you! Should I ever have dared this without the Gods! —Let us go! you must follow me! or, if you do not

wish to do so, I will remain. What matters it to me!
—Drown my soul in your breath! Let my lips be
crushed with kissing your hands!"

"Let me see it!" she said. "Nearer! nearer!"

Day was breaking, and the sheets of talc in the
walls were filled with a vinous colour. Salammbô
leaned fainting against the cushions of the bed.

"I love you!" cried Matho.

"Give it!" she stammered out, and they drew
closer together.

She kept advancing, clothed in her white trailing
simar, and with her large eyes fastened on the veil.
Matho gazed at her, dazzled by the splendours of her
head, and, holding out the zaïmph towards her, was
about to enfold her in an embrace. She was stretching out her arms. Suddenly she stopped, and they
stood looking at each other, open-mouthed.

Then without understanding the meaning of his
solicitation a horror seized upon her. Her delicate
eyebrows rose, her lips opened; she trembled. At
last she struck one of the brass pateras which hung
at the corners of the red mattress, crying:

"To the rescue! to the rescue! Back, sacrilegious
man! infamous and accursed! Help, Taanach, Kroum,
Ewa, Micipsa, Schaoul!"

And the scared face of Spendius, appearing in
the wall between the clay flagons, cried out these
words:

"Fly! they are hastening hither!"

A great tumult came upwards shaking the staircases, and a flood of people, women, serving-men,
and slaves, rushed into the room with stakes, toma-
hawks, cutlasses, and daggers. They were nearly
paralysed with indignation on perceiving a man; the

3—12

female servants uttered funeral wailings, and the eunuchs grew pale beneath their black skins.

Matho was standing behind the balustrades. With the zaïmph which was wrapped about him, he looked like a sidereal god surrounded by the firmament. The slaves were going to fall upon him, but she stopped them:

"Touch it not! It is the mantle of the goddess!"

She had drawn back into a corner; but she took a step towards him, and stretched forth her naked arm:

"A curse upon you, you who have plundered Tanith! Hatred, vengeance, massacre, and grief! May Gurzil, god of battles, rend you! may Mastiman, god of the the dead, stifle you! and may the Other—he who may not be named—burn you!"

Matho uttered a cry as though he had received a sword-thrust. She repeated several times: "Begone! begone!"

The crowd of servants spread out, and Matho, with hanging head, passed slowly through the midst of them; but at the door he stopped, for the fringe of the zaïmph had caught on one of the golden stars with which the flagstones were paved. He pulled it off abruptly with a movement of his shoulder and went down the staircases.

Spendius, bounding from terrace to terrace, and leaping over the hedges and trenches, had escaped from the gardens. He reached the foot of the pharos. The wall was discontinued at this spot, so inaccessible was the cliff. He advanced to the edge, lay down on his back, and let himself slide, feet foremost, down the whole length of it to the bottom; then by swimming he reached the Cape of the Tombs, made a wide circuit of the salt lagoon, and re-entered the camp of the Barbarians in the evening.

The sun had risen; and, like a retreating lion, Matho went down the paths, casting terrible glances around him.

A vague clamor reached his ears. It had started from the palace, and it was beginning afresh in the distance, towards the Acropolis. Some said that the treasure of the Republic had been seized in the temple of Moloch; others spoke of the assassination of a priest. It was thought, moreover, that the Barbarians had entered the city.

Matho, who did not know how to get out of the enclosures, walked straight before him. He was seen, and an outcry was raised. Every one understood; and there was consternation, and then immense wrath.

From the bottom of the Mappalian quarter, from the heights of the Acropolis, from the catacombs, from the borders of the lake, the multitude came in haste. The patricians left their palaces, and the traders left their shops; the women forsook their children; swords, hatchets, and sticks were seized; but the obstacle which had stayed Salammbô stayed them. How could the veil be taken back? The mere sight of it was a crime; it was of the nature of the gods, and contact with it was death.

The despairing priests wrung their hands on the peristyles of the temples. The guards of the Legion galloped about at random; the people climbed upon the houses, the terraces, the shoulders of the colossuses, and the masts of the ships. He went on, nevertheless, and the rage, and the terror also, increased at each of his steps; the streets cleared at his approach, and the torrent of flying men streamed on both sides up to the tops of the walls. Everywhere he could perceive only eyes opened widely as if to devour him, chattering teeth and outstretched fists, and Salammbô's imprecations resounded many times renewed.

Suddenly a long arrow whistled past, then another, and stones began to buzz about him; but the missiles, being badly aimed (for there was the dread of hitting the zaïmph), passed over his head. Moreover, he made a shield of the veil, holding it to the right, to the left, before him and behind him; and they could devise no expedient. He quickened his steps more and more, advancing through the open streets. They were barred with cords, chariots, and snares; and all his windings brought him back again. At last he entered the square of Khamon where the Balearians had perished, and stopped, growing pale as one about to die. This time he was surely lost, and the multitude clapped their hands.

He ran up to the great gate, which was closed. It was very high, made throughout of heart of oak, with iron nails and sheathed with brass. Matho flung himself against it. The people stamped their feet with joy as they saw the impotence of his fury; then he took his sandal, spit upon it, and beat the immovable panels with it. The whole city howled. The veil was forgotten now, and they were about to crush him. Matho gazed with wide vacant eyes upon the crowd. His temples were throbbing with violence enough to stun him, and he felt a numbness as of intoxication creeping over him. Suddenly he caught sight of the long chain used in working the swinging of the gate. With a bound he grasped it, stiffening his arms, and making a buttress of his feet, and at last the huge leaves partly opened.

Then when he was outside he took the great zaïmph from his neck, and raised it as high as possible above his head. The material, upborne by the sea breeze, shone in the sunlight with its colours, its gems, and the figures of its gods. Matho bore it thus across the whole plain as far as the soldiers' tents, and the people on the walls watched the fortune of Carthage depart.

VI.

HANNO.

"I OUGHT to have carried her off!" Matho said in the evening to Spendius. "I should have seized her, and torn her from her house! No one would have dared to touch me!"

Spendius was not listening to him. Stretched on his back he was taking delicious rest beside a large jar filled with honey-coloured water, into which he would dip his head from time to time in order to drink more copiously.

Matho resumed:

"What is to be done? How can we re-enter Carthage?"

"I do not know," said Spendius.

Such impassibility exasperated Matho and he exclaimed:

"Why! the fault is yours! You carry me away, and then you forsake me, coward that you are! Why, pray, should I obey you? Do you think that you are my master? Ah! you prostituter, you slave, you son of a slave!" He ground his teeth and raised his broad hand above Spendius.

The Greek did not reply. An earthen lamp was burning gently against the tent-pole, where the zaïmph shone amid the hanging panoply. Suddenly Matho put on his cothurni, buckled on his brazen jacket of mail, and took his helmet.

"Where are you going?" asked Spendius.

"I am returning! Let me alone! I will bring her back! And if they show themselves I will crush them like vipers! I will put her to death, Spendius! Yes," he repeated, "I will kill her! You shall see, I will kill her!"

But Spendius, who was listening eagerly, snatched up the zaïmph abruptly and threw it into a corner, heaping up fleeces above it. A murmuring of voices was heard, torches gleamed, and Narr' Havas entered, followed by about twenty men.

They wore white woollen cloaks, long daggers, copper necklaces, wooden earrings, and boots of hyena skin; and standing on the threshold they leaned upon their lances like herdsmen resting themselves. Narr' Havas was the handsomest of all; his slender arms were bound with straps ornamented with pearls. The golden circlet which fastened his ample garment about his head held an ostrich feather which hung down behind upon his shoulder; his teeth were displayed in a continual smile; his eyes seemed sharpened like arrows, and there was something observant and airy about his whole demeanour.

He declared that he had come to join the Mercenaries, for the Republic had long been threatening his kingdom. Accordingly he was interested in assisting the Barbarians, and he might also be of service to them.

"I will provide you with elephants (my forests

are full of them), wine, oil, barley, dates, pitch and sulphur for sieges, twenty thousand foot-soldiers and ten thousand horses. If I address myself to you, Matho, it is because the possession of the zaïmph has made you chief man in the army. Moreover," he added, "we are old friends."

Matho, however, was looking at Spendius, who, seated on the sheep-skins, was listening, and giving little nods of assent the while. Narr' Havas continued speaking. He called the gods to witness he cursed Carthage. In his imprecations he broke a javelin. All his men uttered simultaneously a loud howl, and Matho, carried away by so much passion, exclaimed that he accepted the alliance.

A white bull and a black sheep, the symbols of day and night, were then brought, and their throats were cut on the edge of a ditch. When the latter was full of blood they dipped their arms into it. Then Narr' Havas spread out his hand upon Matho's breast, and Matho did the same to Narr' Havas. They repeated the stain upon the canvas of their tents. Afterwards they passed the night in eating, and the remaining portions of the meat were burnt together with the skin, bones, horns, and hoofs.

Matho had been greeted with great shouting when he had come back bearing the veil of the goddess; even those who were not of the Chanaanitish religion were made by their vague enthusiasm to feel the arrival of a genius. As to seizing the zaïmph, no one thought of it, for the mysterious manner in which he had acquired it was sufficient in the minds of the Barbarians to justify its possession; such were the thoughts of the soldiers of the African race. The others, whose hatred was not of such long standing,

did not know how to make up their minds. If they
had had ships they would immediately have departed.

Spendius, Narr' Havas, and Matho despatched men
to all the tribes on Punic soil.

Carthage was sapping the strength of these nations. She wrung exorbitant taxes from them, and
arrears or even murmurings were punished with
fetters, the axe, or the cross. It was necessary to
cultivate whatever suited the Republic, and to furnish
what she demanded; no one had the right of possess-
ing a weapon; when villages rebelled the inhabitants
were sold; governors were esteemed like wine-
presses, according to the quantity which they succeeded in extracting. Then beyond the regions
immediately subject to Carthage extended the allies,
paying only a moderate tribute, and behind the allies
roamed the Nomads, who might be let loose upon
them. By this system the crops were always abundant, the studs skilfully managed, and the plantations
superb.

The elder Cato, a master in the matters of tillage
and slaves, was amazed at it ninety-two years later,
and the death-cry which he repeated continually at
Rome was but the exclamation of jealous greed.

During the last war the exactions had been increased, so that nearly all the towns of Libya
had surrendered to Regulus. To punish them, a
thousand talents, twenty thousand oxen, three hundred bags of gold dust, and considerable advances of
grain had been exacted from them, and the chiefs of
the tribes had been crucified or thrown to the lions.

Tunis especially execrated Carthage! Older than
the metropolis, it could not forgive her her greatness,
and it fronted her walls crouching in the mire on the

water's edge like a venomous beast watching her. Transportations, massacres, and epidemics did not weaken it. It had assisted Archagathas, the son of Agathocles, and the Eaters of Uncleanness found arms there at once.

The couriers had not yet set out when universal rejoicing broke out in the provinces. Without waiting for anything they strangled the comptrollers of the houses and the functionaries of the Republic in the baths; they took the old weapons that had been concealed out of the caves; they forged swords with the iron of the ploughs; the children sharpened javelins at the doors, and the women gave their necklaces, rings, earrings, and everything that could be employed for the destruction of Carthage. Piles of lances were heaped up in the county towns like sheaves of maize. Cattle and money were sent off. Matho speedily paid the Mercenaries their arrears, and owing to this, which was Spendius's idea, he was appointed commander-in-chief—the schalischim of the Barbarians.

Reinforcements of men poured in at the same time. The aborigines appeared first, and were followed by the slaves from the country; caravans of Negroes were seized and armed, and merchants on their way to Carthage, despairing of any more certain profit, mingled with the Barbarians. Numerous bands were continually arriving. From the heights of the Acropolis the growing army might be seen.

But the guards of the Legion were posted as sentries on the platform of the aqueduct, and near them rose at intervals brazen vats, in which floods of asphalt were boiling. Below in the plain the great crowd stirred tumultuously. They were in a state of uncertainty, feeling the embarrassment with which Barbarians are always inspired when they meet with walls.

Utica and Hippo-Zarytus refused their alliance. Phœnician colonies like Carthage, they were self-governing, and always had clauses inserted in the treaties concluded by the Republic to distinguish them from the latter. Nevertheless they respected this stronger sister of theirs who protected them, and they did not think that she could be vanquished by a mass of Barbarians; these would on the contrary be themselves exterminated. They desired to remain neutral and to live at peace.

But their position rendered them indispensable. Utica, at the foot of the gulf, was convenient for bringing assistance into Carthage from without. If Utica alone were taken, Hippo-Zarytus, six hours further distant along the coast, would take its place, and the metropolis, being revictualled in this way, would be impregnable.

Spendius wished the siege to be undertaken immediately. Narr' Havas was opposed to this: an advance should first be made upon the frontier. This was the opinion of the veterans, and of Matho himself, and it was decided that Spendius should go to attack Utica, and Matho Hippo-Zarytus, while in the third place the main body should rest on Tunis and occupy the plain of Carthage, Autaritus being in command. As to Narr' Havas, he was to return to his own kingdom to procure elephants and to scour the roads with his cavalry.

The women cried out loudly against this decision; they coveted the jewels of the Punic ladies. The Libyans also protested. They had been summoned against Carthage, and now they were going away from it! The soldiers departed almost alone. Matho commanded his own companions, together with the Iberians, Lusitanians, and the men of the West, and of the islands; all those who spoke Greek had asked for Spendius on account of his cleverness.

Great was the stupefaction when the army was seen suddenly in motion; it stretched along beneath the mountain of Ariana on the road to Utica beside the sea. A fragment remained before Tunis, the rest disappeared to re-appear on the other shore of the gulf on the outskirts of the woods in which they were lost.

They were perhaps eighty thousand men. The two Tyrian cities would offer no resistance, and they would return against Carthage. Already there was a considerable army attacking it from the base of the isthmus, and it would soon perish from famine, for it was impossible to live without the aid of the provinces, the citizens not paying contributions as they did at Rome. Carthage was wanting in political genius. Her eternal anxiety for gain prevented her from having the prudence which results from loftier ambitions. A galley anchored on the Libyan sands, it was with toil that she maintained her position. The nations roared like billows around her, and the slightest storm shook this formidable machine.

The treasury was exhausted by the Roman war and by all that had been squandered and lost in the bargaining with the Barbarians. Nevertheless soldiers must be had, and not a government would trust the Republic! Ptolemæus had lately refused it two thousand talents. Moreover the rape of the veil disheartened them. Spendius had clearly foreseen this.

But the nation, feeling that it was hated, clasped its money and its gods to its heart, and its patriotism was sustained by the very constitution of its government.

First, the power rested with all, without any one being strong enough to engross it. Private debts were considered as public debts, men of Chanaanitish race had a monopoly of commerce, and by multiplying the profits of piracy with those of usury, by hard dealings in lands and slaves and with the poor, fortunes were sometimes made. These alone opened up all the magistracies, and although authority and money were perpetuated in the same families, people tolerated the oligarchy because they hoped ultimately to share in it.

The societies of merchants, in which the laws were elaborated, chose the inspectors of the exchequer, who on leaving office nominated the hundred members of the Council of the Ancients, themselves dependent on the Grand Assembly, or general gathering of all the rich. As to the two Suffets, the relics of the monarchy and the less than consuls, they were taken from distinct families on the same day. All kinds of enmities were contrived between them, so that they might mutually weaken each other. They could not deliberate concerning war, and when they were vanquished the Great Council crucified them.

The power of Carthage emanated, therefore, from the Syssitia, that is to say, from a large court in the centre of Malqua, at the place, it was said, where the first bark of Phœnician sailors had touched, the sea having retired a long way since then. It was a collection of little rooms of archaic architecture, built of palm trunks with corners of stone, and separated from one another so as to accommodate the various societies separately. The rich crowded there all day to discuss their own concerns and those of the government, from the procuring of pepper to the extermination of Rome. Thrice in a moon they would have their beds brought up to the lofty terrace running along the wall of the court, and they might be seen from below at table in the air, without cothurni or cloaks, with their diamond-covered fingers wandering over the dishes, and their large earrings hanging down among the flagons,—all fat and lusty, half-naked, smiling and eating beneath the blue sky, like great sharks sporting in the sea.

But just now they were unable to dissemble their anxiety; they were too pale for that. The crowd which waited for them at the gates escorted them to their palaces in order to obtain some news from them. As in times of pestilence, all the houses were shut; the streets would fill and suddenly clear again; people ascended the Acropolis or ran to the harbour, and the Great Council deliberated every night. At last the people were convened in the square of Khamon, and it was decided to leave the management of things to Hanno, the conqueror of Hecatompylos.

He was a true Carthaginian, devout, crafty, and pitiless towards the people of Africa. His revenues equalled those of the Barcas. No one had such experience in administrative affairs.

He decreed the enrolment of all healthy citizens, he placed catapults on the towers, he exacted exorbitant supplies of arms, he even ordered the construction of fourteen galleys which were not required, and he desired everything to be registered and care-

fully set down in writing. He had himself conveyed
to the arsenal, the pharos, and the treasuries of the
temples; his great litter was continually to be seen
swinging from step to step as it ascended the staircases of the Acropolis. And then in his palace at
night, being unable to sleep, he would yell out war-
like manœuvres in terrible tones so as to prepare
himself for the fray.

In their extremity of terror all became brave. The
rich ranged themselves in line along the Mappalian
district at cockcrow, and tucking up their robes prac-
tised themselves in handling the pike. But for want
of an instructor they had disputes about it. They
would sit down breathless upon the tombs and then
begin again. Several even dieted themselves. Some
imagined that it was necessary to eat a great deal in
order to acquire strength, while others who were inconvenienced by their corpulence weakened themselves with fasts in order to become thin.

Utica had already called several times upon Carthage for assistance; but Hanno would not set out until the engines of war had been supplied with the last
screw. He lost three moons more in equipping the
one hundred and twelve elephants that were lodged
in the ramparts. They were the conquerors of
Regulus; the people loved them; it was impossible to
treat such old friends too well. Hanno had the brass
plates which adorned their breasts recast, their tusks
gilt, their towers enlarged, and caparisons, edged
with very heavy fringes, cut out of the handsomest
purple. Finally, as their drivers were called Indians
(after the first ones, no doubt, who came from the
Indies) he ordered them all to be costumed after the
Indian fashion; that is to say, with white pads round

their temples, and small drawers of byssus, which with their transverse folds looked like two valves of a shell applied to the hips.

The army under Autaritus still remained before Tunis. It was hidden behind a wall made with mud from the lake, and protected on the top by thorny brushwood. Some Negroes had planted tall sticks here and there bearing frightful faces,—human masks made with birds' feathers, and jackals' or serpents' heads,—which gaped towards the enemy for the purpose of terrifying him; and the Barbarians, reckoning themselves invincible through these means, danced, wrestled, and juggled, convinced that Carthage would perish before long. Any one but Hanno would easily have crushed such a multitude, hampered as it was with herds and women. Moreover, they knew nothing of drill, and Autaritus was so disheartened that he had ceased to require it.

They stepped aside when he passed by rolling his big blue eyes. Then on reaching the edge of the lake he would draw back his sealskin cloak, unfasten the cord which tied up his long red hair, and soak the latter in the water. He regretted that he had not deserted to the Romans along with the two thousand Gauls of the temple of Eryx.

Often the sun would suddenly lose his rays in the middle of the day. Then the gulf and the open sea would seem as motionless as molten lead. A cloud of brown dust stretching perpendicularly would speed whirling along; the palm trees would bend and the sky disappear, while stones would be heard rebounding on the animals' cruppers; and the Gaul, his lips glued against the holes in his tent, would gasp with exhaustion and melancholy. His thoughts would be of the scent of the pastures on autumn mornings, of snowflakes, or of the bellowing of the urus lost in the fog, and closing his eyelids he would in imagination behold the fires in long, straw-roofed cottages flickering on the marshes in the depths of the woods.

Others regretted their native lands as well as he, even though they might not be so far away. Indeed the Carthaginian captives could distinguish the velaria spread over the courtyards of their houses, beyond the gulf on the slopes of Byrsa. But sentries marched round them continually. They were all fastened to a common chain. Each one wore an iron carcanet, and the crowd was never weary of coming to gaze at them. The women would show their little children the handsome robes hanging in tatters on their wasted limbs.

Whenever Autaritus looked at Gisco he was seized with rage at the recollection of the insult that he had received, and he would have killed him but for the oath which he had taken to Narr' Havas. Then he would go back into his tent and drink a mixture of barley and cumin until he swooned away from intoxication, —to awake afterwards in broad day light consumed with horrible thirst.

Matho, meanwhile, was besieging Hippo-Zarytus. But the town was protected by a lake, communicating with the sea. It had three lines of circumvallation, and upon the heights which surrounded it there extended a wall fortified with towers. He had never commanded in such an enterprise before. Moreover, he was beset with thoughts of Salammbô, and he raved in the delight of her beauty as in the sweetness of a vengeance that transported him with pride.

3—13

He felt an acrid, frenzied, permanent want to see her again. He even thought of presenting himself as the bearer of a flag of truce, in the hope that once within Carthage he might make his way to her. Often he would cause the assault to be sounded and waiting for nothing rush upon the mole which it was sought to construct in the sea. He would snatch up the stones with his hands, overturn, strike, and deal sword-thrusts everywhere. The Barbarians would dash on pell-mell; the ladders would break with a loud crash, and masses of men would tumble into the water, causing it to fly up in red waves against the walls. Finally the tumult would subside, and the soldiers would retire to make a fresh beginning.

Matho would go and seat himself outside the tents, wipe his blood-splashed face with his arm, and gaze at the horizon in the direction of Carthage.

In front of him, among the olives, palms, myrtles and planes, stretched two broad ponds which met another lake, the outlines of which could not be seen. Behind one mountain other mountains reared themselves, and in the middle of the immense lake rose an island perfectly black and pyramidal in form. On the left, at the extremity of the gulf, were sand-heaps like arrested waves, large and pale, while the sea, flat as a pavement of lapis-lazuli, ascended by insensible degrees to the edge of the sky. The verdure of the country was lost in places beneath long sheets of yellow; carobs were shining like knobs of coral; vine branches drooped from the tops of the sycamores; the murmuring of the water could be heard; crested larks were hopping about, and the sun's latest fires gilded the carapaces of the tortoises as they came forth from the reeds to inhale the breeze.

Matho would heave deep sighs. He would lie flat on his face, with his nails buried in the soil, and weep; he felt wretched, paltry, forsaken. Never would he possess her, and he was unable even to take a town.

At night when alone in his tent he would gaze upon the zaïmph. Of what use to him was this thing which belonged to the gods?—and doubts crept into the Barbarian's thoughts. Then, on the contrary, it would seem to him that the vesture of the goddess was depending from Salammbô, and that a portion of her soul hovered in it, subtler than a breath; and he would feel it, breathe it in, bury his face in it, and kiss it with sobs. He would cover his shoulders with it in order to delude himself into believing that he was beside her.

Sometimes he would suddenly steal away, stride in the starlight over the sleeping soldiers as they lay wrapped in their cloaks, spring upon a horse on reaching the camp gates, and two hours later be at Utica in Spendius's tent.

At first he would speak of the siege, but his coming was only to ease his sorrow by talking about Salammbô. Spendius exhorted him to be prudent.

"Drive away these trifles from your soul, which is degraded by them! Formerly you were used to obey; now you command an army, and if Carthage is not conquered we shall at least be granted provinces. We shall become kings!"

But how was it that the possession of the zaïmph did not give them the victory? According to Spendius they must wait.

Matho fancied that the veil affected people of Chanaanitish race exclusively, and, in his Barbarian-like subtlety, he said to himself: "The zaïmph will accordingly do nothing for me, but since they have lost it, it will do nothing for them."

Afterwards a scruple troubled him. He was afraid of offending Moloch by worshipping Aptouknos, the god of the Libyans, and he timidly asked Spendius to which of the gods it would be advisable to sacrifice a man.

"Keep on sacrificing!" laughed Spendius.

Matho, who could not understand such indifference, suspected the Greek of having a genius of whom he would not speak.

All modes of worship, as well as all races, were to be met with in these armies of Barbarians, and consideration was had to the gods of others, for they too, inspired fear. Many mingled foreign practices with their native religion. It was to no purpose that they did not adore the stars; if a constellation were fatal or helpful, sacrifices were offered to it; an unknown amulet found by chance at a moment of peril became a divinity; or it might be a name and nothing more, which would be repeated without any attempt to understand its meaning. But after pillaging temples, and seeing numbers of nations and slaughters, many ultimately ceased to believe in anything but destiny and death;— and every evening these would fall asleep with the placidity of wild beasts. Spendius had spit upon the images of Jupiter Olympius; nevertheless he dreaded to speak aloud in the dark, nor did he fail every day to put on his right boot first.

He reared a long quadrangular terrace in front of Utica, but in proportion as it ascended the rampart was also heightened, and what was thrown down by the one side was almost immediately raised again by

the other. Spendius took care of his men; he dreamed
of plans and strove to recall the stratagems which he
had heard described in his travels. But why did Narr'
Havas not return? There was nothing but anxiety.

Hanno had at last concluded his preparations. One
night when there was no moon he transported his
elephants and soldiers on rafts across the gulf of Carthage. Then they wheeled round the mountain of
the Hot Springs so as to avoid Autaritus, and continued their march so slowly that instead of surprising
the Barbarians in the morning, as the Suffet had calculated, they did not reach them until it was broad
daylight on the third day.

Utica had on the east a plain which extended to
the large lagoon of Carthage; behind it a valley ran
at right angles between two low and abruptly terminated mountains; the Barbarians were encamped further to the left in such a way as to blockade the
harbour; and they were sleeping in their tents (for on
that day both sides were too weary to fight and were
resting) when the Carthaginian army appeared at the
turning of the hills.

Some camp followers furnished with slings were
stationed at intervals on the wings. The first line
was formed of the guards of the Legion in golden
scale-armour, mounted on their big horses, which
were without mane, hair, or ears, and had silver
horns in the middle of their foreheads to make them
look like rhinoceroses. Between their squadrons were
youths wearing small helmets and swinging an ashen
javelin in each hand. The long files of the heavy infantry marched behind. All these traders had piled as
many weapons upon their bodies as possible. Some
might be seen carrying an axe, a lance, a club, and

two swords all at once; others bristled with darts like porcupines, and their arms stood out from their cuirasses in sheets of horn or iron plates. At last the scaffoldings of the lofty engines appeared: carroba-listas, onagers, catapults and scorpions, rocking on chariots drawn by mules and quadrigas of oxen; and in proportion as the army drew out, the captains ran panting right and left to deliver commands, close up the files, and preserve the intervals. Such of the An-cients as held commands had come in purple cassocks, the magnificent fringes of which tangled in the white straps of their cothurni. Their faces, which were smeared all over with vermilion, shone beneath enor-mous helmets surmounted with images of the gods; and, as they had shields with ivory borders covered with precious stones, they might have been taken for suns passing over walls of brass.

But the Carthaginians manœuvred so clumsily that the soldiers in derision urged them to sit down. They called out that they were just going to empty their big stomachs, to dust the gilding of their skin, and to give them iron to drink.

A strip of green cloth appeared at the top of the pole planted before Spendius's tent: it was the signal. The Carthaginian army replied to it with a great noise of trumpets, cymbals, flutes of asses' bones, and tympanums. The Barbarians had already leaped out-side the palisades, and were facing their enemies within a javelin's throw of them.

A Balearic slinger took a step forward, put one of his clay bullets into his thong, and swung round his arm. An ivory shield was shivered, and the two armies mingled together.

The Greeks made the horses rear and fall back upon

their masters by pricking their nostrils with the points
of their lances. The slaves who were to hurl stones
had picked such as were too big, and they accordingly fell close to them. The Punic foot-soldiers
exposed the right side in cutting with their long
swords. The Barbarians broke their lines; they
slaughtered them freely; they stumbled over the dying
and dead, quite blinded by the blood that spirted
into their faces. The confused heap of pikes, helmets,
cuirasses and swords turned round about, widening
out and closing in with elastic contractions. The gaps
increased more and more in the Carthaginian cohorts,
the engines could not be got out of the sand; and
finally the Suffet's litter (his grand litter with crystal
pendants), which from the beginning might have been
seen tossing among the soldiers like a bark on the
waves, suddenly foundered. He was no doubt dead.
The Barbarians found themselves alone.

The dust around them fell and they were beginning
to sing, when Hanno himself appeared on the top of
an elephant. He sat bare-headed beneath a parasol
of byssus which was carried by a negro behind him.
His necklace of blue plates flapped against the flowers
on his black tunic; his huge arms were compressed
within circles of diamonds, and with open mouth he
brandished a pike of inordinate size, which spread out
at the end like a lotus, and flashed more than a mirror. Immediately the earth shook,— and the Barbarians saw all the elephants of Carthage, with their gilt
tusks and blue-painted ears, hastening up in single
line, clothed with bronze and shaking the leathern
towers which were placed above their scarlet caparisons, in each one of which were three archers bending large bows.

The soldiers were barely in possession of their arms; they had taken up their positions at random. They were frozen with terror; they stood undecided.

Javelins, arrows, phalaricas, and masses of lead were already being showered down upon them from the towers. Some clung to the fringes of the caparisons in order to climb up, but their hands were struck off with cutlasses and they fell backwards upon the swords' points. The pikes were too weak and broke, and the elephants passed through the phalanxes like wild boars through tufts of grass; they plucked up the stakes of the camp with their trunks, and traversed it from one end to the other, overthrowing the tents with their breasts. All the Barbarians had fled. They were hiding themselves in the hills bordering the valley by which the Carthaginians had come.

The victorious Hanno presented himself before the gates of Utica. He had a trumpet sounded. The three Judges of the town appeared in the opening of the battlements on the summit of a tower.

But the people of Utica would not receive such well-armed guests. Hanno was furious. At last they consented to admit him with a feeble escort.

The streets were too narrow for the elephants. They had to be left outside.

As soon as the Suffet was in the town the principal men came to greet him. He had himself taken to the vapour baths, and called for his cooks.

Three hours afterward he was still immersed in the oil of cinnamomum with which the basin had been filled; and while he bathed he ate flamingoes tongues with honied poppy-seeds on a spread ox-hide.

Beside him was his Greek physician, motionless, in a
long yellow robe, directing the re-heating of the bath
from time to time, and two young boys leaned over
the steps of the basin and rubbed his legs. But attention to his body did not check his love for the
commonwealth, for he was dictating a letter to be
sent to the Great Council, and as some prisoners had
just been taken he was asking himself what terrible
punishment could be devised.

"Stop!" said he to a slave who stood writing in
the hollow of his hand. "Let some of them be
brought to me! I wish to see them!"

And from the bottom of the hall, full of a whitish
vapour on which the torches cast red spots, three
Barbarians were thrust forward: a Samnite, a Spartan,
and a Cappadocian.

"Proceed!" said Hanno.

"Rejoice, light of the Baals! your Suffet has exterminated the ravenous hounds! Blessings on the
Republic! Give orders for prayers!" He perceived
the captives and burst out laughing: "Ah! ha! my
fine fellows of Sicca! You are not shouting so loudly
to-day! It is I! Do you recognize me? And where
are your swords? What really terrible fellows!" and
he pretended to be desirous to hide himself as if
he were afraid of them. "You demanded horses,
women, estates, magistracies, no doubt, and priest-
hoods! Why not? Well, I will provide you with
the estates, and such as you will never come out of!
You shall be married to gibbets that are perfectly
new! Your pay? it shall be melted into your mouths
in leaden ingots! and I will put you into good and
very exalted positions among the clouds, so as to
bring you close to the eagles!"

The three long-haired and ragged Barbarians looked at him without understanding what he said. Wounded in the knees, they had been seized by having ropes thrown over them, and the ends of the great chains on their hands trailed upon the pavement. Hanno was indignant at their impassibility.

"On your knees! on your knees! jackals! dust! vermin! excrements! And they make no reply! Enough! be silent! Let them be flayed alive! No! presently!"

He was breathing like a hippopotamus and rolling his eyes. The perfumed oil overflowed beneath the mass of his body, and clinging to the scales on his skin, made it look pink in the light of the torches.

He resumed:

"For four days we suffered greatly from the sun. Some mules were lost in crossing the Macaras. In spite of their position, the extraordinary courage——Ah! Demonades! how I suffer! Have the bricks reheated, and let them be red-hot!"

A noise of rakes and furnaces was heard. The incense smoked more strongly in the large perfuming-pans, and the shampooers, who were quite naked and were sweating like sponges, crushed a paste composed of wheat, sulphur, black wine, bitch's milk, myrrh, galbanum and storax upon his joints. He was consumed with incessant thirst, but the yellow-robed man did not yield to this inclination, and held out to him a golden cup in which viper broth was smoking.

"Drink!" said he, "that the strength of sun-born serpents may penetrate into the marrow of your bones, and take courage, O reflection of the gods! You know, moreover, that a priest of Eschmoun watches those cruel stars round the Dog from which your malady is derived. They are growing pale like the spots on your skin, and you are not to die from them."

"Oh! yes, that is so, is it not?" repeated the Suffet, "I am not to die from them!" And his violaceous lips gave forth a breath more nauseous than the exhalation from a corpse. Two coals seemed to burn in the place of his eyes, which had lost their eyebrows; a mass of wrinkled skin hung over his forehead; both his ears stood out from his head and were beginning to increase in size; and the deep lines forming semicircles round his nostrils gave him a strange and terrifying appearance, the look of a wild beast. His unnatural voice was like a roar; he said:

"Perhaps you are right, Demonades. In fact there are many ulcers here which have closed. I feel robust. Here! look how I am eating!"

And less from greediness than from ostentation, and the desire to prove to himself that he was in good health, he cut into the forcemeats of cheese and marjoram, the boned fish, gourds, oysters with eggs, horse-radishes, truffles, and brochettes of small birds. As he looked at the prisoners he revelled in the imagination of their tortures. Nevertheless he remembered Sicca, and the rage caused by all his woes found vent in the abuse of these three men.

"Ah! traitors! ah! wretches! infamous, accursed creatures! And you outraged me!—me! the Suffet! Their services, the price of their blood, say they! Ah! yes! their blood! their blood!" Then speaking to himself:—"All shall perish! not one shall be sold! It would be better to bring them to Carthage! I should be seen—but, doubtless, I have not brought chains enough? Write: Send me—How many of them are there? go and ask Muthumbal! Go! no pity! and let all their hands be cut off and brought to me in baskets!"

But strange cries at once hoarse and shrill penetrated into the hall above Hanno's voice and the rattling of the dishes that were being placed around him. They increased, and suddenly the furious trumpeting of the elephants burst forth as if the battle were beginning again. A great tumult was going on around the town.

The Carthaginians had not attempted to pursue the Barbarians. They had taken up their quarters at the foot of the walls with their baggage, mules, serving men, and all their train of satraps; and they made merry in their beautiful pearl-bordered tents, while the camp of the Mercenaries was now nothing but a heap of ruins in the plain. Spendius had recovered his courage. He despatched Zarxas to Matho, scoured the woods, rallied his men (the losses had been inconsiderable),— and they were re-forming their lines, enraged at having been conquered without a fight, when they discovered a vat of petroleum which had no doubt been abandoned by the Carthaginians. Then Spendius had some pigs carried off from the farms, smeared them with bitumen, set them on fire, and drove them towards Utica.

The elephants were terrified by the flames and fled. The ground sloped upwards, javelins were thrown at them, and they turned back;— and with great blows of ivory and trampling of feet they ripped up the Carthaginians, stifled them, flattened them. the Barbarians descended the hill behind them; the Punic camp, which was without entrenchments was sacked at the first rush, and the Carthaginians were

crushed against the gates, which were not opened
through fear of the Mercenaries.

Day broke, and Matho's foot-soldiers were seen
coming up from the west. At the same time horsemen appeared; they were Narr' Havas with his Numidians. Leaping ravines and bushes they ran down
the fugitives like greyhounds pursuing hares. This
change of fortune interrupted the Suffet. He called
out to be assisted to leave the vapour bath.

The three captives were still before him. Then a
Negro (the same who had carried his parasol in the
battle) leaned over to his ear.

"Well?" replied the Suffet slowly. "Ah! kill
them!" he added in an abrupt tone.

The Ethiopian drew a long dagger from his girdle
and the three heads fell. One of them rebounded
among the remains of the feast, and leaped into the
basin, where it floated for some time with open
mouth and staring eyes. The morning light entered
through the chinks in the wall; the three bodies
streamed with great bubbles like three fountains, and
a sheet of blood flowed over the mosaics with their
powdering of blue dust. The Suffet dipped his
hand into this hot mire and rubbed his knees with
it: it was a cure.

When evening had come he stole away from the
town with his escort, and made his way into the
mountain to rejoin his army.

He succeeded in finding the remains of it.

Four days afterward he was on the top of a defile
at Gorza, when the troops under Spendius appeared below. Twenty stout lances might easily have checked
them by attacking the head of their column, but the
Carthaginians watched them pass by in a state of

stupefaction.   Hanno recognised the king of the
Numidians in the rearguard; Narr' Havas bowed to
him, at the same time making a sign which he did
not understand.

The return to Carthage took place amid all kinds
of terrors.   They marched only at night, hiding in
the olive woods during the day.   There were deaths
at every halting-place; several times they believed
themselves lost.   At last they reached Cape Hermæum,
where vessels came to receive them.

Hanno was so fatigued, so desperate — the loss of
the elephants in particular overwhelmed him — that he
demanded poison from Demonades in order to put an
end to it all.   Moreover he could already feel himself
stretched upon the cross.

Carthage had not strength enough to be indignant
with him.   Its losses had amounted to one hundred
thousand nine hundred and seventy-two shekels of
silver, fifteen thousand six hundred and twenty-three
shekels of gold, eighteen elephants, fourteen members
of the Great Council, three hundred of the rich, eight
thousand citizens, corn enough for three moons, a
considerable quantity of baggage, and all the engines
of war!   The defection of Narr' Havas was certain,
and both sieges were beginning again.   The army
under Autaritus now extended from Tunis to Rhades.
From the top of the Acropolis long columns of smoke
might be seen in the country ascending to the sky;
they were the mansions of the rich, which were on
fire.

One man alone could have saved the Republic.
People repented that they had slighted him, and the
peace party itself voted holocausts for Hamilcar's return.

The sight of the zaïmph had upset Salammbô. At night she thought that she could hear the footsteps of the goddess, and she would awake terrified and shrieking. Every day she sent food to the temples. Taanach was worn out with executing her orders, and Schahabarim never left her.

VII.

HAMILCAR BARCA.

HE Announcer of the Moons, who watched on the summit of the temple of Eschmoun every night in order to signal the disturbances of the planet with his trumpet, one morning perceived towards the west something like a bird skimming the surface of the sea with its long wings.

It was a ship with three tiers of oars and with a horse carved on the prow. The sun was rising; the Announcer of the Moons put up his hand before his eyes, and then grasping his clarion with outstretched arms sounded a loud brazen cry over Carthage.

People came out of every house; they would not believe what was said; they disputed with one another; the mole was covered with people. At last they recognised Hamilcar's trireme.

It advanced in fierce and haughty fashion, cleaving the foam around it, the lateen-yard quite square and the sail bulging down the whole length of the mast; its gigantic oars kept time as they beat the water; every now and then the extremity of the keel, which was shaped like a plough-share, would appear, and the ivory-headed horse, rearing both its feet beneath

the spur which terminated the prow, would seem to
be speeding over the plains of the sea.

As it rounded the promontory the wind ceased,
the sail fell, and a man was seen standing bareheaded
beside the pilot. It was he, Hamilcar, the Suffet!
About his sides he wore gleaming sheets of steel; a
red cloak, fastened to his shoulders, left his arms
visible; two pearls of great length hung from his ears,
and his black, bushy beard rested on his breast.

The galley, however, tossing amid the rocks, was
proceeding along the side of the mole, and the crowd
followed it on the flag-stones, shouting:

"Greeting! blessing! Eye of Khamon! ah! deliver us! 'Tis the fault of the rich! they want to put
you to death! Take care of yourself, Barca!"

He made no reply, as if the loud clamour of
oceans and battles had completely deafened him.
But when he was below the staircase leading down
from the Acropolis, Hamilcar raised his head, and
looked with folded arms upon the temple of Eschmoun. His gaze mounted higher still, to the great
pure sky; he shouted an order in a harsh voice to his
sailors; the trireme leaped forward; it grazed the idol
set up at the corner of the mole to stay the storms;
and in the merchant harbour, which was full of filth,
fragments of wood, and rinds of fruit, it pushed aside
and crushed against the other ships moored to stakes and
terminating in crocodiles' jaws. The people hastened
thither, and some threw themselves into the water to
swim to it. It was already at the very end before
the gate which bristled with nails. The gate rose,
and the trireme disappeared beneath the deep arch.

The Military Harbour was completely separated
from the town; when ambassadors arrived, they had

to proceed between two walls through a passage which had its outlet on the left in front of the temple of Khamoun. This great expanse of water was as round as a cup, and was bordered with quays on which sheds were built for sheltering the ships. Before each of these rose two pillars bearing the horns of Ammon on their capitals and forming continuous porticoes all round the basin. On an island in the centre stood a house for the marine Suffet.

The water was so limpid that the bottom was visible with its paving of white pebbles. The noise of the streets did not reach so far, and Hamilcar as he passed recognised the triremes which he had formerly commanded.

Not more than twenty perhaps remained, under shelter on the land, leaning over on their sides or standing upright on their keels, with lofty poops and swelling prows, and covered with gildings and mystic symbols. The chimæras had lost their wings, the Pataec Gods their arms, the bulls their silver horns;—and half-painted, motionless, and rotten as they were, yet full of associations, and still emitting the scent of voyages, they all seemed to say to him, like mutilated soldiers on seeing their master again, "'Tis we! 'tis we! and *you* too are vanquished!"

No one excepting the marine Suffet might enter the admiral's house. So long as there was no proof of his death he was considered as still in existence. In this way the Ancients avoided a master the more, and they had not failed to comply with the custom in respect to Hamilcar.

The Suffet proceeded into the deserted apartments. At every step he recognised armour and furniture—familiar objects which nevertheless astonished him, and in a perfuming-pan in the vestibule there even remained the ashes of the perfumes that had been kindled at his departure for the conjuration of Melkarth. It was not thus that he had hoped to return. Everything that he had done, everything that he had seen, unfolded itself in his memory: assaults, conflagrations, legions, tempests, Drepanum, Syracuse, Lilybæum, Mount Etna, the plateau of Eryx, five years of battles, —until the fatal day when arms had been laid down and Sicily had been lost. Then he once more saw the woods of citron-trees, and herdsmen with their goats on gray mountains; and his heart leaped at the thought of the establishment of another Carthage down yonder. His projects and his recollections buzzed through his head, which was still dizzy from the pitching of the vessel; he was overwhelmed with anguish, and, becoming suddenly weak, he felt the necessity of drawing near to the gods.

Then he went up to the highest story of his house, and taking a nail-studded staple from a golden shell, which hung on his arm, he opened a small oval chamber.

It was softly lighted by means of delicate black discs let into the wall and as transparent as glass. Between the rows of these equal discs, holes, like those for the urns in columbaria, were hollowed out. Each of them contained a round dark stone, which appeared to be very heavy. Only people of superior understanding honoured these abaddirs, which had fallen from the moon. By their fall they denoted the stars, the sky, and fire; by their colour dark night, and by their density the cohesion of terrestrial things. A stifling atmosphere filled this mystic place. The round stones lying in the niches were whitened somewhat with sea-sand which the wind had no doubt driven through the door. Hamilcar counted them one after the other with the tip of his finger; then he hid his face in a saffron-coloured veil, and, falling on his knees, stretched himself on the ground with both arms extended.

The daylight outside was beginning to strike on the folding shutters of black lattice-work. Arborescences, hillocks, eddies, and ill-defined animals appeared in their diaphanous thickness; and the light came terrifying and yet peaceful as it must be behind the sun in the dull spaces of future creations. He strove to banish from his thoughts all forms, and all symbols and appellations of the gods, that he might the better apprehend the immutable spirit which outward appearances took away. Something of the planetary vitalities penetrated him, and he felt withal a wiser and more intimate scorn of death and of every accident. When he rose he was filled with serene fearlessness and was proof against pity or dread, and as his chest was choking he went to the top of the tower which overlooked Carthage.

The town sank downwards in a long hollow curve, with its cupolas, its temples, its golden roofs, its houses, its clusters of palm trees here and there, and its glass balls with streaming rays, while the ramparts formed, as it were, the gigantic border of this horn of plenty which poured itself out before him. Far below he could see the harbours, the squares, the interiors of the courts, the plan of the streets, and the people, who seemed very small and but little above the level of the pavement. Ah! if Hanno had not arrived too late on the morning of the Aegatian islands! He fastened his eyes on the

extreme horizon and stretched forth his quivering
arms in the direction of Rome.

The steps of the Acropolis were occupied by the
multitude. In the square of Khamon the people were
pressing forward to see the Suffet come out, and the
terraces were gradually being loaded with people; a
few recognised him, and he was saluted; but he retired in order the better to excite the impatience of
the people.

Hamilcar found the most important men of his
party below in the hall: Istatten, Subeldia, Hictamon,
Yeoubas and others. They related to him all that
had taken place since the conclusion of the peace:
the greed of the Ancients, the departure of the soldiers, their return, their demands, the capture of
Gisco, the theft of the zaïmph, the relief and subsequent abandonment of Utica; but no one ventured to
tell him of the events which concerned himself. At
last they separated, to meet again during the night at
the assembly of the Ancients in the temple of Moloch.

They had just gone out when a tumult arose outside the door. Some one was trying to enter in
spite of the servants; and as the disturbance was increasing Hamilcar ordered the stranger to be shown in.

An old negress made her appearance, broken,
wrinkled, trembling, stupid-looking, wrapped to the
heels in ample blue veils. She advanced face to face
with the Suffet, and they looked at each other for
some time; suddenly Hamilcar started; at a wave of
his hand the slaves withdrew. Then, signing to her
to walk with precaution, he drew her by the arm
into a remote apartment.

The negress threw herself upon the floor to kiss
his feet; he raised her brutally.

"Where have you left him, Iddibal?"

"Down there, Master;" and extricating herself from her veils, she rubbed her face with her sleeve; the black colour, the senile trembling, the bent figure disappeared, and there remained a strong old man whose skin seemed tanned by sand, wind, and sea. A tuft of white hair rose on his skull like the crest of a bird; and he indicated his disguise, as it lay on the ground, with an ironic glance.

"You have done well, Iddibal! 'Tis well!" Then piercing him, as it were, with his keen gaze: "No one yet suspects?"

The old man swore to him by the Kabiri that the mystery had been kept. They never left their cottage, which was three days' journey from Hadrumetum, on a shore peopled with turtles, and with palms on the dune. "And in accordance with your command, O Master! I teach him to hurl the javelin and to drive a team."

"He is strong, is he not?"

"Yes, Master, and intrepid as well! He has no fear of serpents, or thunder, or phantoms. He runs barefooted like a herdsman along the brinks of precipices."

"Speak! speak!"

"He invents snares for wild beasts. Would you believe it, that last moon he surprised an eagle; he dragged it away, and the bird's blood and the child's were scattered in the air in large drops like driven roses. The animal in its fury enwrapped him in the beating of its wings; he strained it against his breast, and as it died his laughter increased, piercing and proud like the clashing of swords."

Hamilcar bent his head, dazzled by such presages of greatness.

"But he has been for some time restless and disturbed. He gazes at the sails passing far out at sea; he is melancholy, he rejects bread, he inquires about the gods, and he wishes to become acquainted with Carthage."

"No, no! not yet!" exclaimed the Suffet.

The old slave seemed to understand the peril which alarmed Hamilcar, and he resumed:

"How is he to be restrained? Already I am obliged to make him promises, and I have come to Carthage only to buy him a dagger with a silver handle and pearls all around it." Then he told how, having perceived the Suffet on the terrace, he had passed himself off on the warders of the harbour as one of Salammbô's women, so as to make his way in to him.

Hamilcar remained for a long time apparently lost in deliberation; at last he said:

"To-morrow you will present yourself at sunset behind the purple factories in Megara, and imitate a jackal's cry three times. If you do not see me, you will return to Carthage on the first day of every moon. Forget nothing! Love him! You may speak to him now about Hamilcar."

The slave resumed his costume, and they left the house and the harbour together.

Hamilcar went on his way alone on foot and without an escort, for the meetings of the Ancients were, under extraordinary circumstances, always secret, and were resorted to mysteriously.

At first he went along the western front of the Acropolis, and then passed through the Green Market, the galleries of Kinisdo, and the Perfumers' suburb. The scattered lights were being extinguished, the broader streets grew still, then shadows glided through the darkness. They followed him, others appeared, and like him they all directed their course towards the Mappalian district.

The temple of Moloch was built at the foot of a steep defile in a sinister spot. From below nothing could be seen but lofty walls rising indefinitely like those of a monstrous tomb. The night was gloomy, a greyish fog seemed to weigh upon the sea, which beat against the cliff with a noise as of death-rattles and sobs; and the shadows gradually vanished as if they had passed through the walls.

But as soon as the doorway was crossed one found oneself in a vast quadrangular court bordered by arcades. In the centre rose a mass of architecture with eight equal faces. It was surmounted by cupolas which thronged around a second story supporting a kind of rotunda, from which sprang a cone with a re-entrant curve and terminating in a ball on the summit.

Fires were burning in cylinders of filigree-work fitted upon poles, which men were carrying to and fro. These lights flickered in the gusts of wind and reddened the golden combs which fastened their plaited hair on the nape of the neck. They ran about calling to one another to receive the Ancients.

Here and there on the flag-stones huge lions were couched like sphinxes, living symbols of the devouring Sun. They were slumbering with half-closed eyelids. But roused by the footsteps and voices they rose slowly, came towards the Ancients, whom they recognised by their dress, and rubbed themselves against their thighs, arching their backs with sonorous yawns; the vapour of their breath passed across the light of the torches. The stir increased, doors closed, all the priests fled, and the Ancients disappeared beneath the columns which formed a deep vestibule round the temple.

These columns were arranged in such a way that their circular ranks, which were contained one within another, showed the Saturnian period with its years, the years with their months, and the months with their days, and finally reached to the walls of the sanctuary.

Here it was that the Ancients laid aside their sticks of narwhal's horn,—for a law which was always observed inflicted the punishment of death upon any one entering the meeting with any kind of weapon. Several wore a rent repaired with a strip of purple at the bottom of their garment, to show that they had not been economical in their dress when mourning for their relatives, and this testimony to their affliction prevented the slit from growing larger. Others had their beards inclosed in little bags of violet skin, and fastened to their ears by two cords. They all accosted one another by embracing breast to breast. They surrounded Hamilcar with congratulations; they might have been taken for brothers meeting their brother again.

These men were generally thick-set, with curved noses like those of the Assyrian colossi. In a few, however, the more prominent cheek-bone, the taller figure, and the narrower foot, betrayed an African origin and nomad ancestors. Those who lived continually shut up in their counting-houses had pale faces; others showed in theirs the severity of the desert, and strange jewels sparkled on all the fingers of their hands, which were burnt by unknown suns.

The navigators might be distinguished by their rolling gait, while the men of agriculture smelt of the wine-press, dried herbs, and the sweat of mules. These old pirates had lands under tillage, these money-grubbers would fit out ships, these proprietors of cultivated lands supported slaves who followed trades. All were skilled in religious discipline, expert in strategy, pitiless and rich. They looked wearied of prolonged cares. Their flaming eyes expressed distrust, and their habits of travelling and lying, trafficking and commanding, gave an appearance of cunning and violence, a sort of discreet and convulsive brutality to their whole demeanour. Further, the influence of the god cast a gloom upon them.

They first passed through a vaulted hall which was shaped like an egg. Seven doors, corresponding to the seven planets, displayed seven squares of different colours against the wall. After traversing a long room they entered another similar hall.

A candelabrum completely covered with chiselled flowers was burning at the far end, and each of its eight golden branches bore a wick of byssus in a diamond chalice. It was placed upon the last of the long steps leading to a great altar, the corners of which terminated in horns of brass. Two lateral staircases led to its flattened summit; the stones of it could not be seen; it was like a mountain of heaped cinders, and something indistinct was slowly smoking on the top of it. Then further back, higher than the candelabrum, and much higher than the altar, rose the Moloch, all of iron, and with gaping apertures in his human breast. His outspread wings were stretched upon the wall, his tapering hands reached down to the ground; three black stones bordered by yellow circles

represented three eyeballs on his brow, and his bull's
head was raised with a terrible effort as if in order
to bellow.

Ebony stools were ranged round the apartment.
Behind each of them was a bronze shaft resting on
three claws and supporting a torch. All these lights
were reflected in the mother-of-pearl lozenges which
formed the pavement of the hall. So lofty was the
latter that the red colour of the walls grew black as
it rose towards the vaulted roof, and the three eyes
of the idol appeared far above like stars half lost in
the night.

The Ancients sat down on the ebony stools after
putting the trains of their robes over their heads.
They remained motionless with their hands crossed
inside their broad sleeves, and the mother-of-pearl
pavement seemed like a luminous river streaming
from the altar to the door and flowing beneath their
naked feet.

The four pontiffs had their places in the centre,
sitting back to back on four ivory seats which formed
a cross, the high-priest of Eschmoun in a hyacinth
robe, the high-priest of Tanith in a white linen robe,
the high-priest of Khamon in a tawny woollen robe,
and the high-priest of Moloch in a purple robe.

Hamilcar advanced towards the candelabrum. He
walked all round it, looking at the burning wicks;
then he threw a scented powder upon them, and
violet flames appeared at the extremities of the
branches.

Then a shrill voice rose; another replied to it,
and the hundred Ancients, the four pontiffs, and Hamilcar, who remained standing, simultaneously in-
toned a hymn, and their voices — ever repeating the

same syllables and strengthening the sounds — rose, grew loud, became terrible, and then suddenly were still.

There was a pause for some time. At last Hamilcar drew from his breast a little three-headed statuette, as blue as sapphire, and placed it before him. It was the image of Truth, the very genius of his speech. Then he replaced it in his bosom, and all, as if seized with sudden wrath, cried out:

"They are good friends of yours, are the Barbarians! Infamous traitor! You come back to see us perish, do you not? Let him speak! — No! no!"

They were taking their revenge for the constraint to which political ceremonial had just obliged them; and even though they had wished for Hamilcar's return, they were now indignant that he had not anticipated their disasters, or rather that he had not endured them as well as they.

When the tumult had subsided, the pontiff of Moloch rose:

"We ask you why you did not return to Carthage?"

"What is that to you?" replied the Suffet disdainfully.

Their shouts were redoubled.

"Of what do you accuse me? I managed the war badly perhaps! You have seen how I order my battles, you who conveniently allow Barbarians ——"

"Enough! enough!"

He went on in a low voice so as to make himself the better listened to:

"Oh! that is true! I am wrong, lights of the Baals; there are intrepid men among you! Gisco, rise!" And surveying the step of the altar with half-closed eyelids, as if he sought for some one, he repeated:

"Rise, Gisco! You can accuse me; they will protect you! But where is he?" Then, as if he remembered himself: "Ah! in his house, no doubt! surrounded by his sons, commanding his slaves, happy, and counting on the wall the necklaces of honour which his country has given to him!"

They moved about raising their shoulders as if they were being scourged with thongs. "You do not even know whether he is living or dead!" And without giving any heed to their clamours he said that in deserting the Suffet they had deserted the Republic. So, too, the peace with Rome, however advantageous it might appear to them, was more fatal than twenty battles. A few — those who were the least rich of the Council and were suspected of perpetual leanings towards the people or towards tyranny — applauded. Their opponents, chiefs of the Syssitia and administrators, triumphed over them in point of numbers; and the more eminent of them had ranged themselves close to Hanno, who was sitting at the other end of the hall before the lofty door, which was closed by a hanging of hyacinth colour.

He had covered the ulcers on his face with paint. But the gold dust on his hair had fallen upon his shoulders, where it formed two brilliant sheets, so that his hair appeared whitish, fine, and frizzled like wool. His hands were enveloped in linen soaked in a greasy perfume, which dripped upon the pavement, and his disease had no doubt considerably increased, for his eyes were hidden beneath the folds of his eyelids. He had thrown back his head in order to see.

His partisans urged him to speak. At last in a hoarse and hideous voice he said:

"Less arrogance, Barca! We have all been vanquished! Each one supports his own misfortune! Be resigned!"

"Tell us rather," said Hamilcar, smiling, "how it was that you steered your galleys into the Roman fleet?"

"I was driven by the wind," replied Hanno.

"You are like a rhinoceros trampling on his dung: you are displaying your own folly! be silent!" And they began to indulge in recriminations respecting the battle of the Aegatian islands.

Hanno accused him of not having come to meet him.

"But that would have left Eryx undefended. You ought to have stood out from the coast; what prevented you? Ah! I forgot! all elephants are afraid of the sea!"

Hamilcar's followers thought this jest so good that they burst out into loud laughter. The vault rang with it like the beating of tympanums.

Hanno denounced the unworthiness of such an insult; the disease had come upon him from a cold taken at the siege of Hecatompylos, and tears flowed down his face like winter rain on a ruined wall.

Hamilcar resumed:

"If you had loved me as much as him there would be great joy in Carthage now! How many times did I not call upon you! and you always refused me money!"

"We had need of it," said the chiefs of the Syssitia.

"And when things were desperate with me — we drank mules' urine and ate the straps of our sandals;

when I would fain have had the blades of grass soldiers, and made battalions with the rottenness of our dead, you recalled the vessels that I had left!"

"We could not risk everything," replied Baat-Baal, who possessed gold mines in Darytian Gætulia.

"But what did you do here, at Carthage, in your houses, behind your walls? There are Gauls on the Eridanus who ought to have been roused, Chanaanites at Cyrene who would have come, and while the Romans send ambassadors to Ptolemæus——"

"Now he is extolling the Romans to us!" Some one shouted out to him: "How much have they paid you to defend them?"

"Ask that of the plains of Bruttium, of the ruins of Locri, of Metapontum, and of Heraclea! I have burnt all their trees, I have pillaged all their temples, and even to the death of their grandchildren's grandchildren——"

"Why! you declaim like a rhetor!" said Kapouras, a very illustrious merchant. "What is it that you want?"

"I say that we must be more ingenious or more terrible! If the whole of Africa rejects your yoke the reason is, my feeble masters, that you do not know how to fasten it upon her shoulders! Agathocles, Regulus, Cœpio, any bold man has only to land and capture her; and when the Libyans in the east concert with the Numidians in the west, and the Nomads come from the south, and the Romans from the north"—a cry of horror rose—"Oh! you will beat your breasts, and roll in the dust, and tear your cloaks! No matter! you will have to go and turn the mill-stone in the Suburra, and gather grapes on the hills of Latium."

They smote their right thighs to mark their sense of the scandal, and the sleeves of their robes rose like large wings of startled birds. Hamilcar, carried away by a spirit, continued his speech, standing on the highest step of the altar, quivering and terrible; he raised his arms, and the rays from the candelabrum which burned behind him passed between his fingers like javelins of gold.

"You will lose your ships, your country seats, your chariots, your hanging beds, and the slaves who rub your feet! The jackal will couch in your palaces, and the ploughshare will upturn your tombs. Nothing will be left but the eagles' scream and a heap of ruins. Carthage, thou wilt fall!"

The four pontiffs spread out their hands to avert the anathema. All had risen. But the marine Suffet, being a sacerdotal magistrate under the protection of the Sun, was inviolable so long as the assembly of the rich had not judged him. Terror was associated with the altar. They drew back.

Hamilcar had ceased speaking, and was panting with eye fixed, his face as pale as the pearls of his tiara, almost frightened at himself, and his spirit lost in funereal visions. From the height on which he stood, all the torches on the bronze shafts seemed to him like a vast crown of fire laid level with the pavement; black smoke issuing from them mounted up into the darkness of the vault; and for some minutes the silence was so profound that they could hear in the distance the sound of the sea.

Then the Ancients began to question one another. Their interests, their existence, were attacked by the Barbarians. But it was impossible to conquer them without the assistance of the Suffet, and in spite of

their pride this consideration made them forget every
other. His friends were taken aside. There were interested reconciliations, understandings, and promises.
Hamilcar would not take any further part in any government. All conjured him. They besought him; and
as the word treason occurred in their speech, he fell
into a passion. The sole traitor was the Great Council, for as the enlistment of the soldiers expired with
the war, they became free as soon as the war was
finished; he even exalted their bravery and all the
advantages which might be derived from interesting
them in the Republic by donations and privileges.

Then Magdassin, a former provincial governor, said,
as he rolled his yellow eyes:

"Truly Barca, with your travelling you have become a Greek, or a Latin, or something! Why speak
you of rewards for these men? Rather let ten thousand Barbarians perish than a single one of us!"

The Ancients nodded approval, murmuring: —
"Yes, is there need for so much trouble? They can
always be had!"

"And they can be got rid of conveniently, can
they not? They are deserted as they were by you in
Sardinia. The enemy is apprised of the road which
they are to take, as in the case of those Gauls in
Sicily, or perhaps they are disembarked in the middle
of the sea. As I was returning I saw the rock quite
white with their bones!"

"What a misfortune!" said Kapouras impudently.

"Have they not gone over to the enemy a hundred times?" cried the others.

"Why, then," exclaimed Hamilcar, "did you recall them to Carthage, notwithstanding your laws?
And when they are in your town, poor and numerous

3—15

amid all your riches, it does not occur to you to weaken them by the slightest division! Afterwards you dismiss the whole of them with their women and children, without keeping a single hostage! Did you expect that they would murder themselves to spare you the pain of keeping your oaths? You hate them because they are strong! You hate me still more, who am their master! Oh! I felt it just now when you were kissing my hands and were all putting a constraint upon yourselves not to bite them!"

If the lions that were sleeping in the court had come howling in, the uproar could not have been more frightful. But the pontiff of Eschmoun rose, and, standing perfectly upright, with his knees close together, his elbows pressed to his body, and his hands half open, he said:

"Barca, Carthage has need that you take the general command of the Punic forces against the Mercenaries!"

"I refuse," replied Hamilcar.

"We will give you full authority," cried the chiefs of the Syssitia.

"No!"

"With no control, no partition, all the money that you want, all the captives, all the booty, fifty zereths of land for every enemy's corpse."

"No! no! because it is impossible to conquer with you!"

"He is afraid!"

"Because you are cowardly, greedy, ungrateful, pusillanimous and mad!"

"He is careful of them!"

"In order to put himself at their head," said some one.

"And return against us," said another; and from the bottom of the hall Hanno howled:

"He wants to make himself king!"

Then they bounded up, overturning the seats and the torches: the crowd of them rushed towards the altar; they brandished daggers. But Hamilcar dived into his sleeves and drew from them two broad cutlasses; and half stooping, his left foot advanced, his eyes flaming and his teeth clenched, he defied them as he stood there beneath the golden candelabrum.

Thus they had brought weapons with them as a precaution; it was a crime; they looked with terror at one another. As all were guilty, every one became quickly reassured; and by degrees they turned their backs on the Suffet and came down again maddened with humiliation. For the second time they recoiled before him. They remained standing for some time. Several who had wounded their fingers put them to their mouths or rolled them gently in the hem of their mantles, and they were about to depart when Hamilcar heard these words:

"Why! it is a piece of delicacy to avoid distressing his daughter!"

A louder voice was raised:

"No doubt, since she takes her lovers from among the Mercenaries!"

At first he tottered, then his eyes rapidly sought for Shahabarim. But the priest of Tanith had alone remained in his place; and Hamilcar could see only his lofty cap in the distance. All were sneering in his face. In proportion as his anguish increased their joy redoubled, and those who were behind shouted amid the hootings:

"He was seen coming out of her room!"

"One morning in the month of Tammouz!"

"It was the thief who stole the zaïmph!"

"A very handsome man!"

"Taller than you!"

He snatched off his tiara, the ensign of his rank —his tiara with its eight mystic rows, and with an emerald shell in the centre — and with both hands and with all his strength dashed it to the ground; the golden circles rebounded as they broke, and the pearls rang upon the pavement. Then they saw a long scar upon the whiteness of his brow; it moved like a serpent between his eyebrows; all his limbs trembled. He ascended one of the lateral staircases which led on to the altar, and walked upon the latter! This was to devote himself to the god, to offer himself as a holocaust. The motion of his mantle agitated the lights of the candelabrum, which was lower than his sandals, and the fine dust raised by his footsteps surrounded him like a cloud as high as the waist. He stopped between the legs of the brass colossus. He took up two handfuls of the dust, the mere sight of which made every Carthaginian shudder with horror, and said:

"By the hundred torches of your Intelligences! by the eight fires of the Kabiri! by the stars, the meteors, and the volcanoes! by everything that burns! by the thirst of the desert and the saltness of the ocean! by the cave of Hadrumetum and the empire of Souls! by extermination! by the ashes of your sons and the ashes of the brothers of your ancestors with which I now mingle my own! — you, the Hundred of the Council of Carthage, have lied in your accusation of my daughter! And I, Hamilcar Barca, marine Suffet, chief of the rich and ruler of the people, in the presence of bull-headed Moloch, I swear"— they expected something frightful, but he resumed in a loftier and calmer tone—"that I will not even speak to her about it!"

The sacred servants entered wearing their golden combs, some with purple sponges and others with branches of palm. They raised the hyacinth curtain which was stretched before the door; and through the opening of this angle there was visible behind the other halls the great pink sky which seemed to be a continuation of the vault and to rest at the horizon upon the blue sea. The sun was issuing from the waves and mounting upwards. It suddenly struck upon the breast of the brazen colossus, which was divided into seven compartments closed by gratings. His red-toothed jaws opened in a horrible yawn; his enormous nostrils were dilated, the broad daylight animated him, and gave him a terrible and impatient aspect, as if he would fain have leaped without to mingle with the star, the god, and together traverse the immensities.

The torches, however, which were scattered on the ground, were still burning, while here and there on the mother-of-pearl pavement was stretched from them what looked like spots of blood. The Ancients were reeling from exhaustion; they filled their lungs inhaling the freshness of the air; the sweat flowed down their livid faces; they had shouted so much that they could now scarcely make their voices heard. But their wrath against the Suffet was not at all abated; they hurled menaces at him by way of farewells, and Hamilcar answered them again.

"Until the next night, Barca, in the temple of Eschmoun!"

"I shall be there!"

"We will have you condemned by the rich!"

"And I you by the people!"

"Take care that you do not end on the cross!"

"And you that you are not torn to pieces in the streets!"

As soon as they were on the threshold of the court they again assumed a calm demeanor.

Their runners and coachmen were waiting for them at the door. Most of them departed on white mules. The Suffet leaped into his chariot and took the reins; the two animals, curving their necks, and rhythmically beating the rebounding pebbles, went up the whole of the Mappalian Way at full gallop, and the silver vulture at the extremity of the pole seemed to fly, so quickly did the chariot pass along.

The road crossed a field planted with slabs of stone, which were pointed on the top like pyramids, and had open hands carved out in the centre as if all the dead men lying beneath had stretched them out towards heaven to demand something. Next there came scattered cabins built of earth, branches, and bulrush-hurdles, and all of a conical shape. These dwellings, which became constantly denser as the road ascended towards the Suffet's gardens, were irregularly separated from one another by little pebble walls, trenches of spring water, ropes of esparto-grass, and nopal hedges. But Hamilcar's eyes were fastened on a great tower, the three storys of which formed three monster cylinders—the first being built of stone, the second of brick, and the third all of cedar—supporting a copper cupola upon twenty-four pillars of juniper, from which slender interlacing chains of brass

hung down after the manner of garlands. This lofty
edifice overlooked the buildings—the emporiums and
mercantile houses—which stretched to the right, while
the women's palace rose at the end of the cypress
trees, which were ranged in line like two walls of
bronze.

When the echoing chariot had entered through the
narrow gateway it stopped beneath a broad shed in
which there were shackled horses eating from heaps
of chopped grass.

All the servants hastened up. They formed quite
a multitude, those who worked on the country estates
having been brought to Carthage through fear of the
soldiers. The labourers, who were clad in animals'
skins, had chains riveted to their ankles and trailing
after them; the workers in the purple factories had
arms as red as those of executioners; the sailors wore
green caps; the fishermen coral necklaces; the hunts-
men carried nets on their shoulders; and the people
belonging to Megara wore black or white tunics,
leathern drawers, and caps of straw, felt or linen,
according to their service or their different occupations.

Behind pressed a tattered populace. They lived
without employment remote from the apartments,
slept at night in the gardens, ate the refuse from the
kitchens,—a human mouldiness vegetating in the
shadow of the palace. Hamilcar tolerated them from
foresight even more than from scorn. They had all
put a flower in the ear in token of their joy, and many
of them had never seen him.

But men with head-dresses like the Sphinx's, and
furnished with great sticks, dashed into the crowd,
striking right and left. This was to drive back the
slaves, who were curious to see their master, so that

he might not be assailed by their numbers or inconvenienced by their smell.

Then they all threw themselves flat on the ground, crying:

"Eye of Baal, may your house flourish!" And through these people as they lay thus on the ground in the avenue of cypress trees, Abdalonim, the Steward of the stewards, waving a white mitre, advanced towards Hamilcar with a censer in his hand.

Salammbô was then coming down the galley staircase. All her slave women followed her; and, at each of her steps, they also descended. The heads of the Negresses formed big black spots on the line of the bands of the golden plates clasping the foreheads of the Roman women. Others had silver arrows, emerald butterflies, or long bodkins set like suns in their hair. Rings, clasps, necklaces, fringes, and bracelets shone amid the confusion of white, yellow, and blue garments; a rustling of light material became audible; the pattering of sandals might be heard together with the dull sound of naked feet as they were set down on the wood;—and here and there a tall eunuch, head and shoulders above them, smiled with his face in air. When the shouting of the men had subsided they hid their faces in their sleeves, and together uttered a strange cry like the howling of a she-wolf, and so frenzied and strident was it that it seemed to make the great ebony staircase, with its thronging women, vibrate from top to bottom like a lyre.

The wind lifted their veils, and the slender stems of the papyrus plants rocked gently. It was the month of Schebaz and the depth of winter. The flowering pomegranates swelled against the azure of the sky, and the sea appeared through the branches with an island in the distance half lost in the mist.

Hamilcar stopped on perceiving Salammbô. She had come to him after the death of several male children. Moreover, the birth of daughters was considered a calamity in the religions of the Sun. The gods had afterwards sent him a son; but he still felt something of the betrayal of his hope, and the shock, as it were, of the curse which he had uttered against her. Salammbô, however, continued to advance.

Long bunches of various-coloured pearls fell from her ears to her shoulders, and as far as her elbows. Her hair was crisped so as to simulate a cloud. Round her neck she wore little quadrangular plates of gold, representing a woman between two rampant lions; and her costume was a complete reproduction of the equipment of the goddess. Her broad-sleeved hyacinth robe fitted close to her figure, widening out below. The vermilion on her lips gave additional whiteness to her teeth, and the antimony on her eyelids greater length to her eyes. Her sandals, which were cut out in bird's plumage, had very high heels, and she was extraordinarily pale, doubtless on account of the cold.

At last she came close to Hamilcar, and without looking at him, without raising her head, said to him:

"Greeting, eye of Baalim, eternal glory! triumph! leisure! satisfaction! riches! Long has my heart been sad and the house drooping. But the returning master is like reviving Tammouz; and beneath your gaze, O father, joyfulness and a new existence will everywhere prevail!"

And taking from Taanach's hands a little oblong vase wherein smoked a mixture of meal, butter, cardamom, and wine: "Drink freely," said she, "of the returning cup, which your servant has prepared!"

He replied: "A blessing upon you!" and he mechanically grasped the golden vase which she held out to him.

He scanned her, however, with such harsh attention, that Salammbô was troubled and stammered out:

"They have told you, O Master!"

"Yes! I know!" said Hamilcar in a low voice.

Was this a confession, or was she speaking of the Barbarians? And he added a few vague words upon the public embarrassments which he hoped by his own sole efforts to clear away.

"O father!" exclaimed Salammbô, "you will not obliterate what is irreparable!"

Then he drew back and Salammbô was astonished at his amazement; for she was not thinking of Carthage but of the sacrilege in which she found herself implicated. This man, who made legions tremble and whom she hardly knew, terrified her like a god; he had guessed, he knew all, something awful was about to happen. "Pardon!" she cried.

Hamilcar slowly bowed his head.

Although she wished to accuse herself she dared not open her lips; and yet she felt stifled with the need of complaining and being comforted. Hamilcar was struggling against a longing to break his oath. He kept it out of pride or from the dread of putting an end to his uncertainty; and he looked into her face with all his might so as to lay hold on what she kept concealed at the bottom of her heart.

By degrees the panting Salammbô, crushed by such heavy looks, let her head sink below her shoulders. He was now sure that she had erred in the embrace of a Barbarian; he shuddered and raised both his fists. She uttered a shriek and fell down among her women, who crowded around her.

Hamilcar turned on his heel. All the stewards followed him.

The door of the emporiums was opened, and he entered a vast round hall from which long passages leading to other halls branched off like the spokes from the nave of a wheel. A stone disc stood in the centre with balustrades to support the cushions that were heaped up upon carpets.

The Suffet walked at first with rapid strides; he breathed noisily, he struck the ground with his heel, and drew his hand across his forehead like a man annoyed by flies. But he shook his head, and as he perceived the accumulation of his riches he became calm; his thoughts, which were attracted by the vistas in the passages, wandered to the other halls that were full of still rarer treasures. Bronze plates, silver ingots, and iron bars alternated with pigs of tin brought from the Cassiterides over the Dark Sea; gums from the country of the Blacks were running over their bags of palm bark; and gold dust heaped up in leathern bottles was insensibly creeping out through the worn-out seams. Delicate filaments drawn from marine plants hung amid flax from Egypt, Greece, Taprobane and Judæa; madrepores bristled like large bushes at the foot of the walls; and an indefinable odour—the exhalation from perfumes, leather, spices, and ostrich feathers, the latter tied in great bunches at the very top of the vault—floated through the air. An arch was formed above the door before each passage with elephants' teeth placed upright and meeting together at the points.

At last he ascended the stone disc. All the stewards stood with arms folded and heads bent while Abdalonim reared his pointed mitre with a haughty air.

Hamilcar questioned the Chief of the Ships. He was an old pilot with eyelids chafed by the wind, and white locks fell to his hips as if dashing foam of the tempests had remained on his beard.

He replied that he had sent a fleet by Gades and Thymiamata to try to reach Eziongaber by doubling the Southern Horn and the promontory of Aromata.

Others had advanced continuously towards the west for four moons without meeting with any shore; but the ships' prows became entangled in weeds, the horizon echoed continually with the noise of cataracts, blood-coloured mists darkened the sun, a perfume-laden breeze lulled the crews to sleep; and their memories were so disturbed that they were now unable to tell anything. However, expeditions had ascended the rivers of the Scythians, had made their way into Colchis, and into the countries of the Jugrians and of the Estians, had carried off fifteen hundred maidens in the Archipelago, and sunk all the strange vessels sailing beyond Cape Oestrymon, so that the secret of the routes should not be known. King Ptolemæus was detaining the incense from Schesbar; Syracuse, Elathia, Corsica, and the islands had furnished nothing, and the old pilot lowered his voice to announce that a trireme was taken at Rusicada by the Numidians,—"for they are with them, Master."

Hamilcar knit his brows; then he signed to the Chief of the Journeys to speak. This functionary was enveloped in a brown, ungirdled robe, and had his head covered with a long scarf of white stuff which passed along the edge of his lips and fell upon his shoulder behind.

The caravans had set out regularly at the winter equinox. But of fifteen hundred men directing their course towards the extreme boundaries of Ethiopia with excellent camels, new leathern bottles, and supplies of painted cloth, but one had reappeared at Carthage—the rest having died of fatigue or become mad through the terror of the desert;—and he said that far beyond the Black Harousch, after passing the Atarantes and the country of the great apes, he had seen immense kingdoms, wherein the pettiest utensils were all of gold, a river of the colour of milk and as broad as the sea, forests of blue trees, hills of aromatics, monsters with human faces vegetating on the rocks with eyeballs which expanded like flowers to look at you; and then crystal mountains supporting the sun behind lakes all covered with dragons. Others had returned from India with peacocks, pepper, and new textures. As to those who go by way of the Syrtes and the temple of Ammon to purchase chalcedony, they had no doubt perished in the sands. The caravans from Gaetulia and Phazzana had furnished their usual supplies; but he, the Chief of the Journeys, did not venture to fit one out just now.

Hamilcar understood; the Mercenaries were in occupation of the country. He leaned upon his other elbow with a hollow groan; and the Chief of the Farms was so afraid to speak that he trembled horribly in spite of his thick shoulders and his big red eyeballs. His face, which was as snub-nosed as a mastiff's, was surmounted by a net woven of threads of bark; he wore a waist-belt of hairy leopard's skin, wherein gleamed two formidable cutlasses.

As soon as Hamilcar turned away he began to cry aloud and invoke all the Baals. It was not his fault! he could not help it! He had watched the temperature, the soil, the stars, had planted at the winter solstice and pruned at the waning of the moon, had inspected the slaves and had been careful of their clothes.

But Hamilcar grew angry at this loquacity. He clacked his tongue, and the man with the cutlasses went on in rapid tones:

"Ah, Master! they have pillaged everything! sacked everything! destroyed everything! Three thousand trees have been cut down at Maschala, and at Ubada the granaries have been looted and the cisterns filled up! At Tedes they have carried off fifteen hundred gomors of meal; at Marrazana they have killed the shepherds, eaten the flocks, burnt your house—your beautiful house with its cedar beams, which you used to visit in the summer! The slaves at Tuburbo who were reaping barley fled to the mountains; and the asses, the mules both great and small, the oxen from Taormina, and the antelopes,—not a single one left! all carried away! It is a curse! I shall not survive it!" He went on again in tears: "Ah! if you knew how full the cellars were, and how the ploughshares shone! Ah! the fine rams! ah! the fine bulls!——"

Hamilcar's wrath was choking him. It burst forth:

"Be silent! Am I a pauper, then? No lies! speak the truth! I wish to know all that I have lost to the last shekel, to the last cab! Abdalonim, bring me the accounts of the ships, of the caravans, of the farms, of the house! And if your consciences are not clear, woe be on your heads! Go out!"

All the stewards went out walking backwards, with their fists touching the ground.

Abdalonim went up to a set of pigeon-holes in the wall, and from the midst of them took out knotted cords, strips of linen or papyrus, and sheeps' shoulder-blades inscribed with delicate writing. He laid them at Hamilcar's feet, placed in his hands a wooden frame furnished on the inside with three threads on which balls of gold, silver, and horn were strung, and began:

"One hundred and ninety-two houses in the Mappalian district let to the New Carthaginians at the rate of one bekah a moon."

"No! it is too much! be lenient towards the poor people! and you will try to learn whether they are attached to the Republic, and write down the names of those who appear to you to be the most daring! What next?"

Abdalonim hesitated in surprise at such generosity.

Hamilcar snatched the strips of linen from his hands.

"What is this? three palaces around Khamon at twelve kesitahs a month! Make it twenty! I do not want to be eaten up by the rich."

The Steward of the stewards, after a long salutation, resumed:

"Lent to Tigillas until the end of the season two kikars at three per cent., maritime interest; to Bar-Malkarth fifteen hundred shekels on the security of thirty slaves. But twelve have died in the salt-marshes."

"That is because they were not hardy," said the Suffet, laughing. "No matter! if he is in want of money, satisfy him! We should always lend, and at different rates of interest, according to the wealth of the individual."

Then the servant hastened to read all that had been brought in by the iron-mines of Annaba, the coral fisheries, the purple factories, the farming of the tax on the resident Greeks, the export of silver to Arabia, where it had ten times the value of gold, and the captures of vessels, deduction of a tenth being made for the temple of the goddess. "Each time I declared a quarter less, Master!" Hamilcar was reckoning with the balls; they rang beneath his fingers.

"Enough! What have you paid?"

"To Stratonicles of Corinth, and to three Alexandrian merchants, on these letters here (they have been realised), ten thousand Athenian drachmas, and twelve Syrian talents of gold. The food for the crews, amounting to twenty minae a month for each trireme ——"

"I know! How many lost?"

"Here is the account on these sheets of lead," said the Steward. "As to the ships chartered in common, it has often been necessary to throw the cargoes into the seas, and so the unequal losses have been divided among the partners. For the ropes which were borrowed from the arsenals, and which it was impossible to restore, the Syssitia exacted eight hundred kesitahs before the expedition to Utica."

"They again!" said Hamilcar, hanging his head; and he remained for a time as if quite crushed by the weight of all the hatreds that he could feel upon him. "But I do not see the Megara expenses?"

Clade Victor Dwiggins

Abdalonim, turning pale, went to another set of pigeon-holes, and took from them some planchettes of sycamore wood strung in packets on leathern strings.

Hamilcar, curious about these domestic details, listened to him and grew calm with the monotony of the tones in which the figures were enumerated. Abdalonim became slower. Suddenly he let the wooden sheets fall to the ground and threw himself flat on his face with his arms stretched out in the position of a condemned criminal. Hamilcar picked up the tablets without any emotion; and his lips parted and his eyes grew larger when he perceived an exorbitant consumption of meat, fish, birds, wines, and aromatics, with broken vases, dead slaves, and spoiled carpets set down as the expense of a single day.

Abdalonim, still prostrate, told him of the feast of the Barbarians. He had not been able to avoid the command of the Ancients. Moreover, Salammbô desired money to be lavished for the better reception of the soldiers.

At his daughter's name Hamilcar leaped to his feet. Then with compressed lips he crouched down upon the cushions, tearing the fringes with his nails, and panting with staring eyes.

"Rise!" said he; and he descended.

Abdalonim followed him; his knees trembled. But seizing an iron bar he began like one distraught to loosen the paving stones. A wooden disc sprang up and soon there appeared throughout the length of the passage several of the large covers employed for stopping up the trenches in which grain was kept.

"You see, Eye of Baal," said the servant, trembling, "they have not taken everything yet! and these

3—16

are each fifty cubits deep and filled up to the brim! During your voyage I had them dug out in the arsenals, in the gardens, everywhere! your house is full of corn as your heart is of wisdom."

A smile passed over Hamilcar's face. "It is well, Abdalonim!" Then bending over to his ear: "You will have it brought from Etruria, Brutium, whence you will, and no matter at what price! Heap it and keep it! I alone must possess all the corn in Carthage."

Then when they were at the extremity of the passage, Abdalonim, with one of the keys hanging at his girdle, opened a large quadrangular chamber divided in the centre by pillars of cedar. Gold, silver, and brass coins were arranged on tables or packed into niches, and rose as high as the joists of the roof along the four walls. In the corners there were huge baskets of hippopotamus skin supporting whole rows of smaller bags; there were hillocks formed of heaps of bullion on the pavement; and here and there a pile that was too high had given way and looked like a ruined column. The large Carthaginian pieces, representing Tanith with a horse beneath a palm-tree, mingled with those from the colonies, which were marked with a bull, star, globe, or crescent. Then there might be seen pieces of all values, dimensions, and ages arranged in unequal amounts — from the ancient coins of Assyria, slender as the nail, to the ancient ones of Latium, thicker than the hand, with the buttons of Egina, the tablets of Bactriana, and the short bars of Lacedæmon; many were covered with rust, or had grown greasy, or, having been taken in nets or from among the ruins of captured cities, were green with the water or

blackened by fire. The Suffet had very speedily calculated whether the sums present corresponded with
the gains and losses which had just been read to
him; and he was going away when he perceived
three brass jars completely empty. Abdalonim turned
away his head to mark his horror, and Hamilcar, re-
signing himself to it, said nothing.

They crossed other passages and other halls, and
at last reached a door where, to ensure its better
protection and in accordance with a Roman custom
lately introduced into Carthage, a man was fastened
by the waist to a long chain let into the wall. His
beard and nails had grown to an immoderate length,
and he swayed himself from right to left with that
continual oscillation which is characteristic of captive
animals. As soon as he recognised Hamilcar he
darted towards him, crying:

"Pardon, Eye of Baal! pity! kill me! For ten
years I have not seen the sun! In your father's
name, pardon!"

Hamilcar, without answering him, clapped his
hands and three men appeared; and all four simultaneously stiffening their arms, drew back from its
rings the enormous bar which closed the door. Hamilcar took a torch and disappeared into the darkness.

This was believed to be the family burying-place;
but nothing would have been found in it except a
broad well. It was dug out merely to baffle robbers,
and it concealed nothing. Hamilcar passed along beside it; then stooping down he made a very heavy
millstone turn upon its rollers, and through this aperture entered an apartment which was built in the
shape of a cone.

The walls were covered with scales of brass; and in the centre, on a granite pedestal, stood the statue of one of the Kabiri called Aletes, the discoverer of the mines in Celtiberia. On the ground, at its base, and arranged in the form of a cross, were large gold shields and monster close-necked silver vases, of extravagant shape and unfitted for use; for it was customary to cast quantities of metal in this way, so that dilapidation and even removal should be almost impossible.

With his torch he lit a miner's lamp which was fastened to the idol's cap, and green, yellow, blue, violet, wine-coloured, and blood-coloured fires suddenly illuminated the hall. It was filled with gems which were either in gold calabashes fastened like sconces upon sheets of brass, or were ranged in native masses at the foot of the wall. There were callaides shot away from the mountains with slings, carbuncles formed by the urine of the lynx, glossopetræ which had fallen from the moon, tyanos, diamonds, sandastra, beryls, with the three kinds of rubies, the four kinds of sapphires, and the twelve kinds of emeralds. They gleamed like splashes of milk, blue icicles, and silver dust, and shed their light in sheets, rays, and stars. Ceraunia, engendered by the thunder, sparkled by the side of chalcedonies, which are a cure for poison. There were topazes from Mount Zabarca to avert terrors, opals from Bactriana to prevent abortions, and horns of Ammon, which are placed under the bed to induce dreams.

The fires from the stones and the flames from the lamp were mirrored in the great golden shields. Hamilcar stood smiling with folded arms, and was

less delighted by the sight of his riches than by the
consciousness of their possession. They were inaccessible, exhaustless, infinite. His ancestors sleeping
beneath his feet transmitted something of their eter-
nity to his heart. He felt very near to the subterranean
deities. It was as the joy of one of the Kabiri; and
the great luminous rays striking upon his face looked
like the extremity of an invisible net linking him
across the abysses with the centre of the world.

A thought came which made him shudder, and
placing himself behind the idol he walked straight up
to the wall. Then among the tattooings on his arm
he scrutinised a horizontal line with two other per-
pendicular ones which in Chanaanitish figures expressed the number thirteen. Then he counted as far
as the thirteenth of the brass plates and again raised
his ample sleeve; and with his right hand stretched
out he read other more complicated lines on his arm,
at the same time moving his fingers daintily about
like one playing on a lyre. At last he struck seven
blows with his thumb, and an entire section of the
wall turned about in a single block.

It served to conceal a sort of cellar containing
mysterious things which had no name and were of
incalculable value. Hamilcar went down the three
steps, took up a llama's skin which was floating on
a black liquid in a silver vat, and then re-ascended.

Abdalonim again began to walk before him. He
struck the pavement with his tall cane, the pommel
of which was adorned with bells, and before every
apartment cried aloud the name of Hamilcar amid
eulogies and benedictions.

Along the walls of the circular gallery, from
which the passages branched off, were piled little

beams of algummim, bags of Lawsonia, cakes of Lemnos-earth, and tortoise carapaces filled with pearls. The Suffet brushed them with his robe as he passed without even looking at some gigantic pieces of amber, an almost divine material formed by the rays of the sun.

A cloud of odourous vapour burst forth.

"Push open the door!"

They went in.

Naked men were kneading pastes, crushing herbs, stirring coals, pouring oil into jars, and opening and shutting the little ovoid cells which were hollowed out all round in the wall, and were so numerous that the apartment was like the interior of a hive. They were brimful of myrobalan, bdellium, saffron, and violets. Gums, powders, roots, glass phials, branches of filipendula, and rose-petals were scattered about everywhere, and the scents were stifling in spite of the cloud-wreaths from the styrax shrivelling on a brazen tripod in the centre.

The Chief of the Sweet Odours, pale and long as a waxen torch, came up to Hamilcar to crush a roll of metopion in his hands, while two others rubbed his heels with leaves of baccharis. He repelled them; they were Cyreneans of infamous morals, but valued on account of the secrets which they possessed.

To show his vigilance the Chief of the Odours offered the Suffet a little malobathrum to taste in an electrum spoon; then he pierced three Indian bezoars with an awl. The master, who knew the artifices employed, took a horn full of balm, and after holding it near the coals inclined it over his robe. A brown spot appeared; it was a fraud. Then he gazed fixedly at the Chief of the Odours, and without saying anything flung the gazelle's horn full in his face.

However indignant he might be at adulterations made to his own prejudice, when he perceived some parcels of nard which were being packed up for countries beyond the sea, he ordered antimony to be mixed with it so as to make it heavier.

Then he asked where three boxes of psagdas designed for his own use were to be found.

The Chief of the Odours confessed that he did not know; some soldiers had come howling in with knives and he had opened the boxes for them.

"So you are more afraid of them than of me!" cried the Suffet; and his eyeballs flashed like torches through the smoke upon the tall, pale man who was beginning to understand. "Abdalonim! you will make him run the gauntlet before sunset: tear him!"

This loss, which was less than the others, had exasperated him; for in spite of his efforts to banish them from his thoughts he was continually coming again across the Barbarians. Their excesses were blended with his daughter's shame, and he was angry with the whole household for knowing of the latter and for not speaking of it to him. But something impelled him to bury himself in his misfortune; and in an inquisitorial fit he visited the sheds behind the mercantile house to see the supplies of bitumen, wood, anchors and cordage, honey and wax, the cloth warehouse, the stores of food, the marble yard and the silphium barn.

He went to the other side of the gardens to make an inspection in their cottages, of the domestic artisans whose productions were sold. There were tailors embroidering cloaks, others making nets, others painting cushions or cutting out sandals, and Egyptian workmen polished papyrus with a shell, while the weavers' shuttles rattled and the armourers' anvils rang.

Hamilcar said to them:

"Beat away at the swords! I shall want them." And he drew the antelope's skin that had been steeped in poisons from his bosom to have it cut into a cuirass more solid than one of brass and unassailable by steel or flame.

As soon as he approached the workmen, Abdalonim, to give his wrath another direction, tried to anger him against them by murmured disparagement of their work. "What a performance! It is a shame! The Master is indeed too good." Hamilcar moved away without listening to him.

He slackened his pace, for the paths were barred by great trees calcined from one end to the other, such as may be met with in woods where shepherds have encamped; and the palings were broken the water in the trenches was disappearing, while fragments of glass and the bones of apes were to be seen amid the miry puddles. A scrap of cloth hung here and there from the bushes, and the rotten flowers formed a yellow muck-heap beneath the citron trees. In fact, the servants had neglected everything, thinking that the master would never return.

At every step he discovered some new disaster, some further proof of the thing which he had forbidden himself to learn. Here he was soiling his purple boots as he crushed the filth under-foot; and he had not all these men before him at the end of a catapult to make them fly into fragments! He felt humiliated at having defended them; it was a delusion and a piece of treachery; and as he could not revenge himself upon the soldiers, or the Ancients, or Salammbô, or anybody, and his wrath required some victim, he condemned all the slaves of the gardens to the mines at a single stroke.

Abdalonim shuddered each time that he saw him approaching the parks. But Hamilcar took the path towards the mill, from which there might be heard issuing a mournful melopœia.

The heavy mill-stones were turning amid the dust. They consisted of two cones of porphyry laid the one upon the other — the upper one of the two, which carried a funnel, being made to revolve upon the second by means of strong bars. Some men were pushing these with their breasts and arms, while others were yoked to them and were pulling them. The friction of the straps had formed purulent scabs round about their armpits such as are seen on asses' withers, and the end of the limp black rag, which scarcely covered their loins, hung down and flapped against their hams like a long tail. Their eyes were red, the irons on their feet clanked, and all their breasts panted rhythmically. On their mouths they had muzzles fastened by two little bronze chains to render it impossible for them to eat the flour, and their hands were enclosed in gauntlets without fingers, so as to prevent them from taking any.

At the master's entrance the wooden bars creaked still more loudly. The grain grated as it was being crushed. Several fell upon their knees; the others, continuing their work, stepped across them.

He asked for Giddenem, the governor of the slaves, and that personage appeared, his rank being displayed in the richness of his dress. His tunic, which was slit up the sides, was of fine purple; his ears were weighted with heavy rings; and the strips of cloth enfolding his legs were joined together with a lacing of gold which extended from his ankles to his hips, like a serpent winding about a tree. In his fingers, which were laden with rings, he held a necklace of jet beads, so as to recognise the men who were subject to the sacred disease.

Hamilcar signed to him to unfasten the muzzles. Then with the cries of famished animals they all rushed upon the flour, burying their faces in the heaps of it and devouring it.

"You are weakening them!" said the Suffet.

Giddenem replied that such treatment was necessary in order to subdue them.

"It was scarcely worth while sending you to the slaves' school at Syracuse. Fetch the others!"

And the cooks, butlers, grooms, runners, and litter-carriers, the men belonging to the vapour-baths, and the women with their children, all ranged themselves in a single line in the garden from the mercantile house to the deer park. They held their breath. An immense silence prevailed in Megara. The sun was lengthening across the lagoon at the foot of the cata-combs. The peacocks were screeching. Hamilcar walked along step by step.

"What am I to do with these old creatures?" he said. "Sell them! There are too many Gauls: they are drunkards! and too many Cretans: they are liars! Buy me some Capadocians, Asiatics, and Ne-groes."

He was astonished that the children were so few. "The house ought to have births every year, Giddenem. You will leave the huts open every night to let them mingle freely."

He then had the thieves, the lazy, and the mutinous shown to him. He distributed punishments, with reproaches to Giddenem; and Giddenem, ox-like, bent his low forehead, with its two broad intersecting eyebrows.

"See, Eye of Baal," he said, pointing out a sturdy Libyan, "here is one who was caught with the rope round his neck."

"Ah! you wish to die?" said the Suffet scornfully.

"Yes!" replied the slave in an intrepid tone.

Then, without heeding the precedent or the pecuniary loss, Hamilcar said to the serving-men:

"Away with him!"

Perhaps in his thoughts he intended a sacrifice. It was a misfortune which he inflicted upon himself in order to avert more terrible ones.

Giddenem had hidden those who were mutilated behind the others. Hamilcar perceived them:

"Who cut off your arm?"

"The soldiers, Eye of Baal."

Then to a Samnite who was staggering like a wounded heron:

"And you, who did that to you?"

It was the governor, who had broken his leg with an iron bar.

This silly atrocity made the Suffet indignant; he snatched the jet necklace out of Giddenem's hands.

"Cursed be the dog that injures the flock! Gracious Tanith, to cripple slaves! Ah! you ruin your master! Let him be smothered in the dunghill. And those that are missing? Where are they? Have you helped the soldiers to murder them?"

His face was so terrible that all the women fled. The slaves drew back and formed a large circle around them; Giddenem was frantically kissing his sandals; Hamilcar stood upright with his arms raised above him.

But with his understanding as clear as in the sternest of his battles, he recalled a thousand odious things, ignominies from which he had turned aside; and in the gleaming of his wrath he could once more see all his disasters simultaneously as in the lightnings of a storm. The governors of the country estates had fled through terror of the soldiers, perhaps through collusion with them; they were all deceiving him; he had restrained himself too long.

"Bring them here!" he cried; "and brand them on the forehead with red-hot irons as cowards!"

Then they brought and spread out in the middle of the garden, fetters, carcanets, knives, chains for those condemned to the mines, cippi for fastening the legs, numellæ for confining the shoulders, and scorpions or whips with triple thongs terminating in brass claws.

All were placed facing the sun, in the direction of Moloch the Devourer, and were stretched on the ground on their stomachs or on their backs, those, however, who were sentenced to be flogged standing upright against the trees with two men beside them, one counting the blows and the other striking.

In striking he used both his arms, and the whistling thongs made the bark of the plane-trees fly. The blood was scattered like rain upon the foliage, and red masses writhed with howls at the foot of the trees. Those who were under the iron tore their faces with their nails. The wooden screws could be heard creaking; dull knockings resounded; sometimes a sharp cry would suddenly pierce the air. In the direction of the kitchens, men were brisking up burning coals with fans amid tattered garments and scattered hair, and a smell of burning flesh was perceptible. Those who were under the scourge, swooning, but kept in their positions by the bonds on their arms, rolled their heads upon their shoulders and closed their eyes. The others who were watching them began to shriek with terror, and the lions, remembering the feast perhaps, stretched themselves out yawning against the edge of the dens.

Then Salammbô was seen on the platform of her terrace. She ran wildly about it from left to right. Hamilcar perceived her. It seemed to him that she was holding up her arms towards him to ask for pardon; with a gesture of horror he plunged into the elephants' park.

These animals were the pride of the great Punic houses. They had carried their ancestors, had triumphed in the wars, and they were reverenced as being the favourites of the Sun.

Those of Megara were the strongest in Carthage. Before he went away Hamilcar had required Abdalonim to swear that he would watch over them. But they had died from their mutilations; and only three remained, lying in the middle of the court in the dust before the ruins of their manger.

They recognised him and came up to him.

One had its ears horribly slit, another had a large wound in its knee, while the trunk of the third was cut off.

They looked sadly at him, like reasonable creatures; and the one that had lost its trunk tried by stooping its huge head and bending its hams to stroke him softly with the hideous extremity of its stump.

At this caress from the animal two tears started into his eyes. He rushed at Abdalonim.

"Ah! wretch! the cross! the cross!"

Abdalonim fell back swooning upon the ground.

The bark of a jackal rang from behind the purple factories, the blue smoke of which was ascending slowly into the sky; Hamilcar paused.

The thought of his son had suddenly calmed him like the touch of a god. He caught a glimpse of a prolongation of his might, an indefinite continuation of his personality, and the slaves could not understand whence this appeasement had come upon him.

As he bent his steps towards the purple factories he passed before the ergastulum, which was a long house of black stone built in a square pit with a small pathway all round it and four staircases at the corners.

Iddibal was doubtless waiting until the night to finish his signal. "There is no hurry yet," thought Hamilcar; and he went down into the prison. Some cried out to him: "Return;" the boldest followed him.

The open door was flapping in the wind. The twilight entered through the narrow loopholes, and in the interior broken chains could be distinguished hanging from the walls.

This was all that remained of the captives of war!

Then Hamilcar grew extraordinarily pale, and those who were leaning over the pit outside saw him resting one hand against the wall to keep himself from falling.

But the jackal uttered its cry three times in succession. Hamilcar raised his head; he did not speak a word nor make a gesture. Then when the sun had completely set he disappeared behind the nopal hedge, and in the evening he said as he entered the assembly of the rich in the temple of Eschmoun :

"Luminaries of the Baalim, I accept the command of the Punic forces against the army of the Barbarians!"

VIII.

The Battle of the Macaras.

N THE following day he drew two hundred and twenty-three thousand kikars of gold from the Syssitia, and decreed a tax of fourteen shekels upon the rich. Even the women contributed; payment was made in behalf of the children, and he compelled the colleges of priests to furnish money — a monstrous thing, according to Carthaginian customs.

He demanded all the horses, mules, and arms. A few tried to conceal their wealth, and their property was sold; and, to intimidate the avarice of the rest, he himself gave sixty suits of armour, and fifteen hundred gomers of meal, which was as much as was given by the Ivory Company.

He sent into Liguria to buy soldiers, three thousand mountaineers accustomed to fight with bears; they were paid for six moons in advance at the rate of four minæ a day.

Nevertheless an army was wanted. But he did not, like Hanno, accept all the citizens. First he rejected those engaged in sedentary occupations, and

then those who were big-bellied or had a pusillanimous look; and he admitted those of ill-repute, the
scum of Malqua, sons of Barbarians, freed men. For
reward he promised some of the New Carthaginians
complete rights of citizenship.

His first care was to reform the Legion. These
handsome young fellows, who regarded themselves as
the military majesty of the Republic, governed themselves. He reduced their officers to the ranks; he
treated them harshly, made them run, leap, ascend
the declivity of the Byrsa at a single burst, hurl
javelins, wrestle together, and sleep in the squares at
night. Their families used to come to see them and
pity them.

He ordered shorter swords and stronger buskins.
He fixed the number of serving-men, and reduced the
amount of baggage; and as there were three hundred
Roman pila kept in the temple of Moloch, he took
them in spite of the pontiff's protests.

He organised a phalanx of seventy-two elephants
with those which had returned from Utica, and others
which were private property, and rendered them
formidable. He armed their drivers with mallet and
chisel to enable them to split their skulls in the fight
if they ran away.

He would not allow his generals to be nominated
by the Grand Council. The Ancients tried to urge
the laws in objection, but he set them aside; no one
ventured to murmur again, and everything yielded to
the violence of his genius.

He assumed sole charge of the war, the government, and the finances; and as a precaution against
accusations he demanded the Suffet Hanno as ex-
aminer of his accounts.

3—17

He set to work upon the ramparts, and had the old and now useless inner walls demolished in order to furnish stones. But difference of fortune, replacing the hierarchy of race, still kept the sons of the vanquished and those of the conquerors apart; thus the patricians viewed the destruction of these ruins with an angry eye, while the plebeians, scarcely knowing why, rejoiced.

The troops defiled under arms through the streets from morning till night; every moment the sound of trumpets was heard; chariots passed bearing shields, tents, and pikes; the courts were full of women engaged in tearing up linen; the enthusiasm spread from one to another, and Hamilcar's soul filled the Republic.

He had divided his soldiers into even numbers, being careful to place a strong man and a weak one alternately throughout the length of his files, so that he who was less vigorous or more cowardly might be at once led and pushed forward by two others. But with his three thousand Ligurians, and the best in Carthage, he could form only a simple phalanx of four thousand and ninety-six hoplites, protected by bronze helmets, and handling ashen sarissæ fourteen cubits long.

There were two thousand young men, each equipped with a sling, a dagger, and sandals. He reinforced them with eight hundred others armed with round shields and Roman swords.

The heavy cavalry was composed of the nineteen hundred remaining guardsmen of the Legion, covered with plates of vermilion bronze, like the Assyrian Clinabarians. He had further four hundred mounted archers, of those that were called Tarentines, with caps of weasel's skin, two-edged axes, and leathern tunics. Finally there were twelve hundred Negroes from the quarter of the caravans, who were mingled with the Clinabarians, and were to run beside the stallions with one hand resting on the manes. All was ready, and yet Hamilcar did not start.

Often at night he would go out of Carthage alone and make his way beyond the lagoon towards the mouths of the Macaras. Did he intend to join the Mercenaries? The Ligurians encamped in the Mappalian district surrounded his house.

The apprehensions of the rich appeared justified when, one day, three hundred Barbarians were seen approaching the walls. The Suffet opened the gates to them; they were deserters; drawn by fear or by fidelity, they were hastening to their master.

Hamilcar's return had not surprised the Mercenaries; according to their ideas the man could not die. He was returning to fulfil his promise; — a hope by no means absurd, so deep was the abyss between Country and Army. Moreover they did not believe themselves culpable; the feast was forgotten.

The spies whom they surprised undeceived them. It was a triumph for the bitter; even the lukewarm grew furious. Then the two sieges overwhelmed them with weariness; no progress was being made; a battle would be better! Thus many men had left the ranks and were scouring the country. But at news of the arming they returned; Matho leaped for joy. "At last! at last!" he cried.

Then the resentment which he cherished against Salammbô was turned against Hamilcar. His hate could now perceive a definite prey; and as his vengeance grew easier of conception he almost believed that he had realised it and he revelled in it already. At the same time he was seized with a loftier tenderness, and consumed by more acrid desire. He saw himself alternately in the midst of the soldiers brandishing the Suffet's head on a pike, and then in the room with the purple bed, clasping the maiden in his arms, covering her face with kisses, passing his hands over her long, black hair; and the imagination of this, which he knew could never be realised, tortured him. He swore to himself that, since his companions had appointed him schalishim, he would conduct the war; the certainty that he would not return from it urged him to render it a pitiless one.

He came to Spendius and said to him:

"You will go and get your men! I will bring mine! Warn Autaritus! We are lost if Hamilcar attacks us! Do you understand me? Rise!"

Spendius was stupefied before such an air of authority. Matho usually allowed himself to be led, and his previous transports had quickly passed away. But just now he appeared at once calmer and more terrible; a superb will gleamed in his eyes like the flame of sacrifice.

The Greek did not listen to his reasons. He was living in one of the Carthaginian pearl-bordered tents, drinking cool beverages from silver cups, playing at the cottabos, letting his hair grow, and conducting the siege with slackness. Moreover, he had entered into communications with some in the town and would not leave, being sure that it would open its gates before many days were over.

Narr' Havas, who wandered about among the three armies, was at that time with him. He supported his opinion, and even blamed the Libyan for wishing in his excess of courage to abandon their enterprise.

"Go, if you are afraid!" exclaimed Matho; "you promised us pitch, sulphur, elephants, foot-soldiers, horses! where are they?"

Narr' Havas reminded him that he had exterminated Hanno's last cohorts;—as to the elephants, they were being hunted in the woods, he was arming the foot-soldiers, the horses were on their way; and the Numidian rolled his eyes like a woman and smiled in an irritating manner as he stroked the ostrich feather which fell upon his shoulder. In his presence Matho was at a loss for a reply.

But a man who was a stranger entered, wet with perspiration, scared, and with bleeding feet and loosened girdle; his breathing shook his lean sides enough to have burst them, and speaking in an unintelligible dialect he opened his eyes wide as if he were telling of some battle. The king sprang outside and called his horsemen.

They ranged themselves in the plain before him in the form of a circle. Narr' Havas, who was mounted, bent his head and bit his lips. At last he separated his men into two equal divisions, and told the first to wait; then with an imperious gesture he carried off the others at a gallop and disappeared on the horizon in the direction of the mountains.

"Master!" murmured Spendius, "I do not like these extraordinary chances—the Suffet returning, Narr' Havas going away——"

"Why! what does it matter?" said Matho disdainfully.

It was a reason the more for anticipating Hamilcar by uniting with Autaritus. But if the siege of the towns were raised, the inhabitants would come out and attack them in the rear, while they would have the Carthaginians in front. After much talking the following measures were resolved upon and immediately executed.

Spendius proceeded with fifteen thousand men as far as the bridge built across the Macaras, three miles from Utica; the corners of it were fortified with four huge towers provided with catapults; all the paths and gorges in the mountains were stopped up with trunks of trees, pieces of rock, interlacings of thorn, and stone walls; on the summits heaps of grass were made which might be lighted as signals, and shepherds who were able to see at a distance were posted at intervals.

No doubt Hamilcar would not, like Hanno, advance by the mountain of the Hot Springs. He would think that Autaritus, being master of the interior, would close the route against him. Moreover, a check at the opening of the campaign would ruin him, while if he gained a victory he would soon have to make a fresh beginning, the Mercenaries being further off. Again, he could disembark at Cape Grapes and march thence upon one of the towns. But he would then find himself between the two armies, an indiscretion which he could not commit with his scanty forces. Accordingly he must proceed along the base of Mount Ariana, then turn to the left to avoid the mouths of the Macaras, and come straight to the bridge. It was there that Matho expected him.

At night he used to inspect the pioneers by torchlight. He would hasten to Hippo-Zarytus or to the works on the mountains, would come back again,

would never rest. Spendius envied his energy; but
in the management of spies, the choice of sentries,
the working of the engines and all means of defence,
Matho listened docilely to his companion. They spoke
no more of Salammbô,—one not thinking about her,
and the other being prevented by a feeling of shame.

Often he would go towards Carthage, striving to
catch sight of Hamilcar's troops. His eyes would
dart along the horizon; he would lie flat on the
ground, and believe that he could hear an army in
the throbbing of his arteries.

He told Spendius that if Hamilcar did not arrive
within three days he would go with all his men to
meet him and offer him battle. Two further days
elapsed. Spendius restrained him; but on the morning of the sixth day he departed.

The Carthaginians were no less impatient for war
than the Barbarians. In tents and in houses there
was the same longing and the same distress; all were
asking one another what was delaying Hamilcar.

From time to time he would mount to the cupola
of the temple of Eschmoun beside the Announcer of
the Moons and take note of the wind.

One day—it was the third of the month of Tibby
—they saw him descending from the Acropolis
with hurried steps. A great clamour arose in the
Mappalian district. Soon the streets were astir, and
the soldiers were everywhere beginning to arm surrounded by weeping women who threw themselves
upon their breasts; then they ran quickly to the
square of Khamon to take their places in the ranks.
No one was allowed to follow them or even to speak
to them, or to approach the ramparts; for some min-

3

utes the whole town was as silent as a great tomb. The soldiers as they leaned on their lances were thinking, and the others in the houses were sighing.

At sunset the army went out by the western gate; but instead of taking the road to Tunis or making for the mountains in the direction of Utica, they continued their march along the edge of the sea; and they soon reached the Lagoon, where round spaces quite whitened with salt glittered like gigantic silver dishes forgotten on the shore.

Then the pools of water multiplied. The ground gradually became softer, and the feet sank in it. Hamilcar did not turn back. He went on still at their head; and his horse, which was yellow-spotted like a dragon, advanced into the mire flinging froth around him, and with great straining of the loins. Night—a moonless night—fell. A few cried out that they were about to perish; he snatched their arms from them, and gave them to the serving-men. Nevertheless the mud became deeper and deeper. Some had to mount the beasts of burden; others clung to the horses' tails; the sturdy pulled the weak, and the Ligurian corps drove on the infantry with the points of their pikes. The darkness increased. They had lost their way. All stopped.

Then some of the Suffet's slaves went on ahead to look for the buoys which had been placed at intervals by his order. They shouted through the darkness, and the army followed them at a distance.

At last they felt the resistance of the ground. Then a whitish curve became dimly visible, and they found themselves on the bank of the Macaras. In spite of the cold no fires were lighted

In the middle of the night squalls of wind arose. Hamilcar had the soldiers roused, but not a trumpet was sounded: their captains tapped them softly on the shoulder.

A man of lofty stature went down into the water. It did not come up to his girdle; it was possible to cross.

The Suffet ordered thirty-two of the elephants to be posted in the river a hundred paces further on, while the others, lower down, would check the lines of men that were carried away by the current; and holding their weapons above their heads they all crossed the Macaras as though between two walls. He had noticed that the western wind had driven the sand so as to obstruct the river and form a natural causeway across it.

He was now on the left bank in front of Utica, and in a vast plain, the latter being advantageous for his elephants, which formed the strength of his army.

This feat of genius filled the soldiers with enthusiasm. They recovered extraordinary confidence. They wished to hasten immediately against the Barbarians; but the Suffet made them rest for two hours. As soon as the sun appeared they moved into the plain in three lines — first came the elephants, and then the light infantry with the cavalry behind it, the phalanx marching next.

The Barbarians encamped at Utica, and the fifteen thousand about the bridge were surprised to see the ground undulating in the distance. The wind, which was blowing very hard, was driving tornadoes of sand before it; they rose as though snatched from the soil, ascended in great light-coloured strips, then parted asunder and began again, hiding the Punic army the while from the Mercenaries. Owing to the horns, which stood up on the edge of the helmets, some thought that they could perceive a herd of oxen; others, deceived by the motion of the cloaks, pretended that they could distinguish wings, and those who had travelled a good deal shrugged their shoulders and explained everything by the illusions of the mirage. Nevertheless something of enormous size continued to advance. Little vapours, as subtle as the breath, ran across the surface of the desert; the sun, which was higher now, shone more strongly: a harsh light, which seemed to vibrate, threw back the depths of the sky, and permeating objects, rendered distance incalculable. The immense plain expanded in every direction beyond the limits of vision; and the almost insensible undulations of the soil extended to the extreme horizon, which was closed by a great blue line which they knew to be the sea. The two armies, having left their tents, stood gazing; the people of Utica were massing on the ramparts to have a better view.

At last they distinguished several transverse bars bristling with level points. They became thicker, larger; black hillocks swayed to and fro; square thickets suddenly appeared; they were elephants and lances. A single shout went up: "The Carthaginians!" and without signal or command the soldiers at Utica and those at the bridge ran pell-mell to fall in a body upon Hamilcar.

Spendius shuddered at the name. "Hamilcar! Hamilcar!" he repeated, panting, and Matho was not there! What was to be done? No means of flight! The suddenness of the event, his terror of the Suffet, and above all, the urgent need of forming an immediate resolution, distracted him; he could see himself pierced by a thousand swords, decapitated, dead. Meanwhile he was being called for; thirty thousand men would follow him; he was seized with fury against himself; he fell back upon the hope of victory; it was full of bliss, and he believed himself more intrepid than Epaminondas. He smeared his cheeks with vermilion in order to conceal his paleness, then he buckled on his knemids and his cuirass, swallowed a patera of pure wine, and ran after his troops, who were hastening towards those from Utica.

They united so rapidly that the Suffet had not time to draw up his men in battle array. By degrees he slackened his speed. The elephants stopped; they rocked their heavy heads with their chargings of ostrich feathers, striking their shoulders the while with their trunks.

Behind the intervals between them might be seen the cohorts of the velites, and further on the great helmets of the Clinabarians, with steel heads glancing in the sun, cuirasses, plumes, and waving standards. But the Carthaginian army, which amounted to eleven thousand three hundred and ninety-six men, seemed scarcely to contain them, for it formed an oblong, narrow at the sides and pressed back upon itself.

Seeing them so weak, the Barbarians, who were thrice as numerous, were seized with extravagant joy. Hamilcar was not to be seen. Perhaps he had remained down yonder? Moreover what did it matter? The disdain which they felt for these traders strengthened their courage; and before Spendius could command a manœuvre they had all understood it, and already executed it.

They deployed in a long, straight line, overlapping the wings of the Punic army in order to completely encompass it. But when there was an interval of only three hundred paces between the armies, the elephants turned round instead of advancing; then the Clinabarians were seen to face about and follow them; and the surprise of the Mercenaries increased when they saw the archers running to join them. So the Carthaginians were afraid, they were fleeing! A tremendous hooting broke out from among the Barbarian troops, and Spendius exclaimed from the top of his dromedary: "Ah! I knew it! Forward! forward!"

Then javelins, darts, and sling-bullets burst forth simultaneously. The elephants feeling their croups stung by the arrows began to gallop more quickly; a great dust enveloped them, and they vanished like shadows in a cloud.

But from the distance there came a loud noise of footsteps dominated by the shrill sound of the trumpets, which were being blown furiously. The space which the Barbarians had in front of them, which was full of eddies and tumult, attracted like a whirlpool; some dashed into it. Cohorts of infantry appeared; they closed up; and at the same time all the rest saw the foot-soldiers hastening up with the horsemen at a gallop.

Hamilcar had, in fact, ordered the phalanx to break its sections, and the elephants, light troops, and cavalry to pass through the intervals so as to bring themselves speedily upon the wings, and so well had he calculated the distance from the Barbarians, that at the moment when they reached him, the entire Carthaginian army formed one long straight line.

In the centre bristled the phalanx, formed of syn-

tagmata or full squares having sixteen men on each
side. All the leaders of all the files appeared amid
long, sharp lanceheads, which jutted out unevenly
around them, for the first six ranks crossed their
sarissæ, holding them in the middle, and the ten lower
ranks rested them upon the shoulders of their companions in succession before them. Their faces were all
half hidden beneath the visors of their helmets; their
right legs were all covered with bronze knemids;
broad cylindrical shields reached down to their knees;
and the horrible quadrangular mass moved in a single
body, and seemed to live like an animal and work
like a machine. Two cohorts of elephants flanked it
in regular array; quivering, they shook off the splin-
ters of the arrows that clung to their black skins. The
Indians, squatting on their withers among the tufts of
white feathers, restrained them with their spoon-
headed harpoons, while the men in the towers, who
were hidden up to their shoulders, moved about iron
distaffs furnished with lighted tow on the edges of
their large bended bows. Right and left of the elephants
hovered the slingers, each with a sling around his
loins, a second on his head, and a third in his right
hand. Then came the Clinabarians, each flanked by
a negro, and pointing their lances between the ears of
their horses, which, like themselves, were completely
covered with gold. Afterwards, at intervals, came
the light-armed soldiers with shields of lynx skin,
beyond which projected the points of the javelins
which they held in their left hands; while the Tarentines, each having two coupled horses, relieved this
wall of soldiers at its two extremities.

The army of the Barbarians, on the contrary, had
not been able to preserve its line. Undulations and

blanks were to be found through its extravagant length; all were panting and out of breath with their running.

The phalanx moved heavily along with thrusts from all its sarissæ; and the too slender line of the Mercenaries soon yielded in the centre beneath the enormous weight.

Then the Carthaginian wings expanded in order to fall upon them, the elephants following. The phalanx, with obliquely pointed lances, cut through the Barbarians; there were two enormous, struggling bodies; and the wings with slings and arrows beat them back upon the phalangites. There was no cavalry to get rid of them, except two hundred Numidians operating against the right squadron of the Clinabarians. All the rest were hemmed in, and unable to extricate themselves from the lines. The peril was imminent, and the need of coming to some resolution urgent.

Spendius ordered attacks to be made simultaneously on both flanks of the phalanx so as to pass clean through it. But the narrower ranks glided below the longer ones and recovered their position, and the phalanx turned upon the Barbarians as terrible in flank as it had just been in front.

They struck at the staves of the sarissæ, but the cavalry in the rear embarrassed their attack; and the phalanx, supported by the elephants, lengthened and contracted, presenting itself in the form of a square, a cone, a rhombus, a trapezium, a pyramid. A twofold internal movement went on continually from its head to its rear; for those who were at the lowest part of the files hastened up to the first ranks, while the latter, from fatigue, or on account of the wounded, fell further back. The Barbarians found themselves thronged upon the phalanx. It was impossible for it to advance; there was, as it were, an ocean wherein leaped red crests and scales of brass, while the bright shields rolled like silver foam. Sometimes broad currents would descend from one extremity to the other, and then go up again, while a heavy mass remained motionless in the centre. The lances dipped and rose alternately. Elsewhere there was so quick a play of naked swords that only the points were visible, while turmæ of cavalry formed wide circles which closed again like whirlwinds behind them.

Above the voices of the captains, the ringing of clarions and the grating of lyres, bullets of lead and almonds of clay whistled through the air, dashing the sword from the hand or the brain out of the skull. The wounded, sheltering themselves with one arm beneath their shields, pointed their swords by resting the pommels upon the ground, while others, lying in pools of blood, would turn and bite the heels of those above them. The multitude was so compact, the dust so thick, and the tumult so great that it was impossible to distinguish anything; the cowards who offered to surrender were not even heard. Those whose hands were empty clasped one another close; breasts cracked against cuirasses, and corpses hung with head thrown back between a pair of contracted arms. There was a company of sixty Umbrians who, firm on their hams, their pikes before their eyes, immovable and grinding their teeth, forced two syntagmata to recoil simultaneously. Some Epirote shepherds ran upon the left squadron of the Clinabarians, and whirling their staves, seized the horses by the mane; the animals threw their riders and fled across the plain. The Punic slingers scattered here and there stood gaping. The phalanx began to waver, the captains ran to and fro in distraction, the rearmost in the files were pressing upon the soldiers, and the Barbarians had re-formed; they were recovering; the victory was theirs.

But a cry, a terrible cry broke forth, a roar of pain and wrath: it came from the seventy-two elephants which were rushing on in double line, Hamilcar having waited until the Mercenaries were massed together in one spot to let them loose against them; the Indians had goaded them so vigorously that blood was trickling down their broad ears. Their trunks, which were smeared with minium, were stretched straight out in the air like red serpents; their breasts were furnished with spears and their backs with cuirasses; their tusks were lengthened with steel blades curved like sabres,—and to make them more ferocious they had been intoxicated with a mixture of pepper, wine, and incense. They shook their necklaces of bells, and shrieked; and the elephantarchs bent their heads beneath the stream of phalaricas which was beginning to fly from the tops of the towers.

In order to resist them the better the Barbarians rushed forward in a compact crowd; the elephants flung themselves impetuously upon the centre of it. The spurs on their breasts, like ships' prows, clove through the cohorts, which flowed surging back. They stifled the men with their trunks, or else snatching them up from the ground delivered them over their heads to the soldiers in the towers; with their tusks they disembowelled them, and hurled them into the air, and long entrails hung from their ivory fangs like bundles of ropes from a mast. The Barbarians strove to blind them, to hamstring them;

others would slip beneath their bodies, bury a sword in them up to the hilt, and perish crushed to death; the most intrepid clung to their straps; they would go on sawing the leather amid flames, bullets, and arrows, and the wicker tower would fall like a tower of stone. Fourteen of the animals on the extreme right, irritated by their wounds, turned upon the second rank; the Indians seized mallet and chisel, applied the latter to a joint in the head, and with all their might struck a great blow.

Down sank the huge beasts, falling one above another. It was like a mountain; and upon the heap of dead bodies and armour a monstrous elephant, called "The Fury of Baal," which had been caught by the leg in some chains, stood howling until the evening with an arrow in its eye.

The others, however, like conquerors, delighting in extermination, overthrew, crushed, stamped, and raged against the corpses and the *débris*. To repel the maniples in serried circles around them, they turned about on their hind feet as they advanced, with a continual rotatory motion. The Carthaginians felt their energy increase, and the battle began again.

The Barbarians were growing weak; some Greek hoplites threw away their arms, and terror seized upon the rest. Spendius was seen stooping upon his dromedary, and spurring it on the shoulders with two javelins. Then they all rushed away from the wings and ran towards Utica.

The Clinabarians, whose horses were exhausted, did not try to overtake them. The Ligurians, who were weakened by thirst, cried out for an advance towards the river. But the Carthaginians, who were posted in the centre of the syntagmata, and had suffered less, stamped their feet with longing for the vengeance which was flying from them; and they were already darting forward in pursuit of the Mercenaries when Hamilcar appeared.

He held in his spotted and sweat-covered horse with silver reins. The bands fastened to the horns on his helmet flapped in the wind behind him, and he had placed his oval shield beneath his left thigh. With a motion of his triple-pointed pike he checked the army.

The Tarentines leaped quickly upon their spare horses, and set off right and left towards the river and towards the town.

The phalanx exterminated all the remaining Barbarians at leisure. When the swords appeared they would stretch out their throats and close their eyelids. Others defended themselves to the last, and were knocked down from a distance with flints like mad dogs. Hamilcar had desired the taking of prisoners, but the Carthaginians obeyed him grudgingly, so much pleasure did they derive from plunging their swords into the bodies of the Barbarians. As they were too hot they set about their work with bare arms like mowers; and when they desisted to take breath they would follow with their eyes a horseman galloping across the country after a fleeing soldier. He would succeed in seizing him by the hair, hold him thus for a while, and then fell him with a blow of his axe.

Night fell. Carthaginians and Barbarians had disappeared. The elephants which had taken to flight roamed in the horizon with their fired towers. These burned here and there in the darkness like beacons half lost in the mist; and no movement could be discerned in the plain save the undulation of the river, which was heaped with corpses, and was drifting them away to the sea.

Two hours afterwards Matho arrived. He caught sight in the starlight of long, uneven heaps lying upon the ground.

They were files of Barbarians. He stooped down; all were dead. He called into the distance, but no voice replied.

That very morning he had left Hippo-Zarytus with his soldiers to march upon Carthage. At Utica the army under Spendius had just set out, and the inhabitants were beginning to fire the engines. All had fought desperately. But, the tumult which was going on in the direction of the bridge increasing in an incomprehensible fashion, Matho had struck across the mountain by the shortest road, and as the Barbarians were fleeing over the plain he had encountered nobody.

Facing him were little pyramidal masses rearing themselves in the shade, and on this side of the river and closer to him were motionless lights on the surface of the ground. In fact the Carthaginians had fallen back behind the bridge, and to deceive the Barbarians the Suffet had stationed numerous posts upon the other bank.

Matho, still advancing, thought that he could distinguish Punic ensigns, for horses' heads which did not stir appeared in the air fixed upon the tops of piles of staves which could not be seen; and further off he could hear a great clamour, a noise of songs, and clashing of cups.

Then, not knowing where he was nor how to find Spendius, assailed with anguish, scared, and lost in the darkness, he returned more impetuously by the same road. The dawn was growing grey when from the top of the mountain he perceived the town with the carcasses of the engines blackened by the flames and looking like giant skeletons leaning against the walls.

All was peaceful amid extraordinary silence and heaviness. Among his soldiers on the verge of the tents men were sleeping nearly naked, each upon his back, or with his forehead against his arm which was supported by his cuirass. Some were unwinding bloodstained bandages from their legs. Those who were doomed to die rolled their heads about gently; others dragged themselves along and brought them drink. The sentries walked up and down along the narrow paths in order to warm themselves, or stood in a fierce attitude with their faces turned towards the horizon, and their pikes on their shoulders. Matho found Spendius sheltered beneath a rag of canvas, supported by two sticks set in the ground, his knee in his hands and his head cast down.

They remained for a long time without speaking.

At last Matho murmured: "Conquered!"

Spendius rejoined in a gloomy voice: "Yes, conquered!"

And to all questions he replied by gestures of despair.

Meanwhile sighs and death-rattles reached them. Matho partially opened the canvas. Then the sight of the soldiers reminded him of another disaster on the same spot, and he ground his teeth: "Wretch! once already——"

Spendius interrupted him: "You were not there either."

"It is a curse!" exclaimed Matho. "Nevertheless, in the end I will get at him! I will conquer him! I will slay him! Ah! if I had been there!——" The thought of having missed the battle rendered him even more desperate than the defeat. He snatched up his sword and threw it upon the ground. "But how did the Carthaginians beat you?"

The former slave began to describe the manœuvres. Matho seemed to see them, and he grew angry. The army from Utica ought to have taken Hamilcar in the rear instead of hastening to the bridge.

"Ah! I know!" said Spendius.

"You ought to have made your ranks twice as deep, avoided exposing the velites against the phalanx, and given free passage to the elephants. Everything might have been recovered at the last moment; there was no necessity to fly."

Spendius replied:

"I saw him pass along in his large red cloak, with uplifted arms and higher than the dust, like an eagle flying upon the flank of the cohorts; and at every nod they closed up or darted forward; the throng carried us towards each other; he looked at me, and I felt the cold steel as it were in my heart."

"He selected the day, perhaps?" whispered Matho to himself.

They questioned each other, trying to discover what it was that had brought the Suffet just when circumstances were most unfavourable. They went on to talk over the situation, and Spendius, to extenuate his fault, or to revive his courage, asserted that some hope still remained.

"And if there be none, it matters not!" said Matho; "alone, I will carry on the war!"

"And I too!" exclaimed the Greek, leaping up; he strode to and fro, his eyes sparkling, and a strange smile wrinkling his jackal face.

"We will make a fresh start; do not leave me again! I am not made for battles in the sunlight — the flashing of the swords troubles my sight; it is a disease, I lived too long in the ergastulum. But give me walls to scale at night, and I will enter the citadels, and the corpses shall be cold before cock-crow! Show me any one, anything, an enemy, a treasure, a woman,—a woman," he repeated, "were she a king's daughter, and I will quickly bring your desire to your feet. You reproach me for having lost the battle against Hanno, nevertheless I won it back again. Confess it! my herd of swine did more for us than a phalanx of Spartans." And yielding to the need that he felt of exalting himself and taking his revenge, he enumerated all that he had done for the cause of the Mercenaries. "It was I who urged on the Gaul in the Suffet's gardens! And later, at Sicca, I maddened them all with fear of the Republic! Gisco was sending them back, but I prevented the interpreters speaking. Ah! how their tongues hung out of their mouths! do you remember? I brought you into Carthage; I stole the zaïmph. I led you to her. I will do more yet: you shall see!" He burst out laughing like a madman.

Matho regarded him with gaping eyes. He felt in a measure uncomfortable in the presence of this man, who was at once so cowardly and so terrible.

The Greek resumed in jovial tones and cracking his fingers:

"Evoe! Sun after rain! I have worked in the quarries, and I have drunk Massic wine beneath a golden awning in a vessel of my own like a Ptolemæus. Calamity should help to make us cleverer. By dint of work we may make fortune bend. She loves politicians. She will yield!"

He returned to Matho and took him by the arm.

"Master, at present the Carthaginians are sure of their victory. You have quite an army which has not fought, and your men obey *you*. Place them in the front; mine will follow to avenge themselves. I have still three thousand Carians, twelve hundred slingers and archers, whole cohorts! A phalanx even might be formed; let us return!"

Matho, who had been stunned by the disaster, had hitherto thought of no means of repairing it. He listened with open mouth, and the bronze plates which circled his sides rose with the leapings of his heart. He picked up his sword, crying:

"Follow me; forward!"

But when the scouts returned, they announced that the Carthaginian dead had been carried off, that the bridge was in ruins, and that Hamilcar had disappeared.

IN THE FIELD.

AMILCAR had thought that the Mercenaries would await him at Utica, or that they would return against him; and finding his forces insufficient to make or to sustain an attack, he had struck southwards along the right bank of the river, thus protecting himself immediately from a surprise.

He intended first to wink at the revolt of the tribes and to detach them all from the cause of the Barbarians; then when they were quite isolated in the midst of the provinces he would fall upon them and exterminate them.

In fourteen days he pacified the region comprised between Thouccaber and Utica, with the towns of Tignicabah, Tessourah, Vacca, and others further to the west. Zounghar built in the mountains, Assouras celebrated for its temple, Djeraado fertile in junipers, Thapitis, and Hagour sent embassies to him. The country people came with their hands full of provisions, implored his protection, kissed his feet and those of the soldiers, and complained of the Bar-

(202)

barians. Some came to offer him bags containing
heads of Mercenaries slain, so they said, by themselves, but which they had cut off corpses; for many
had lost themselves in their flight, and were found
dead here and there beneath the olive trees and
among the vines.

On the morrow of his victory, Hamilcar, to dazzle
the people, had sent to Carthage the two thousand
captives taken on the battlefield. They arrived in
long companies of one hundred men each, all
with their arms fastened behind their backs with a
bar of bronze which caught them at the nape of the
neck, and the wounded, bleeding as they still were,
running also along; horsemen followed them, driving
them on with blows of the whip.

Then there was a delirium of joy! People repeated that there were six thousand Barbarians killed;
the others would not hold out, and the war was finished; they embraced one another in the streets, and
rubbed the faces of the Patæc Gods with butter and
cinnamomum to thank them. These, with their big
eyes, their big bodies, and their arms raised as high
as the shoulder, seemed to live beneath their fresh-
ened paint, and to participate in the cheerfulness of
the people. The rich left their doors open; the
city resounded with the noise of the timbrels;
the temples were illuminated every night, and the
servants of the goddess went down to Malqua and
set up stages of sycamore-wood at the corners of
the cross-ways, and prostituted themselves there.
Lands were voted to the conquerors, holocausts to
Melkarth, three hundred gold crowns to the Suffet,
and his partisans proposed to decree to him new
prerogatives and honours.

He had begged the Ancients to make overtures to Autaritus for exchanging all the Barbarians, if necessary, for the aged Gisco, and the other Carthaginians detained like him. The Libyans and Nomads composing the army under Autaritus knew scarcely anything of these Mercenaries, who were men of Italiote or Greek race; and the offer by the Republic of so many Barbarians for so few Carthaginians, showed that the value of the former was nothing and that of the latter considerable. They dreaded a snare. Autaritus refused.

Then the Ancients decreed the execution of the captives, although the Suffet had written to them not to put them to death. He reckoned upon incorporating the best of them with his own troops and of thus instigating defections. But hatred swept away all circumspection.

The two thousand Barbarians were tied to the stelæ of the tombs in the Mappalian quarter; and traders, scullions, embroiderers, and even women,—the widows of the dead with their children—all who would, came to kill them with arrows. They aimed slowly at them, the better to prolong their torture, lowering the weapon and then raising it in turn; and the multitude pressed forward howling. Paralytics had themselves brought thither in hand-barrows; many took the precaution of bringing their food, and remained on the spot until the evening; others passed the night there. Tents had been set up in which drinking went on. Many gained large sums by hiring out bows.

Then all these crucified corpses were left upright, looking like so many red statues on the tombs, and the excitement even spread to the people of Malqua, who were the descendants of the aboriginal families, and were usually indifferent to the affairs of their country. Out of gratitude for the pleasure it had been giving them they now interested themselves in its fortunes, and felt that they were Carthaginians, and the Ancients thought it a clever thing to have thus blended the entire people in a single act of vengeance.

The sanction of the gods was not wanting; for crows alighted from all quarters of the sky. They wheeled in the air as they flew with loud hoarse cries, and formed a huge cloud rolling continually upon itself. It was seen from Clypea, Rhades, and the promontory of Hermæum. Sometimes it would suddenly burst asunder, its black spirals extending far away, as an eagle clove the centre of it, and then departed again; here and there on the terraces the domes, the peaks of the obelisks, and the pediments of the temples there were big birds holding human fragments in their reddened beaks.

Owing to the smell the Carthaginians resigned themselves to unbind the corpses. A few of them were burnt; the rest were thrown into the sea, and the waves, driven by the north wind, deposited them on the shore at the end of the gulf before the camp of Autaritus.

This punishment had no doubt terrified the Barbarians, for from the top of Eschmoun they could be seen striking their tents, collecting their flocks, and hoisting their baggage upon asses, and on the evening of the same day the entire army withdrew.

It was to march to and fro between the mountain of the Hot Springs and Hippo-Zarytus, and so debar the Suffet from approaching the Tyrian towns, and from the possibility of a return to Carthage.

Meanwhile the two other armies were to try to overtake him in the south, Spendius in the east, and Matho in the west, in such a way that all three should unite to surprise and entangle him. Then they received a reinforcement which they had not looked for: Narr' Havas reappeared with three hundred camels laden with bitumen, twenty-five elephants, and six thousand horsemen.

To weaken the Mercenaries the Suffet had judged it prudent to occupy his attention at a distance in his own kingdom. From the heart of Carthage he had to come to an understanding with Masgaba, a Gætulian brigand who was seeking to found an empire. Strengthened by Punic money, the adventurer had raised the Numidian States with promises of freedom. But Narr' Havas, warned by his nurse's son, had dropped into Cirta, poisoned the conquerors with the water of the cisterns, struck off a few heads, set all right again, and had just arrived against the Suffet more furious than the Barbarians.

The chiefs of the four armies concerted the arrangements for the war. It would be a long one, and everything must be foreseen.

It was agreed first to entreat the assistance of the Romans, and this mission was offered to Spendius, but as a fugitive he dared not undertake it. Twelve men from the Greek colonies embarked at Annaba in a sloop belonging to the Numidians. Then the chiefs exacted an oath of complete obedience from all the Barbarians. Every day the captains inspected clothes and boots; the sentries were even forbidden to use a shield, for they would often lean it against their lance

and fall asleep as they stood; those who had any
baggage trailing after them were obliged to get rid
of it; everything was to be carried, in Roman fashion,
on the back. As a precaution against the elephants
Matho instituted a corps of cataphract cavalry, men
and horses being hidden beneath cuirasses of hippopotamus skin bristling with nails; and to protect the
horses' hoofs boots of plaited esparto-grass were made
for them.

It was forbidden to pillage the villages, or to tyr-
annise over the inhabitants who were not of Punic
race. But as the country was becoming exhausted,
Matho ordered the provisions to be served out to the
soldiers individually, without troubling about the
women. At first the men shared with them. Many
grew weak for lack of food. It was the occasion of
incessant quarrels and invectives, many drawing away
the companions of the rest by the bait or even by
the promise of their own portion. Matho commanded
them all to be driven away pitilessly. They took
refuge in the camp of Autaritus; but the Gaulish and
Libyan women forced them by their outrageous treatment to depart.

At last they came beneath the walls of Carthage to
implore the protection of Ceres and Proserpine, for in
Byrsa there was a temple with priests consecrated to
these goddesses in expiation of the horrors formerly
committed at the siege of Syracuse. The Syssitia,
alleging their right to waifs and strays, claimed the
youngest in order to sell them; and some fair Lace-
dæmonian women were taken by New Carthaginians
in marriage.

A few persisted in following the armies. They
ran on the flank of the syntagmata by the side of

the captains. They called to their husbands, pulled them by the cloak, cursed them as they beat their breasts, and held out their little naked and weeping children at arm's length. The sight of them was unmanning the Barbarians; they were an embarrassment and a peril. Several times they were repulsed, but they came back again; Matho made the horsemen belonging to Narr' Havas charge them with the point of the lance; and on some Balearians shouting out to him that they must have women, he replied: "*I* have none!"

Just now he was invaded by the genius of Moloch. In spite of the rebellion of his conscience, he performed terrible deeds, imagining that he was thus obeying the voice of a god. When he could not ravage the fields, Matho would cast stones into them to render them sterile.

He urged Autaritus and Spendius with repeated messages to make haste. But the Suffet's operations were incomprehensible. He encamped at Eidous, Monchar, and Tehent successively; some scouts believed that they saw him in the neighbourhood of Ischiil, near the frontiers of Narr' Havas, and it was reported that he had crossed the river above Tebourba as though to return to Carthage. Scarcely was he in one place when he removed to another. The routes that he followed always remained unknown. The Suffet preserved his advantages without offering battle, and while pursued by the Barbarians seemed to be leading them.

These marches and counter marches were still more fatiguing to the Carthaginians; and Hamilcar's forces, receiving no reinforcements, diminished from day to day. The country people were now more backward in bringing him in provisions. In every direction he encountered taciturn hesitation and hatred; and in spite of his entreaties to the Great Council no succour came from Carthage.

It was said, perhaps it was believed, that he had need of none. It was a trick, or his complaints were unnecessary; and Hanno's partisans, in order to do him an ill turn, exaggerated the importance of his victory. The troops which he commanded he was welcome to; but they were not going to supply all his demands continually in that way. The war was quite burdensome enough! it had cost too much, and from pride the patricians belonging to his faction supported him but slackly.

Then Hamilcar, despairing of the Republic, took by force from the tribes all that he wanted for the war—grain, oil, wood, cattle, and men. But the inhabitants were not long in taking to flight. The villages passed through were empty, and the cabins were ransacked without anything being discerned in them. The Punic army was soon encompassed by a terrible solitude.

The Carthaginians, who were furious, began to sack the provinces; they filled up the cisterns and fired the houses. The sparks, being carried by the wind, were scattered far off, and whole forests were on fire on the mountains; they bordered the valleys with a crown of flames, and it was often necessary to wait in order to pass beyond them. Then the soldiers resumed their march over the warm ashes in the full glare of the sun.

Sometimes they would see what looked like the eyes of a tiger cat gleaming in a bush by the side of the road. This was a Barbarian crouching upon his heels, and smeared with dust, that he might not be distinguished from the colour of the foliage; or perhaps when passing along a ravine those on the wings would suddenly hear the rolling of stones, and raising their eyes would perceive a bare-footed man bounding along through the opening of the gorge.

Meanwhile Utica and Hippo-Zarytus were free since the Mercenaries were no longer besieging them. Hamilcar commanded them to come to his assistance. But not caring to compromise themselves, they answered him with vague words, with compliments and excuses.

He went up again abruptly into the North, determined to open up one of the Tyrian towns, though he were obliged to lay siege to it. He required a station on the coast, so as to be able to draw supplies and men from the islands or from Cyrene, and he coveted the harbour of Utica as being the nearest to Carthage.

The Suffet therefore left Zouitin and turned the lake of Hippo-Zarytus with circumspection. But he was soon obliged to lengthen out his regiments into column in order to climb the mountain which separates the two valleys. They were descending at sunset into its hollow, funnel-shaped summit, when they perceived on the level of the ground before them bronze she-wolves which seemed to be running across the grass.

Suddenly large plumes arose and a terrible song burst forth, accompanied by the rhythm of flutes. It was the army under Spendius; for some Campanians and Greeks, in their execration of Carthage, had assumed the ensigns of Rome. At the same time long pikes, shields of leopard's skin, linen cuirasses, and

naked shoulders were seen on the left. These were
the Iberians under Matho, the Lusitanians, Balearians,
and Gætulians; the horses of Narr' Havas were heard
to neigh; they spread around the hill; then came the
loose rabble commanded by Autaritus — Gauls, Libyans, and Nomads; while the Eaters of Uncleanness
might be recognised among them by the fish bones
which they wore in their hair.

Thus the Barbarians, having contrived their marches
with exactness, had come together again. But themselves surprised, they remained motionless for some
minutes in consultation.

The Suffet had collected his men into an orbicular
mass, in such a way as to offer an equal resistance
in every direction. The infantry were surrounded by
their tall, pointed shields fixed close to one another
in the turf. The Clinabarians were outside and the
elephants at intervals further off. The Mercenaries
were worn out with fatigue; it was better to wait
till next day; and the Barbarians feeling sure of their
victory occupied themselves the whole night in eating.

They lighted large bright fires, which, while dazzling themselves, left the Punic army below them in
the shade. Hamilcar caused a trench fifteen feet
broad and ten cubits deep to be dug in Roman
fashion round his camp, and the earth thrown out
to be raised on the inside into a parapet, on which
sharp interlacing stakes were planted; and at sunrise
the Mercenaries were amazed to perceive all the
Carthaginians thus entrenched as if in a fortress.

They could recognise Hamilcar in the midst of the
tents walking about and giving orders. His person
was clad in a brown cuirass cut in little scales; he

was followed by his horse, and stopped from time to time to point out something with his right arm outstretched.

Then more than one recalled similar mornings when, amid the din of clarions, he passed slowly before them, and his looks strengthened them like cups of wine. A kind of emotion overcame them. Those, on the contrary, who were not acquainted with Hamilcar, were mad with joy at having caught him.

Nevertheless if all attacked at once they would do one another mutual injury in the insufficiency of space. The Numidians might dash through; but the Clinabarians, who were protected by cuirasses, would crush them. And then how were the palisades to be crossed? As to the elephants, they were not sufficiently well trained.

"You are all cowards!" exclaimed Matho.

And with the best among them he rushed against the entrenchment. They were repulsed by a volley of stones; for the Suffet had taken their abandoned catapults on the bridge.

This want of success produced an abrupt change in the fickle minds of the Barbarians. Their extreme bravery disappeared; they wished to conquer, but with the smallest possible risk. According to Spendius they ought to maintain carefully the position that they held, and starve out the Punic army. But the Carthaginians began to dig wells, and as there were mountains surrounding the hill, they discovered water.

From the summit of their palisade they launched arrows, earth, dung, and pebbles which they gathered from the ground, while the six catapults rolled incessantly throughout the length of the terrace.

But the springs would dry up of themselves; the provisions would be exhausted, and the catapults worn out; the Mercenaries, who were ten times as numerous, would triumph in the end. The Suffet devised negotiations so as to gain time, and one morning the Barbarians found a sheep's skin covered with writing within their lines. He justified himself for his victory: the Ancients had forced him into the war, and to show them that he was keeping his word, he offered them the pillaging of Utica or Hippo-Zarytus at their choice; in conclusion, Hamilcar declared that he did not fear them because he had won over some traitors, and thanks to them would easily manage the rest.

The Barbarians were disturbed: this proposal of immediate booty made them consider; they were apprehensive of treachery, not suspecting a snare in the Suffet's boasting, and they began to look upon one another with mistrust. Words and steps were watched; terrors awaked them in the night. Many forsook their companions and chose their army as fancy dictated, and the Gauls with Autaritus went and joined themselves with the men of Cisalpine Gaul, whose language they understood.

The four chiefs met together every evening in Matho's tent, and squatting round a shield, attentively moved backwards and forwards the little wooden figures invented by Pyrrhus for the representation of manœuvres. Spendius would demonstrate Hamilcar's resources, and with oaths by all the gods entreat that the opportunity should not be wasted. Matho would walk about angry and gesticulating. The war against Carthage was his own personal affair; he was indignant that the others should interfere in it without being willing to obey him. Autaritus would divine his speech from his countenance and applaud. Narr' Havas would elevate his chin to mark his disdain; there was not a measure that he did not consider fatal; and he had ceased to smile. Sighs would escape him as though he were thrusting back sorrow for an impossible dream, despair for an abortive enterprise.

While the Barbarians deliberated in uncertainty, the Suffet increased his defences: he had a second trench dug within the palisades, a second wall raised, and wooden towers constructed at the corners; and his slaves went as far as the middle of the outposts to drive caltrops into the ground. But the elephants, whose allowances were lessened, struggled in their shackles. To economise the grass he ordered the Clinabarians to kill the least strong among the stallions. A few refused to do so, and he had them decapitated. The horses were eaten. The recollection of this fresh meat was a source of great sadness to them in the days that followed.

From the bottom of the amphitheatre in which they were confined they could see the four bustling camps of the Barbarians all around them on the heights. Women moved about with leathern bottles on their heads, goats strayed bleating beneath the piles of pikes; sentries were being relieved, and eating was going on around tripods. In fact, the tribes furnished them abundantly with provisions, and they did not themselves suspect how much their inaction alarmed the Punic army.

On the second day the Carthaginians had remarked a troop of three hundred men apart from the rest in the camp of the nomads. These were

the rich who had been kept prisoners since the beginning of the war. Some Libyans ranged them
along the edge of the trench, took their station behind them, and hurled javelins, making themselves a
rampart of their bodies. The wretched creatures could
scarcely be recognised, so completely were their faces
covered with vermin and filth. Their hair had been
plucked out in places, leaving bare the ulcers on their
heads, and they were so lean and hideous that they
were like mummies in tattered shrouds. A few
trembled and sobbed with a stupid look; the rest
cried out to their friends to fire upon the Barbarians.
There was one who remained quite motionless with
face cast down, and without speaking; his long white
beard fell to his chain-covered hands; and the Carthaginians, feeling as it were the downfall of the
Republic in the bottom of their hearts, recognised
Gisco. Although the place was a dangerous one
they pressed forward to see him. On his head had
been placed a grotesque tiara of hippopotamus leather
incrusted with pebbles. It was Autaritus's idea; but
it was displeasing to Matho.

Hamilcar in exasperation, and resolved to cut his
way through in one way or another, had the palisades opened; and the Carthaginians went at a furious rate half way up the hill or three hundred paces.
Such a flood of Barbarians descended upon them that
they were driven back to their lines. One of the
guards of the Legion who had remained outside was
stumbling among the stones. Zarxas ran up to him,
knocked him down, and plunged a dagger into his
throat; he drew it out, threw himself upon the
wound—and gluing his lips to it with mutterings of
joy, and startings which shook him to the heels,

pumped up the blood by breastfuls; then he quietly
sat down upon the corpse, raised his face with his
neck thrown back the better to breathe in the air,
like a hind that has just drunk at a mountain stream,
and in a shrill voice began to sing a Balearic song,
a vague melody full of prolonged modulations, with
interruptions and alternations like echoes answering
one another in the mountains; he called upon his
dead brothers and invited them to a feast;—then he
let his hands fall between his legs, slowly bent his
head, and wept. This atrocious occurrence horrified
the Barbarians, especially the Greeks.

From that time forth the Carthaginians did not attempt to make any sally; and they had no thought
of surrender, certain as they were that they would
perish in tortures.

Nevertheless the provisions, in spite of Hamilcar's
carefulness, diminished frightfully. There was not left
per man more than ten k'hommers of wheat, three
hins of millet, and twelve betzas of dried fruit. No
more meat, no more oil, no more salt food, and not
a grain of barley for the horses, which might be
seen stretching down their wasted necks seeking in
the dust for blades of trampled straw. Often the
sentries on vedette upon the terrace would see in the
moonlight a dog belonging to the Barbarians coming
to prowl beneath the entrenchment among the heaps
of filth; it would be knocked down with a stone,
and then, after a descent had been effected along the
palisades by means of the straps of a shield, it would
be eaten without a word. Sometimes horrible bark-
ings would be heard and the man would not come
up again. Three phalangites, in the fourth dilochia

of the twelfth syntagma, killed one another with knives in a dispute about a rat.

All regretted their families, and their houses; the poor their hive-shaped huts, with the shells on the threshold and the hanging net, and the patricians their large halls filled with bluish shadows, where at the most indolent hour of the day they used to rest listening to the vague noise of the streets mingled with the rustling of the leaves as they stirred in their gardens;—to go deeper into the thought of this, and to enjoy it more, they would half close their eyelids, only to be roused by the shock of a wound. Every minute there was some engagement, some fresh alarm; the towers were burning, the Eaters of Uncleanness were leaping across the palisades; their hands would be struck off with axes; others would hasten up; an iron hail would fall upon the tents. Galleries of rushen hurdles were raised as a protection against the projectiles. The Carthaginians shut themselves up within them and stirred out no more.

Every day the sun coming over the hill used, after the early hours, to forsake the bottom of the gorge and leave them in the shade. The grey slopes of the ground, covered with flints spotted with scanty lichen, ascended in front and in the rear, and above their summits stretched the sky in its perpetual purity, smoother and colder to the eye than a metal cupola. Hamilcar was so indignant with Carthage that he felt inclined to throw himself among the Barbarians and lead them against her. Moreover, the porters, sutlers, and slaves were beginning to murmur, while neither people, nor Great Council, nor any one sent as much as a hope. The situation was intolerable, especially owing to the thought that it would become worse.

At the news of the disaster Carthage had leaped, as it were, with anger and hate; the Suffet would have been less execrated if he had allowed himself to be conquered from the first.

But time and money were lacking for the hire of other Mercenaries. As to a levy of soldiers in the town, how were they to be equipped? Hamilcar had taken all the arms! and then who was to command them? The best captains were down yonder with him! Meanwhile, some men despatched by the Suffet arrived in the streets with shouts. The Great Council were roused by them, and contrived to make them disappear.

It was an unnecessary precaution; every one accused Barca of having behaved with slackness. He ought to have annihilated the Mercenaries after his victory. Why had he ravaged the tribes? The sacrifices already imposed had been heavy enough! and the patricians deplored their contributions of fourteen shekels, and the Syssitia their two hundred and twenty-three thousand gold kikars; those who had given nothing lamented like the rest. The populace was jealous of the New Carthaginians, to whom he had promised full rights of citizenship; and even the Ligurians, who had fought with such intrepidity, were confounded with the Barbarians and cursed like them; their race became a crime, the proof of complicity. The traders on the threshold of their shops, the workmen passing plumb-line in hand, the vendors of pickle rinsing their baskets, the attendants in the vapour baths and the retailers of hot drinks all discussed the operations of the campaign. They would trace battle-plans with their fingers in the dust, and there was not a sorry rascal to be found who could not have corrected Hamilcar's mistakes.

It was a punishment, said the priests, for his long-continued impiety. He had offered no holocausts; he had not purified his troops; he had even refused to take augurs with him; and the scandal of sacrilege strengthened the violence of restrained hate, and the rage of betrayed hopes. People recalled the Sicilian disasters, and all the burden of his pride that they had borne for so long! The colleges of the pontiffs could not forgive him for having seized their treasure, and they demanded a pledge from the Great Council to crucify him should he ever return.

The heats of the month of Eloul, which were excessive in that year, were another calamity. Sickening smells rose from the borders of the Lake, and were wafted through the air together with the fumes of the aromatics that eddied at the corners of the streets. The sounds of hymns were constantly heard. Crowds of people occupied the staircases of the temples; all the walls were covered with black veils; tapers burnt on the brows of the Patæc Gods, and the blood of camels slain for sacrifice ran along the flights of stairs forming red cascades upon the steps. Carthage was agitated with funereal delirium. From the depths of the narrowest lanes, and the blackest dens, there issued pale faces, men with viper-like profiles and grinding their teeth. The houses were filled with the women's piercing shrieks, which, escaping through the gratings, caused those who stood talking in the squares to turn round. Sometimes it was thought that the Barbarians were arriving; they had been seen behind the mountain of the Hot Springs; they were encamped at Tunis; and the voices would multiply and swell, and be blended into one single clamour. Then universal silence would reign, some remaining where they had climbed upon the frontals of the buildings, screening their eyes with their open hand, while the rest lay flat on their faces at the foot of the ramparts straining their ears. When their terror had passed off their anger would begin again. But the conviction of their own impotence would soon sink them into the same sadness as before.

It increased every evening when all ascended the terraces, and bowing down nine times uttered a loud cry in salutation of the sun, as it sank slowly behind the lagoon. and then suddenly disappeared among the mountains in the direction of the Barbarians.

They were waiting for the thrice holy festival when, from the summit of a funeral pile, an eagle flew heavenwards as a symbol of the resurrection of the year, and a message from the people to their Baal; they regarded it as a sort of union, a method of connecting themselves with the might of the Sun. Moreover, filled as they now were with hatred, they turned frankly towards homicidal Moloch, and all forsook Tanith. In fact, Rabbetna, having lost her veil, was as if she had been despoiled of part of her virtue. She denied the beneficence of her waters, she had abandoned Carthage; she was a deserter, an enemy. Some threw stones at her to insult her. But many pitied her while they inveighed against her; she was still beloved, and perhaps more deeply than she had been.

All their misfortunes came, therefore, from the loss of the zaïmph. Salammbô had indirectly participated in it; she was included in the same ill will; she must be punished. A vague idea of immolation spread among the people. To appease the Baalim it was without doubt necessary to offer them something of incalculable worth, a being handsome, young, virgin, of old family, a descendant of the gods, a human star. Every day the gardens of Megara were invaded by strange men; the slaves, trembling on their own account, dared not resist them. Nevertheless, they did not pass beyond the galley staircase. They remained below with their eyes raised to the highest terrace; they were waiting for Salammbô, and they would cry out for hours against her like dogs baying at the moon.